Last Stand
Of Old Heroes

First Published in Great Britain 2015 by Netherworld Books
an imprint of Mirador Publishing

First edition: 2015

*Any reference to real names and places are purely fictional
and are constructs of the author. Any offence the references
produce is unintentional and in no way reflects the reality of
any locations or people involved.*

A copy of this work is available through the British Library.

ISBN : 978-1-910105-53-5

Netherworld Books
Mirador
Wearne Lane
Langport
Somerset
TA10 9HB

LAST STAND OF OLD HEROES

THE CHRONICLES OF ARKADIA
VOL. FOUR

J. JONES

"Love your woman, protect the weak, honour the gods and look your enemy in the eye. Never back down."

(Teren Rad)

Chapter 1

The assassin stole through the neatly ordered rows of tents, a shadow among shadows. A few paces either side of him, his two accomplices silently picked their own way towards the quarry. He could see neither of them, but that was a good thing. If he couldn't see them when he knew they were there, then Sulat willing, the sentries guarding the camp's perimeter were unlikely to notice them either.

The silvery half-moon slid out from behind the dark cloud which had swallowed it up a few moments earlier and once again bathed the camp in pale watery light. The assassin stopped instantly. Tilting his head slightly he listened for any sign that their presence had been noticed, but all he could hear was the rhythmic snoring of some soldiers sleeping in the nearby tents and the occasional howl of a wolf somewhere in the distance.

Satisfied that their presence still remained undetected, the assassin started to creep forward again.

Three men slept in the tent they sought. Teren Rad, the leader of the Remadans, Yarik Holte, the menacing looking Delarite and Brak, the assassin's compatriot who had apparently escaped a Salandori slave camp with Rad and now felt some misplaced loyalty to the man.

The assassin's instructions from Prince Furak, Brak's younger brother, were to kill Rad. If they could, he and his comrades were to kill Holte and Brak too. It would certainly be better for their cause if all three men perished, but it was imperative that Rad died. The other two were influential for sure, but it was Rad to whom men gravitated. He was a natural leader that men would readily follow. He could motivate the most disheartened of soldiers and turn certain defeat into victory. Even now, six months after their resounding defeat at the hands of the Narmidian invaders, men still flocked to the camp seeking Rad's leadership. The free armies of Arkadia had been routed that day, but still men believed that Rad would make things right, that he would ultimately lead them to victory. Their faith in him remained undiminished.

Now the Brelandic Council of Leaders was falling under his spell too. More and more of them were coming round to the idea of joining the war and attacking the Narmidians who despite being strung out along Breland's border, had not yet shown any hostile intent towards them. To Prince Furak and those of a similar mind, attacking the Narmidians and making them an enemy would be a mistake and a fatal one at that. Prince Furak and his allies were not prepared to let that happen, especially as the prince was sure that his father, King Eklan, was on the verge of abdicating. Normally the crown would have passed to Brak him being the eldest, but with Brak gone or disgraced, Furak would be next in line. But if Breland was to go to war there was no way the Council would support Furak's ascension. To fight a war with such a powerful adversary with an untried young king would be utter folly and they would insist that Eklan remain king.

So Prince Furak had ordered three like-minded men, trained in the arts of stealth and killing, to assassinate Rad. He had to die. Rad was the focus for all the talk of war within the Council. Furak believed that when Rad was dead the will of the ragtag army that had sought safe haven in his country would dissipate and they would slowly drift away convinced that all hope was lost. If they didn't then he would order them to leave his country, by force if necessary. At one time Furak had considered trying to capture Rad and the others and then handing them over to the Narmidians in an attempt to buy some good will, but in the end he had decided that was probably too risky and had instead settled on Rad's death. With Rad gone there would be no more talk of war from the Council and he would be free to take his rightful place as king once his father abdicated.

A flicker of movement ahead of him and to his right drew the assassin's attention and he stopped once again. He had fallen behind his comrades. If their plan was to work it was vital that they all arrived at Rad's tent at the same time.

Cursing silently for allowing himself to be distracted yet mindful of the need to remain hidden, he quickened his pace and a few seconds later he stopped once more and crouched down; Rad's tent was now just a few paces ahead. To an untrained eye there was nothing different about this tent to the hundreds of others pitched in straight lines around it. There were no standards or flags fluttering from its poles denoting that the leader of the free people slept inside. No bodyguards keeping a silent vigil outside. Yet this was the tent. The assassin had spent days watching and studying the camp until finally he was sure that this was Rad's billet. Rad would never take the same path back to his tent, almost as if he knew that he was being watched, but it was always to this tent that he returned. On more than one occasion the assassin had caught the big Delarite watching him with those cold murderous eyes of his and had worried that their plan was foiled, but either the Delarite was as stupid as he looked or Rad did not concur with his suspicions.

Unless it's a trap!

That was a worrying thought and one the assassin chose to ignore.

He crept forward until he was just a few paces from the front of the tent. To his left he heard the softest of footfalls. Most men would not have noticed them, but he had. An assassin should never be seen or heard. He would have to rebuke his young accomplice in the morning. It was the young man's first mission but in the assassination business, there were no second chances. One errant noise could cost them all their lives.

He gave the young assassin a withering look that spoke volumes before quickly glancing to his right where his other accomplice, a veteran of many missions, squatted, poised to move at his comrade's nod.

Reaching inside his loose fitting tunic the assassin pulled out a dagger. Unlike most daggers, the assassin's weapon of choice had a long thin blade. It was designed to pierce the body deeply with a small entry hole, but to cause much internal bleeding. Often the victim would not realise the extent of their wound until it was too late.

After a cursory nod at his two comrades he silently approached the loose tent flaps, the sound of gentle snoring coming from within as he neared. Carefully and deliberately he peeled back one of the canvas entrance flaps and manoeuvred his body to plug the gap so that no sudden gust of chilled wind would wake the inhabitants and alert them to his presence. He waited a few seconds for his eyes to adjust to the subtle change in light and then silently entered the tent, his dagger poised to strike at the slightest indication that he had been seen.

At the rear of the tent he could now make out the heavily bearded and rugged looking face of Teren Rad as he lay on his back snoring. Either side of the tent were two more makeshift beds, their bulging blankets testament to the fact that they were occupied. Both men appeared to have their backs to him and he could not therefore tell which one was Brak and which one was Holte.

Satisfied that all three men were soundly asleep he adjusted his hold on the dagger and began to cautiously edge towards the slumbering Teren Rad. His two comrades would follow in behind him and deal with the others.

A bead of perspiration began to trickle down the assassin's forehead and he had to fight the urge to wipe it away as he closed on his target.

He froze when Rad made a snorting noise and briefly stirred, but after a few seconds the Remadan settled down again and resumed his snoring. The assassin found himself wondering how the others slept with such a noise assailing their ears night after night. Perhaps it would be a mercy in more ways than one killing this man.

He edged forward some more until finally he was looming over the Remadan. Rad was an old man, that much was true, but even asleep his face exuded power and determination. The assassin did not doubt that the stories he had heard over the years of the man's courage and his acts of valour were all true. He would not have relished the prospect of facing him in open combat. But all men must die and now was Rad's time.

He slowly began to position his dagger for cutting Rad's throat when a sudden gust of cold wind hit his back.

The young fool has not closed the tent flap after following us in, thought the assassin. *Anyone walking by might become suspicious and come to investigate and that would spell the end for us all.*

He turned to gesture for the boy to close the flap, but was surprised to find that he wasn't in the tent. Neither was Dak, the third assassin. Alarm bells began to ring in the assassin's mind. Had his comrades been discovered? Had they been killed or captured? Perhaps they had misunderstood the plan and were keeping guard outside and had assumed that he was taking care of all the tent's occupants. That last possibility was unlikely. The boy might be so stupid, but Dak wasn't. Even as his uncertainty and nerves began to churn the contents of his stomach into liquid, he knew that he had come too far to quit. Besides, even if he did manage to withdraw unnoticed without killing Rad, Prince Furak would in all likelihood have him killed, either for failing him or to keep his complicity in the plan secret.

He would kill Rad and then withdraw to find out what had happened. Rad's two companions would never realise how close they had come to dying that night.

As he once again turned to face Rad, a sharp scratch under his chin caught him by surprise. He froze, his breath catching in his fast constricting throat; grinning up at him and very much awake, lay Teren Rad. The assassin doubted now that he had ever been asleep. Without moving his head the assassin slowly glanced down and saw that Rad was holding a knife under his chin, the tip of which had just pricked the skin, drawing forth the first drops of blood. His life hung in the balance.

"That's right, lad, I've got the drop on you. Bet you didn't see that coming. Now nice and easy, drop that pretty little toothpick in your right hand, but don't get any ideas. I'm missing my beauty sleep for this and that tends to make me a little cranky. When I'm cranky I start to shake and you don't want me to do that." To illustrate his point and without alleviating the pressure under the assassin's chin, Teren made his hand shake forcing the tip of his knife a little bit deeper into the man's chin, but not deep enough to kill him.

The dagger dropped from the assassin's hand and keeping his own knife firmly under the man's chin, Teren slowly sat up, reached out for the assassin's dagger and then began to examine it.

"Nasty piece of work this, but then that's what I'd expect from cowardly scum who rather than fight a man face to face, would prefer to slit his throat in the dead of night." As he spoke he glanced behind the assassin at the open tent flap through which Brak and Yarik now appeared. "Any trouble?"

"Since when did two little whoresons like them pose a problem to us?" growled Yarik.

The assassin stirred uncomfortably at the insult and glanced over at the other two cots in which he thought Brak and Holte were fast asleep. Teren watched the confused look on the man's face with amusement.

"It was a neat trick wasn't it, making you think they were soundly asleep in their beds when in actual fact they weren't even here?" said Teren.

Brak strode over to one of the cots and pulled back the blankets revealing a small man sized log. He laughed at the look of anger and embarrassment that flashed across the assassin's face.

"Now, now, settle down, or you're going to get yourself hurt," said Teren. Looking back over at his two friends he then asked, "What have you done with the bodies of this fella's accomplices?"

"They're safely hidden in one of the storage tents. They won't be able to stay there long or they'll ruin the supplies and start to stink the place out," replied Brak.

"More than they already do," added Yarik. Clearly he was enjoying baiting the remaining assassin.

"Good," replied Teren. "Is this the one you saw following me the other day?"

Yarik moved round a bit so that he had a better view of the man's face. "That's him."

Teren nodded knowingly and then threw the assassin's knife over to Yarik. "Here, a memento for you."

Yarik briefly examined the weapon and then tucked it into his waistband before offering a small grunt. Teren figured that was probably the closest to a thank you he was going to get.

"My arm is starting to ache so I'm going to remove this

knife in a moment," said Teren staring into the assassin's eyes. "However, please don't try anything stupid because even if I don't manage to kill you, the big, ugly fellow over there with the mean countenance, will gladly rip you apart."

Yarik started to fidget and mumble under his breath, something Brak had noticed he did whenever he didn't understand something.

"It means you're angry and not to be trifled with," said Brak.

"I knew that," snapped Yarik before slowly breaking into a grin, one that was soon matched by Teren. Brak just rolled his eyes to the heavens.

"Now why don't you start by telling us why you were so intent on killing the three of us?" asked Teren as he took his knife away from under the man's chin. The assassin just stared blankly back at Teren. "No? Well how about telling us who's paying you to kill us, assuming I haven't wronged you at some point and this is just about revenge?"

"Now there's a thought, Teren Rad wronging someone, who'd have believed it possible?" said Brak grinning.

Teren gave his friend a withering look and Brak shut up. The assassin still said nothing.

Teren sighed. "You will talk to me, son that much I promise you. Now it can be the easy way here and now like old friends round a camp fire or it can be the hard way, which is always my Delarite friend's preference. I won't lie to you, both ways are going to end in your death, but one will be quick and painless, the other one, not so much. It's your choice." When the assassin remained silent, Teren sighed once again and glanced up at his two friends. "He's all yours, Yarik. Just do whatever needs to be done away from the camp; I don't want his screaming upsetting the men. As soon as he tells you what we need to hear, come and find me."

"It'll be my pleasure," said Yarik grabbing the assassin by the scruff of the neck and dragging him towards the tent flap.

"You're not going with him?" Teren asked Brak when the big northerner made no attempt to follow Yarik.

"I have no stomach for what he has planned."

"You're not going soft on me are you, Brak?"

"No, but there's killing a man in combat and then there's murder. I'll have no part of the latter."

"He and his mates did just try to kill us," said Teren.

"I know and for that they deserve to die; but not the way Yarik has planned."

"We need to know who hired them, Brak otherwise they're likely to send more after us and next time we might not be so lucky," said Teren. "Besides, we did ask him nicely."

"I know. Who do you think sent them?" asked Brak.

Teren scratched his straggly beard as he contemplated his friend's question.

"I don't know. Could be the Narmidian king, Vesla or perhaps we've just outstayed our welcome here."

Brak looked aghast. "You think my people could be behind this?"

"Anything's possible, Brak."

"Assassination is not our way."

"There's an exception to every rule."

"It could just as easily be a Delarite or a Datian or any number of other people you've upset. Sulat only knows how many people have grievances against you."

"The assassins were Brelandic, Brak," said Teren.

"I know that, but anybody could have hired them," replied Brak indignantly.

"And that is why our Delarite friend has got to do what he's got to do. We don't want to be killing the wrong men in wanton acts of revenge."

"You seek revenge?" asked Brak.

"Of course I do. If I take no action to track down and punish those who tried to kill me it will send out the wrong message to our enemies and before we know it they'll be queuing up outside our tent."

"Then I must urge the utmost caution, Teren."

"Why?"

"Because the Teren Rad way of getting things done won't be accepted here; my people are proud and expect their laws and customs to be upheld. You can't just go blustering in swinging your axe at someone you suspect might be behind the assassination attempt."

"So what are you saying; that I should do nothing?" asked Teren tersely.

"No, of course not. I'm merely saying that we need to tread lightly on this one and gather our evidence. Once we have the proof of who hired the assassins we go to my father the king. He will ensure the guilty are severely punished you have my word on it."

Teren stared at his friend weighing up his words. Finally he let out a long low breath and slowly nodded.

"As you wish, Brak but on one condition."

"And what's that?"

"That if Yarik finds out who is behind it tonight courtesy of our assassin friend, we deal with it quickly and quietly ourselves and don't trouble your father with the details." Brak's expression suggested that he wasn't happy with the notion but nodded his approval anyway. "Good. I'm still angry at you by the way."

"What for?" asked Brak, confused by the apparent sudden change of topic.

"For not telling me that you were King Eklan's son."

"Would it have made any difference to how you treated me?" asked Brak.

"It may have. I might have left you in those Salandori slave camps."

"I doubt that. You're a better man than you like people to think."

"Perhaps, but you should still have told me," said Teren.

"What is done is done."

Teren nodded knowingly. Brak was right; he wouldn't have treated the big northerner any different had he known he was royalty. He decided to change the subject again.

"So what is your father's current thinking? I have not heard from him for a few days and our men are growing weary of loitering around in this camp. Every day I hear rumours of men drifting away in the night. If we don't do something I'm afraid I'll wake up one day and it will only be the three of us."

"For every man that slips away under the cover of darkness two more join our ranks in the light of day. Remnants of just about every army are converging on this camp."

That was news to Teren's ears.

"Men are still arriving? That is good. And what of your father?"

Brak slumped down on his makeshift bed and massaged the muscles at the base of his neck.

"He is…was, in favour of taking the fight to the Narmidians, but my brother has begun to gnaw away at his resolve. Furak is in favour of making peace with the Narmidians and living side by side with them. He is slowly starting to persuade my father and some on the Council that Breland's best play is to do nothing to provoke the Narmidians."

"Surely your father can't believe that the Narmidians will remain outside his country for ever? If our scouts' reports are to be believed the Narmidian forces are growing by the day," said Teren.

"They are and I for one agree with you, but Furak has poisoned my father's opinion." Brak cast his eyes down to the ground unable to meet Teren's piercing almost accusatory stare.

"What aren't you telling me, Brak? I can see there's something."

Brak slowly looked up and even managed a small smile.

How did the Remadan know him so well after such a short time?

"Furak is gradually turning my father against us, making him believe that we are the problem not the Narmidians."

"We?" asked Teren sceptically.

"You. You and the other foreigners. He says that the only reason that the Narmidians are here is because of the foreign soldiers and that if we exile you or hand you over, the Narmidians will withdraw."

"And your father believes this nonsense?"

"He's starting to. Furak and Nemar, my father's chief advisor, are whispering hatred in his ear all day long. I fear it won't be long before he caves in," said Brak.

"And what of you; does he not listen to the words of his eldest son?"

"He does, but with less and less interest. Such is the level of distrust Furak has instilled in my father that now even my words are greeted with suspicion."

"How can this be? I thought that your father was on the verge of stepping down and handing the crown to you?" asked Teren.

"So it was said, but the Council has urged him to remain on the throne until this crisis is resolved."

"But then surely he will make you king?"

"Even that is no longer certain. As his eldest son it is my birth right that is true, but Furak's endless whispering in my father's ear has soured my relationship with my father. Furak's jealousy and hatred of me is much greater than I feared."

"Enough to hire assassins to kill us?" asked Teren.

That caught Brak by surprise and he didn't immediately reply as he considered his friend's question.

"Perhaps," he finally admitted, though he didn't like to countenance such a thought.

Teren was about to say something further when the tent flaps suddenly opened. Both men instantly reached for their weapons, staying their hands only when they recognised Yarik's face.

Yarik fixed Teren with a hard stare.

"We need to talk. Now!"

Chapter 2

The light within the tent was poor, yet still good enough for Teren and Brak to see that Yarik's tunic was splattered in blood and Teren's gaze lingered on one particularly large stain. Assuming that the blood wasn't Yarik's evidently the assassin had not given up his secrets lightly. Yarik caught his friend's gaze and briefly glanced down at his own tunic.

"He died well and endured much before he told me what we needed to hear."

"He died bloody you mean," said Brak.

"In his profession that is the only way to die. For his bravery I gave him a quick death once he had told me everything he knew."

"You're all heart," said Brak.

The Delarite scowled as he stared back at his companion, unsure whether or not he was being mocked. Not wishing the situation to turn ugly between his two friends, Teren cut in.

"So what did he tell you that is so important?"

"That we may have a problem," replied Yarik.

"I'm listening," urged Teren. Yarik glanced nervously at Brak as if he was unsure whether he should impart the information in front of the northerner. Teren instantly smelled trouble. "Go on, Yarik, none of us is getting any younger."

"Furak!" said Yarik as if that explained everything.

"What about him?" prompted Brak.

"The assassins were hired by him."

"What?" snapped Teren jumping to his feet.

"Never," snapped Brak, conveniently forgetting that he and Teren had been discussing that very possibility just a few moments before Yarik had returned.

"Are you sure, Yarik?" asked Teren holding up a hand to forestall any protests from Brak.

"I've questioned many men in my time, Teren and know when a man is speaking the truth. He did not give the prince's name up lightly."

"But why; it makes no sense?" said Teren more to himself than the others.

"No, actually it makes perfect sense. With me dead he would naturally become the heir apparent and with you two dead, the free armies would soon fracture and melt away. Furak would get the crown he wants, get rid of the foreigners he despises and hopefully avoid a war with the Narmidians by winning their king's favour," explained Brak.

"That's pretty much what the assassin suggested," said Yarik.

"Your brother would kill you to achieve his goals?" asked Teren.

"He would. We're not that close."

"That much is clear. He's going to be angry when he learns we're still alive,"said Teren.

"He probably already knows," said Brak.

"The question is what are we going to do?" said Yarik.

"No, I think the question is what will he do next?" said Brak.

"It depends on whether he thinks we've got evidence proving that he was behind the attempt on our lives. If he doesn't, he'll probably wait it out and deny everything. If he thinks we do, then he's more than likely to try again to kill us," said Teren.

"Then perhaps we should pay him a visit instead before he gets the chance," suggested Yarik, toying with his sword hilt.

"It's your call, Brak; he's your brother," said Teren.

"I think Yarik's right," said Brak after a few moments consideration, "I think we should pay him a visit and question him at first, before taking the matter to my father."

"And if he resists?" asked Teren.

"Then we will have our admission of guilt and will act accordingly," replied Brak.

"Perhaps you should sit this one out, Brak and let me and the Delarite question him," said Teren.

"No, he is my brother and my life was just as much on the line as yours. If it turns ugly I will be there," replied Brak his left hand nonchalantly reaching down for where his dagger was usually sheathed. The sheath was empty prompting a quizzical look on Brak's face.

"You forgotten to pull your knife from one of the assassin's bodies?" asked Teren when he realised what his friend was looking for.

"No, I used my sword. Strange, I don't remember picking it up earlier tonight, yet I normally don't go anywhere without it."

"It's probably lying around here somewhere," said Teren, glancing around.

"Yes, you're probably right," replied Brak, though he didn't sound convinced.

The sound of several men marching in unison caught their attention and all three automatically reached for their swords. The footsteps came to a halt outside their tent and all three men tensed. The tent flaps were suddenly pulled back and two men stepped in both wearing the uniform of the king's personal guard. The older man Teren recalled having seen before, always at King Eklan's side but he didn't recognise the younger man.

"Where I come from it's customary to ask the occupants for permission to enter their tent before you go barging in fully armed. Saves any unnecessary unpleasantness," said Teren fixing both men with a wary cold stare. Yarik grunted his approval.

"You are on King Eklan's land and his Royal Bodyguard need nobody's permission when they are doing his bidding. Perhaps you should go back to wherever it is that you do come from," replied the younger of the two men.

Yarik snarled and took a pace forward, but a gentle restraining hand from Teren stayed his motion.

"Silence! Nobody gave you permission to speak," said the older of the two guards to his companion. "Apologies for the intrusion, Rad, but as my ignorant subordinate rightly says we are here on the king's business and as such are beholding to no man."

Teren nodded his approval of the man's respectful apology.

"Tharl Marit, what can I do for you?" asked Brak releasing his grip on his sword when he recognised the older of the two men as his father's Captain of the Royal Bodyguard. He pointedly didn't acknowledge the other man, making Teren smirk. Yarik, however, continued to glare at the younger man. Teren had seen that look many times and it didn't bode well for the other man's health.

Tharl Marit drew himself up to his full height, his helmet brushing the roof of the tent.

"Prince Brak, by order of Prince Furak and the Council of Leaders, I am here to place you under arrest and to escort you before a special hearing of the Council. You will surrender your sword and come with me now," said Marit.

Teren's and Yarik's swords were unsheathed in a moment and both stood poised to attack the other two men. Cries of alarm from the other guards waiting outside as they drew their own weapons filled the air. Their presence would have been noticed by Teren's men by now. One wrong move and the camp could explode into a maelstrom of violence.

"Hold!" said Brak gesturing for his two friends to lower their weapons. "Prince Furak has no authority to arrest me," he added turning to face Marit. "And on what charge anyway?"

"As acting king he does have the authority especially when backed by the Council," replied Marit.

"What do you mean, acting king? Where is my father?" asked Brak his gaze constantly darting between Marit and Teren.

"Do not pretend that you don't know, Prince Brak," the younger of the two officers said sneering.

"Hold your tongue, worm. If I have to tell you again I will personally cut it out for you," snapped Marit. This time Yarik grinned. Marit turned to face Brak again. "I regret to inform you, Prince Brak that your father was murdered earlier tonight. You are to be charged with his murder."

"What? My father is dead?" asked Brak incredulously. Marit nodded. "How?"

"I regret that I am forbidden to discuss the details with you; I am merely to escort you to the Council for an immediate trial."

"You're not thinking of going are you, lad? You've clearly been set up," asked Teren, his mind already awash with thoughts as to how he and his men could escape the camp with as little bloodshed as possible.

"Yes, I am going. Honour dictates it. Besides, we all know that it is a lie. It will not take me long to disprove their evidence if they even have any." Brak turned his sword around and handed it handle first to Marit.

"Thank you, Prince Brak."

"This is a mistake, Brak, but it's not one we're going to let you make alone. We're coming with you," said Teren sheathing his sword.

"We are?" asked Yarik surprised.

"Yes, we are."

The big Delarite mumbled to himself as he reluctantly sheathed his own weapon.

"Actually I'm afraid you're not," said Marit apologetically.

"Oh and why is that?" asked Teren.

"You are both to remain right here under house arrest until such time as the Council calls for you or says otherwise."

"You are accusing us now?" asked Teren. There was a subtle menace to his voice which did not go unnoticed by Marit.

"You deny it?" asked Marit's companion. "Your uncouth friend is covered in blood."

Again Yarik moved to confront the young officer and once more, albeit reluctantly, Teren restrained him.

A look of pure anger crossed Marit's face and Teren was sure that he was about to strike his younger comrade, but then Marit's gaze settled on the fast drying blood splattered down Yarik's tunic and he seemed to change his mind.

"I think in the circumstances it would be better if you were to remain here, Rad," said Marit.

Rad glanced at Brak who nodded to his friend.

"Very well. But we're not surrendering our weapons."

Marit opened his mouth to protest but then seemed to think better of it. Not only did he not fancy a confrontation with the Remadan, a man for whom he had huge respect, but there was also the small matter of several thousand armed men camped outside. By now they would be aware that something was going on and might react badly if they heard their leaders had been disarmed and placed under arrest. The situation was extremely volatile.

"No, I don't see any necessity for that. Shall we go, Prince Brak? The Council is waiting."

"I'll be fine, Teren. You and Yarik remain here and try and stay out of trouble until I return," said Brak.

"As you wish," replied Teren.

After giving his friend what he hoped was a reassuring smile, Brak turned and exited the tent, quickly followed by Marit. The other bodyguard grinned maliciously at Teren and Yarik and then turned and left.

"I've got a bad feeling about this, Teren," said Yarik.

Teren turned to look at his friend in surprise. Yarik rarely referred to Teren by his name, preferring instead to just call him 'Remadan' or whatever his insult of the day happened to be. Clearly the big man was worried about Brak.

"Me too, Yarik, me too."

Chapter 3

Despite his subordinate's protestations, on the way to the Council hall Marit had agreed that Brak could briefly stop to view his dead father's body. He had been instructed not to tell Brak anything about the circumstances of the king's death, but they had said nothing about not showing him. It was a fine line Marit knew, but he no longer cared particularly if it annoyed his vile, conniving subordinate whose loyalties Marit questioned.

The more Marit saw and heard the less he was willing to believe that the young prince was responsible for his father's murder. He had known Brak and his brother Furak all their lives and had watched almost with a father's pride as both had grown into fine young men. When Brak had announced that he was leaving his father's court to explore Arkadia for a few years, he had found the prince's parting almost as painful to bear as King Eklan himself had. It had been then that he had noticed the changes in Furak. The younger of the two brothers, Furak had always been bitter about the fact that he would in all likelihood never ascend to the throne unless something terrible happened to Brak. When news had reached the court that Brak had been taken captive somewhere in the east by Salandori tribesmen it had broken the king's heart. Outwardly at least, Furak had appeared devastated but Marit had seen the glint in his eyes when the news first broke. The ramifications and consequences of Brak's disappearance had not been lost on Furak.

Brak's face was one of shock as he stood staring at his father's lifeless body stretched out on a stone altar covered in bear furs. There were no obvious signs of trauma and Brak immediately began to consider the possibility that his father had been poisoned. Had the Narmidians somehow got to him? Had they poisoned him to throw the allies' plans into disarray rather than wait to see whether he decided to remain neutral or not? If their plan had been to sow distrust amongst the allies then their plan had succeeded. Perhaps it wasn't the Narmidians at all. Perhaps the killer had been much closer to home and had a different agenda. Whoever it was, Brak silently vowed to bring them to swift justice.

"I'm sorry, Prince Brak, we really must be going; the Council will become suspicious if we linger much longer," said Marit.

Nodding, Brak straightened up and wiped at a tear that slowly meandered down his cheek. Marit looked away to save the young prince's dignity. He either was an extremely good actor or he genuinely had nothing to do with the murder. Marit was positive now that it was the latter and began to worry that he was escorting his prince to an unjust trial and likely death.

Marit led the way out and Brak followed, drawing suspicious and curious glances from those whom they passed. They soon arrived at the doors leading into King Eklan's great hall.

"I thought the Council wanted to see me?" said Brak turning to face Marit.

"They do, but at Prince Furak's insistence the hearing is to be conducted in the great hall so that all might attend."

"A public trial then?"

"So it would seem, my Prince," replied Marit.

"Then let's get this farce over with shall we?"

Marit nodded at the two guards posted outside to open the doors. The heavy oak doors swung open and Brak's small party were immediately greeted by a cacophony of sound which quickly dissipated as all eyes turned their way.

Straightening his back and without waiting for Marit to lead the way, Brak strode confidently into the hall past hundreds of people all of whom were watching his every move. Some stared at him with open hostility, their minds clearly already made up regarding his guilt, but others looked concerned, embarrassed even. Some looked angry and either nodded at Brak or saluted him as he walked past them.

I am not alone then, thought Brak as he came to a halt a few paces in front of the throne where Furak sat flanked on either side by members of the Council of Leaders.

"What is the meaning of this insult, Furak? What gives you

the right to accuse me of our father's murder and to assume the throne?" barked Brak.

"Prince Furak came to us after your father's body was discovered requesting that you be arrested and that he temporarily assume the throne until this matter was settled," said Nemar, King Eklan's chief advisor who was sitting directly to Furak's right.

"Once my father's body was discovered I should have been informed and assumed the throne, not Furak."

"Ordinarily, Prince Brak you would be correct, but this was not ordinary."

"How so?" asked Brak.

"Because of the manner of your father's death," said Nemar.

"Go on."

The Councillor leant forward and started to unwrap something that was lying on the table before him. When it was clear of the rags he carefully lifted it up so that all in the hall might see it.

"Do you recognise this, Prince Brak?"

"Of course I do; it's my dagger."

A ripple of shocked murmuring swept across the great hall.

"There, out of his own mouth, an admission of guilt," bellowed Furak triumphantly, leaping to his feet.

"I admit to nothing other than that is my dagger, though how it comes to be in your possession is a mystery," said Brak.

"Because that is the weapon that was used to stab King Eklan in the back," said Raglan, one of the other five Council Leaders.

"What? That's impossible," said Brak.

"Yet you admit that it is yours and we have several witnesses including myself and Egor," he nodded to another of the Councillors sitting to his left, "who will attest to the fact that we found this very dagger buried in King Eklan's back when we were summoned," said Councillor Raglan.

"It may well be my dagger, Councillor Raglan, but it does not mean that I am the one who used it to kill my father. Why would I?"

"Because he was starting to see through your plan to wage war against the Narmidians and was about to expel your foreign friends," said Furak with a sneer. "You didn't like that so you killed him."

"That is a lie. Whatever my father's decision had been about the Narmidians I would have respected it," said Brak.

"Then how do you account for the fact that your knife was used to kill your father?" asked Voric, another of the Councillors and a true friend to King Eklan.

"I can't, Councillor, other than the fact that I had noticed it was missing just a short while ago." As he spoke, the officer who had accompanied Tharl Marit to arrest him sidled up to Prince Furak and whispered in his ear. Brak watched as his brother's face broke into a malevolent grin and started to nod. Behind him Brak noticed Tharl Marit shuffling uncomfortably, obviously irritated by his subordinate's overt bias.

"Captain Renik informs me that when he and Tharl Marit arrived at your tent to arrest you, at least one of your companions, the uncouth Delarite, was covered in blood. Should we be arresting him for assisting in the murder of our king?" asked Furak.

A wave of discontentment reverberated around the great hall and Brak sensed that the level of support for him had just diminished. Opinion as to whether to join the war against the Narmidian invader was split and whilst reinforcements continued to arrive daily from the Brelandic colonies oversea, no decision had yet been taken. Such accusations would not help the cause of those advocating joining the war.

"Well, Prince Brak, what have you to say to that?" asked Councillor Nemar.

"None of my friends had anything to do with my father's murder either."

"Then how do you explain the blood which apparently this man was covered in?"

"Earlier tonight three assassins, Brelandic men, attempted to kill myself, Teren Rad and Yarik Holte. They did not succeed and paid for the attempt with their lives. Before he died, their leader confessed that they had been hired by Prince Furak," said Brak.

27

The great hall erupted in turmoil as men shouted and accusations flew. For a moment Brak thought that he saw a look of panic sweep across his younger brother's face.

"Silence!" Councillor Voric bellowed before thumping his tankard down on the table so hard that it shattered splashing him and Councillor Egor with ale and shards of clay. "You can prove this, Prince Brak?"

"No I cannot. Yarik Holte and some of his men disposed of the bodies in the river; they will be many miles downstream by now."

"How convenient," said Councillor Nemar.

"Convenient or not, it is the truth Councillors," said Brak glaring at his brother. At that moment in time Brak wanted nothing more than to climb on the dais upon which the throne sat and wipe the conceited smirk off his brother's face, but to do so would have served no purpose other than to play further into his brother's hands.

"So to summarise you admit that the weapon that killed your father is your own dagger, yet you claim that you don't know how it got there and that you misplaced it. You also claim that your brother, Prince Furak, hired three assassins to kill you and your friends yet you cannot prove this either as you claim that their bodies were dumped into the river and are now halfway to the Cold Sea. Despite assassins being renowned for their ability to withstand pain and being prepared to die rather than divulge their sponsor, you claim that before he passed on their leader informed you that Prince Furak had hired them? Have I missed anything?" said Councillor Nemar grinning like a man who knew he had the upper hand.

Brak didn't like the stifled laughs that seemed to come from all around him and he glanced about, his gaze briefly falling on Tharl Marit. The old bodyguard met his gaze, his eyes a mass of conflicting emotions. Not everybody was against Brak it seemed, but was it enough?

"No, that is pretty much it," replied Brak.

Councillor Voric nodded. "The Council will now briefly adjourn to consider what they have heard," and with that he stood and turned to walk away followed by the other Council members. When Prince Furak rose to follow them, Councillor Voric asked him to remain seated as he was not part of the Council. Furak did not look pleased. He clearly wanted to be involved in the Council's deliberations and Brak allowed himself a small smile at his brother's humiliation. He pitied Councillor Voric though as this public rebuttal would not be forgotten regardless of the outcome of the trial, and Brak did not doubt that one night soon, Councillor Voric would suffer a fatal accident.

Brak had witnessed many Council meetings before, although none to consider such serious crimes as the murder of a king and none of them had been lengthy affairs. He was not surprised then when Councillor Voric led his fellow Councillors back into the great hall a little over ten minutes later. They resumed their places either side of Prince Furak and with no tankard left to hammer into the table for silence, Voric instead struck its surface with his fist. Instantly the room fell silent.

"Prince Brak, the Council has considered the evidence before us in the matter of the murder of King Eklan and have arrived at a decision." The hall was deathly silent and Brak felt that he could imagine the hundreds of men crammed in behind him shuffling forward so that they could hear what was said more clearly. However, Councillor Voric possessed a deep and commanding voice which easily reached the far corners of the great hall.

Brak straightened his back and looked Councillor Voric in the eye, momentarily unsettling the man. "And what is your verdict, Councillor Voric?"

"It is the decision of this Council that although the evidence is not conclusive, there is enough to reasonably believe that you have murdered your father." Muffled and muted conversations broke out around the hall, prompting Voric to bellow out a call for silence which was immediately heeded. "As you know the punishment for such a crime is death." More animated discussions erupted around the hall and a few shouted out, some in support of the sentence others against. "However, we have decided on this occasion to commute the sentence."

"What? Why? I demand the death penalty!" shouted Furak once again leaping to his feet.

"You have no say in this matter, Prince Furak," said Councillor Voric.

"It will soon be King Furak, old man, something you would do well to remember."

The veiled threat was not lost on Councillor Voric and the look that crossed his face made Brak wonder whether he was now having second thoughts about finding him guilty in the first place given Furak's reaction.

"As I was saying, on this occasion the Council has decided to commute the sentence, firstly because the evidence is not as cut and dried as some of us would like to believe." He quickly glanced over at a glowering Furak. "And secondly we do not know how Prince Brak's companions will react to his execution. As we all know there are several thousand men from a dozen different nations camped outside the city that follow Prince Brak and his friend Teren Rad. I fear the execution of Prince Brak will provoke them to action and whilst I believe we have enough of our own men to put such an uprising down, it would be extremely costly to both sides. In addition to that, we do not know how the Narmidians would react if they learned that we had turned on one another. They may very well wait until it's all over and then sweep in and finish the rest of us off." That thought seemed to provoke much deliberation and more animated conversations broke out around the hall. This time Voric waited for most of them to die down of their own accord before speaking again.

"It is therefore the decision of the Council that Prince Brak be stripped of his title and sent into exile never to return. The foreigners camped outside our city gates will also be ordered to leave."

"What? If they leave you'll make Breland vulnerable to attack," cried Brak.

"The men of Breland have been fighting and defeating invaders for thousands of years; the Narmidians will meet the same fate if they attempt to attack us," replied Councillor Nemar.

"I care not for myself, but what of the men you are sending

30

away? They came here seeking refuge and protection, but if you send them away they will surely be attacked and slaughtered. Whatever happened to Brelandic hospitality and honour?" said Brak.

"It is no longer our concern what happens to the foreigners; we didn't ask them to come here or to bring their war with them. Whatever happens to them is not on us," said Councillor Nemar.

"You are mistaken, Councillor Nemar, but it is. If you order those men out of our country and they're slaughtered as they're sure to be, Arkadia will never forget. One day there will be a reckoning."

"Perhaps, but you will not be here to see it. You are to leave this place by dawn tomorrow, Brak, never to return. Tharl Marit?"

"Councillor?" answered the Tharl stepping forward and snapping smartly to attention.

"You are to inform the foreigners that they are to all have departed by sun down tomorrow. I suggest that you muster enough armed men to demonstrate that the request is not negotiable," said Councillor Nemar.

"I will, Councillor," replied the Tharl.

Behind him Captain Renik stood grinning.

"Good. Then this meeting is over."

Chapter 4

News of Brak's exile and the imminent expulsion of the entire foreign garrison camped outside the city, soon spread and it was not long before tempers started to fray. The Brelandic warriors appeared split over Brak's treatment, some indignant at the harsh treatment of what they considered a loyal son of the crown, whilst others were angry at the leniency of his punishment. In their eyes the law was the law and needed to be upheld regardless of the consequences.

When Brak returned to his tent under armed guard, he found an increasingly agitated Teren waiting for him. Yarik on the other hand was quiet almost contemplative and Brak knew that wasn't a good sign. It usually meant the big man was seething inside and that an outbreak of uncontrolled violence was imminent.

"They've done what?" shouted Teren when Brak finished telling them about the trial and the punishment meted out. "Are they mad? What you had doesn't sound like any trial I've ever witnessed."

"It is the Brelandic way. We are not big on detail," said Brak almost apologetically.

"Nor fact by the sound of things," replied Teren caustically.

"It is what it is. It could have gone worse. Many such as my brother wish it had. Exile is by far the best I could have hoped for in the circumstances."

"But you're innocent, man. Doesn't that count for anything?"

"I cannot prove it and they have my dagger," replied Brak.

"So what? Obviously one of Furak's cronies came into our tent and stole it at some point and it was then given to whoever carried out the assassination of Eklan to make it look like you," said Teren.

"Quite probably, but as I said, we cannot prove it," said Brak.

"Then we'll make them reconsider," said Yarik hoisting his

sword and accidentally piercing the tent roof with his powerful thrust.

"You mean well, Yarik, I know that, but hundreds would perish on both sides. Not everyone agrees with the Council's ruling and I cannot run the risk of those sympathetic to my cause getting killed." Brak glanced up at the torn tent roof and smiled. "Besides, now we've got to move on; some idiot's gone and put a hole in the roof and it's supposed to be raining tomorrow."

Brak and Teren started to laugh and looked over at their friend encouraging him to join in, but there was no evidence he was ever going to.

Yarik shook his head slowly. "I will never understand you people. Are you not angry at what they have done to you, Brak? Do you not wish for revenge?"

"Make no mistake, Yarik, my heart burns with anger at the injustice and craves vengeance, but there is a time and a place for everything and this is neither."

"I can't see why not. We're here and we have an army outside which will follow us. Let's take our vengeance now. You say not everyone is against you; well they will have the chance to rally to us."

"You make it sound so simple, Yarik."

"Because it is."

"No, it's not. What if the Narmidians came sweeping in and caught us all unawares? What if they wait until one side wins and then invade? Either way it would be a slaughter and I for one do not want to be the cause of that. I will have my vengeance and I will reclaim my throne, but not today. Today we leave," said Brak.

Yarik looked to Teren for support, but the Remadan just looked back and shrugged.

"It's his call, Yarik. Now let it go. It will be dawn soon, so let's just try and grab some sleep before we have to leave; I know I could use some."

"You expect us to sleep when assassins have this very night attempted to take our lives?" asked Yarik.

"Why not? They're dead aren't they?" said Teren.

"Very, but what if there are more of them?" asked Yarik.

"There won't be."

"I don't think I'll trust your gut instinct on this one, old man," said Yarik. "I will sit up and keep watch."

"Suit yourself, but if you're going to stand guard at least do it properly. Don't go falling asleep," said Teren.

"A Delarite takes his duty seriously, Remadan. Sleep in peace knowing that I am watching over you weaklings."

"I'm sure we'll both sleep like babies knowing the great Yarik Holte has our backs," said Teren winking at Brak as he rolled over and closed his eyes.

Brak too lay down though he doubted sleep would come, his thoughts were in turmoil and not at all conducive to sleep. Behind him he could hear the Delarite mumbling and grumbling to himself and smiled. He might have lost much this night but he still had two good friends. There was much to be grateful for. He had also meant what he had said to the others about taking his revenge, but first he needed a plan. He was still considering that fact when his eyes closed and he slipped off into a dreamless sleep.

***

Sleep had eluded Teren, his mind constantly playing out the various scenarios that could befall his men the following morning. When the rudiments of a plan finally formed in his mind and he realised that no matter how much he willed it he was never going to sleep, Teren rose from his makeshift bed and stretched noisily. To his surprise Brak was not in his bed but Yarik was, still heartily snoring as if he didn't have a care in the world. Teren kicked the big Delarite in the side.

"Time to get up you lazy whoreson; the northerner's left."

Yarik, who had woken immediately and had rolled into a sitting position brandishing a knife in Teren's direction, stared at his friend incredulously. "Gone?"

"That's what I said," replied Teren. "You can put that thing away now," he added, nodding towards Yarik's knife which was still pointing in his direction.

"I would, but somebody keeps kicking me awake every morning and I'm getting tired of it," replied Yarik, finally laying the knife down and slowly climbing out of his own makeshift bed.

"Maybe that's because you said you were going to sit up and keep watch for us," said Teren.

"I did…for a while, but when I thought about it I realised you were probably right and that we were unlikely to be attacked twice in the same night," replied Yarik looking more than a little embarrassed.

Teren was pleased to see that the old Delarite warrior seemed to struggle as much as he did first thing in the morning, the ravages of time and old age showing no favouritism. The cracks and clicks as various joints sought to free themselves told Teren that Yarik's body was suffering every bit as much as his own. It made him feel better about himself.

"You all right, old man? Do you need a sit down?" asked Teren smirking.

"There's nothing wrong with me, Remadan, I've got years left. You worry about your own aging carcass."

"Believe me I do."

"So where's he gone?" asked Yarik.

Teren was about to reply when the flaps of the tent lifted and in strolled Brak.

"Where's who gone?" asked the northerner.

"Never mind," replied Teren.

Brak looked quizzically at Yarik.

"Our sentimental Remadan friend was worried you'd left us early without giving him a goodbye kiss."

Brak laughed. "I never knew you cared so much, Teren."

"I don't," snapped Teren, before all three started to laugh. "It's good that you're up though as I have a mind to leave early. How long would you say it is until dawn, Brak?"

"Not long. Long enough to put a few leagues between us and here before the sun rises," Brak replied.

"Good, that is what I hoped. If we leave now the Narmidians won't be expecting us."

"You hope," said Yarik.

"They won't. Even if they have been tipped off, they won't be expecting us to attempt a break out until at least first light. We have until dusk to leave remember."

"But we won't be able to see where we're going; we could march right into the centre of their army," said Yarik.

"We know the disposition of most of their forces…"

"But not all of them," interrupted Yarik.

"No, not all of them," conceded Teren, trying to calm his irritation. The big Delarite wasn't usually this negative; perhaps he was still cranky from his rude awakening. "The plan's not fool proof, Yarik, I know that, but given the time constraints it's the best I can come up with. Brak knows the countryside, we'll be fine."

"So your plan is to charge out of here and hope to catch the Narmidians unaware and get far enough away before they can muster any sort of pursuit?" asked Yarik.

"Pretty much, although there's one additional detail," said Teren.

"And what's that?" asked Brak.

"That we send a small diversionary force out to the east to distract them."

"But that's suicide. The bulk of Vesla's army is stationed to the east," said Brak.

"I know."

"It's suicide," Brak repeated, shaking his head.

"I never said it was a good plan," said Teren apologetically.

"This diversionary force will be vastly outnumbered, in great danger and have the opportunity for a glorious death?" asked Yarik.

"Yes."

"When do I leave?" asked the big Delarite, grinning.

"Soon," replied Teren also grinning. He'd known that the Delarite would be unable to decline the opportunity to write his name into legend once again.

"You can't be serious, Yarik? There has to be another way," said Brak.

"If there is I'm willing to hear it," said Teren as he strapped on his sword, "but you'd better make it quick. Time is against us." Brak stared blankly back at him. "No? Then we go with my plan. Have the men ready to move out imminently and stress the need for silence."

"Don't worry, northerner, perhaps there will be a little bit of glory left for you after I've finished killing every Narmidian dog I can find," said Yarik.

36

"Yarik, you're a diversion, not a sacrifice. You're not going there to die in a blaze of glory. There'll be other opportunities for that. Your job is to draw as many eyes away from our camp as possible to increase our chances of breaking through their lines. When you are no more than twenty leagues from here swing south-west and Sulat willing, we should rendezvous south-west of the Great Forest near the town of Vila..."

"Vilatica," Brak finished.

"Yes, there," said Teren.

"You know it's probably occupied don't you?" said Brak.

"Probably, but only by a small garrison and they won't be expecting us. Anyway, hopefully when we meet up outside the forest they'll see the size of our force and will let us pass. I won't fight them unless I have to. Now enough talk; get the men up and let's do this. Tell your men to swaddle the hooves of their horses, Yarik. Silence is imperative," said Teren.

Yarik nodded and after strapping on his own weapons, left the tent.

"Teren, I'm your friend and I'll follow you anywhere, but this is..."

"It's all we have, Brak. We're not strong enough to face the Narmidians in an open battle and even if we were I wouldn't trust your countrymen not to stab us in the back and attack our rear. No offence."

"None taken. Your fears are not without foundation. However, they're not all against us, Teren. Whilst I was outside earlier I overheard a couple of sentries talking. They said that Vork is coming at the head of an army. They seemed to think he was expected any day."

"I thought Vork died years ago?"

"So did many of us, but he yet draws breath. He would be a vital ally."

"That's assuming he sided with us and not your brother," said Teren.

"He was my father's best friend and will seek vengeance when he hears about his death, but he was already on his way here when my father was killed. That means that he's come to join the war."

"Or maybe just to bolster the garrison here," suggested Teren.

"Vork is no guard. Trust me if he's come across the Cold Sea and brought his Malerians with him, he's come to fight."

"Then that is good news indeed. Unfortunately it does not help us today. Now go and prepare the men. We leave as soon as I can get the blood circulating in these old legs again."

Brak nodded and left the tent and Teren watched him go. If Vork truly was coming then hope was renewed. Teren had never met the man, but the stories of his heroism and courage were legendary. He would be a worthy ally indeed. Before then Teren had an important job; he had to keep what remained of his army alive. They looked to him for leadership and hope. He prayed that he was worthy of such faith and loyalty.

Chapter 5

The initial part of the plan worked like a dream. Starting off a short while before the bulk of the army, Yarik and his small group of men had taken the slumbering Narmidian army completely by surprise and had ridden through their camp causing panic and havoc. Thinking they were under a major attack, troops from other parts of the Narmidian force which had encircled the Brelandic capital, had quickly moved to the east to aid their comrades, realising all too late that it was but a couple of hundred men wreaking havoc. Even then they did not realise what was truly happening. Having been tipped off by their informant in the city that Rad and the others had been ordered to leave, their initial thoughts were that Teren and the other leaders had tried to make an early break for it. Whilst the Narmidian king's ultimate goal was the total destruction of Rad's army, the thought of managing to capture Teren and the other ringleaders was a temptation too much. Every effort was therefore dedicated to the capture of the small band of horsemen who were now making a run for it towards the east.

It was only when a messenger arrived at his command tent and informed the king and his generals that a large force of soldiers had attacked the far western tip of his besieging force that Starik Vesla realised the true extent of the deception. Under the cover of darkness a large force of allies had penetrated his camp, butchering the sentries and anyone else who stirred before making a break for the south. Before leaving they had released and scattered the Narmidian horses, further adding to the mayhem. Then as the still dazed troops tried to round up their horses in order to mount a pursuit, a small force of allied cavalry had hit them in the flank, killing many and once again scattering the horses, before they too rode south providing a screen for their comrades on foot.

The plan was good, Vesla realised. No not good; brilliant and nothing less than what he had come to expect from Teren

Rad over the preceding weeks and months. The cleverness of his plan was only matched by the fury building up inside Vesla, a fury that demanded release. Without warning Vesla struck out as quick as a cobra, the small dagger in his hand slicing delicately across the unsuspecting messenger's throat leaving a gaping wound.

Vesla watched impassively as the blood spurted out of the man's throat and through the fingers of the hand he had clamped around his neck in a desperate attempt to stem the flow. When finally the man slumped forward onto the fur rugs laid at the foot of the makeshift throne, Vesla cast his gaze towards the cluster of generals and commanders gathered sheepishly to his right. He stared at them for long lingering seconds, taking pleasure in the obvious terror they were feeling. To their credit they all met his gaze, but he was not fooled and could see the fear in their eyes. None was certain of the king's favour and any could be the next to suffer his wrath. That was good. That stopped them from becoming complacent and from conspiring against him. If they couldn't trust one another for fear of being reported to the king, then his position was secure.

"General Kulash."

The general almost blanched with fear and Vesla fancied he could hear the sighs of relief from the other officers when their names weren't called out.

General Kulash clasped his trembling hands behind his back and stepped hesitantly forward. Behind Kulash a couple of Vesla's personal bodyguard stirred as if sensing that their skills were about to be called upon.

"My King."

"General, you promised me did you not, that this city of northern barbarians was tied up tighter than a hangman's noose?"

"Yes, my King," replied General Kulash, a rising tide of dread seeping into his guts as he sensed a trap being set for him.

Vesla nodded. "Instead it turns out to be as loose as a whore's skirts. Why is that, Kulash?"

"My King, when news of the allied horsemen attacking our

eastern flank reached their ears, many of our men rushed east to aid their comrades."

"I know what happened, Kulash, I want to know why. Did you give the order, General?"

"No, my King."

"So your men disobeyed you?" asked Vesla with a malevolent glint in his eye.

A trickle of perspiration began to meander down Kulash's face and he licked his lips nervously. He knew that he was being trapped and knew what the punishment would be if the trap was sprung.

"In the heat of the moment they…"

"Yes or no, Kulash; did they disobey you?" roared Vesla.

"Yes, my King."

"There, that wasn't so hard was it, Kulash?" The king's face and tone had immediately warmed and for a brief moment of joy, Kulash began to believe that he was going to survive the king's wrath. He would probably be demoted, but he would live. He was still revelling in that possibility when the sword point emerged from his abdomen before disappearing back where it had come from. Kulash slowly looked down at the ever widening patch of red on his white tunic before glancing up to face his king one last time. Then he collapsed onto the fur rugs close to the still bleeding body of the messenger. Behind him the bodyguard sheathed his sword and stepped back a couple of paces.

"Let that be a warning to all of you. A general who cannot control his men even in a time of panic, is of no use to me. Those who are of no use to me don't get to breathe the same air. General Zibla."

"My King," said a tall confident warrior with a long jagged scar running the length of his left cheek.

"Find out what is happening and report back to me as soon as you can. We have lost enough time already and I don't want to let this ragtag army elude me again," commanded Vesla.

"Are we to pursue both parties, my King?"

"The attack to the east was just a diversion. I doubt that more than one of their leaders rides with them; perhaps the northerner or the Delarite and so they are of little worth. Send

41

a couple of hundred of your Wotogi riders after them. The real prize Rad is with the bulk of their army heading south. We shall pursue them."

"And what of the northerners in the city, my King?"

Vesla stroked his trimmed beard as he contemplated his general's question. "I don't think they will venture out; they don't have the stomach for a fight, that's why they evicted Rad and his scum in an attempt to appease us. Still, it suits me to keep them penned up until I am ready to deal with them. Leave five thousand warriors here under Commander Agrran. The rest will accompany us in the pursuit of Rad and his mongrels."

"As you command, my King," said Zibla, before slowly backing away and departing to carry out the king's orders.

"General Rhot."

"My King."

"Get the army ready to move out as soon as General Zibla has reported back to me," said Vesla.

"Immediately, my King."

"Oh and, Rhot." The general turned back to face his king. "Have someone clean this filth up," said Vesla waving his hand nonchalantly in the direction of the two dead bodies lying in front of him.

"At once," replied Rhot.

A movement out of the corner of his eye drew Vesla's attention and he looked up in time to see his queen walking towards him, two hand maidens in close attendance.

"Ah, Surita, my dear. You finally have your wish, we are leaving this place."

"Really? Are we returning to Narmidia?" asked Surita her tone full of hope.

"Narmidia? No. I still have much to accomplish here in Arkadia. Once the conquest is over there will be plenty of time to return to Narmidia."

"But I tire of these endless camps and long for a proper bed and familiar surroundings," said Surita taking a seat next to her husband and glancing at the two dead bodies in disgust.

"If you are not comfortable you must impress on those around you the need to please you. You are Queen of Narmidia and deserve the best," said Vesla.

42

"You are too kind, husband, but I will endure as you endure. So tell me, where are we heading now?"

"The allies have been forced to leave the city of the northerners. Rad and his mongrels have fled south. We are to pursue them and run them down."

Vesla watched her face for any sign of reaction. Eight years earlier she had been captured by slavers in Remada and brought to the east. Vesla's overseer had bought her as a slave but it had not taken long for her to come to Vesla's attention and he was soon beguiled by her beauty and fiery hair. He had married her shortly after, a wife among many but even then she had not been satisfied. Slowly but surely she had schemed and manipulated her way up the pecking order until eventually by the time that Queen Faris had died in mysterious circumstances, she was the king's favourite. After a brief period of mourning that decency had demanded, he had made her his new queen. But before all that, before she was captured, she had been another man's wife. And not just any man's. Teren Rad had been her husband. It was said that he had searched for Valla, her Remadan name, for many years in the east. Some said that he searched still. Despite her overt affection towards Vesla, he did not know for certain whether or not she still harboured feelings for her former husband, which is why he had ensured that one of her hand maidens was also a skilled assassin. One sign of betrayal by her and Surita's life would be forfeit despite his genuine affection for her.

Vesla had shown her nothing but kindness and generosity since he met her and though he would not admit it to anyone else, his feelings for her were strong, much more so than any of his other seven wives. Or was it eight? He could no longer remember. Whether that kindness and generosity would be enough to keep her by his side if Rad ever got close to her he did not know.

Rad's and Surita's paths had crossed briefly when Vesla had sent his queen to a meeting of Salandori chieftains to try and secure their allegiance whilst he invaded the west. At that time Rad had been a prisoner of the Salandori having been captured whilst he was in the east searching for his wife. Like many of his fellow captives Rad had been forced to fight in an arena for the Salandoris' pleasure, but he had orchestrated a rebellion and had slaughtered all of their Salandori captors. Surita had managed to escape but whether she saw Rad and turned her back on him or had not realised that he was among the slaves and missed out on the chance to be reunited, Vesla did not know. Her behaviour when she returned had been strange and distant, though she had insisted that nothing was amiss. However, her demeanour was enough for Vesla to no longer fully trust her and it had been then that he had infiltrated one of his female assassins into her retinue of maidens.

"You're sure that Teren is among them?" asked Surita disturbing his train of thought.

"I am sure. Does that bother you, my dear?" asked Vesla.

"No, of course not. Once upon a time it would have, but not now. Now I am Queen of the Narmidians and belong to the king." The split-second's hesitation before replying did nothing to ease his fears and suspicions.

"Good. You will have a front row seat when we eventually catch up with that Remadan dog and put him to death. I may even let you choose the manner of his passing."

"You are too kind, husband."

"So I am told."

"When do we leave to give chase?" asked Surita.

"Soon. My generals are at this moment reorganising my forces so that we can both besiege this city and pursue Rad." Vesla noted the look of hope that flashed across her face as she realised the delay might give Rad enough time to put some distance between the two armies. "But don't worry yourself, my dear. The bulk of Rad's men are on foot whilst we will pursue on horseback; they won't get very far. In fact it might please me to let them think they've escaped my clutches and then spring a trap on them. Witnessing the look on Rad's face when the net finally closes in on him extinguishing any last hope he might have had, would bring me a great deal of pleasure." He smiled inwardly at the look of despair that she struggled to hide. "Now, if you'll excuse me, my dear, I have much to prepare," and without another word he strode out of the tent flanked by two of his royal bodyguards.

Chapter 6

The blade swished harmlessly over his head and Teren immediately stepped forward and plunged his own blade into the exposed midriff of his attacker. Without bothering to check that the man was no longer a threat, he quickly withdrew his sword before sweeping it in a powerful arc to his right where the blade chopped into the right leg of a young warrior, severing it just below the knee. Then his sword was up in a flash blocking the downward chop of a wild-eyed warrior with dark skin, before kicking the man's knee and causing him to stumble. Teren's blade immediately chopped down into the man's neck partly severing his head.

Teren pushed on and found himself confronted by two warriors, both armed with curved swords. They eyed him warily, perhaps having just witnessed the easy way in which he had just despatched three of their comrades and didn't want to go the same way. For his part, Teren was glad for the brief respite. He was caught in the blood haze, the fog of war, that wonderful feeling that a warrior feels when he is lost in the maelstrom of battle. But every man has his limits and Teren was fast reaching his.

"Either of you ladies going to attack or are we just going to dance all night?" growled Teren.

Both men began to cautiously move towards him but right in front of his eyes, the man to Teren's left suddenly grunted and stumbled backwards a couple of paces, his hands feebly clawing at a spear shaft embedded in his stomach. It had taken Teren as much by surprise as it had the dead man's comrade, but Teren was the first to react and had thrust his sword point into the man's throat before he realised what had happened.

A grinning Datian warrior came up alongside Teren and retrieved his spear. "That was a nice throw, my friend," said Teren.

"Not really," replied the powerfully built man, "I was aiming for his companion."

Teren stared at the man unsure whether to be grateful or worried. By the time he had decided it was a little of both the man had already moved on.

"We're almost through, Teren," said a familiar voice nearby.

Teren turned to see Brak, covered in blood, none of which appeared to be his, standing to his right.

"Good. Keep them moving, Brak. If we stop, we're dead. It won't be long before Vesla realises what's going on and organises a proper pursuit. He suddenly barged Brak out of the way and parried a series of quick but predictable sword thrusts from a young and inexperienced warrior, before launching his own attack which resulted in Teren opening the man's throat.

"Thanks," said Brak grinning.

"Don't worry, Prince, I'm keeping count," replied Teren who was also grinning. "Now get them moving."

Brak nodded and after briefly stopping to thrust his sword into the back of one of two Narmidians who were fighting a Cardellan, he moved forward shouting for the others to follow.

The sound of a horse reining in to his left startled Teren and he whirled round with his sword raised above his head ready to strike, but lowered it again when he recognised Sergeant Nim, the Delarite he had put in charge of the few mounted men they possessed.

"You need to hurry them along, Teren; my men can't hold them forever."

"I know, Nim, but it's not as if they're just letting us walk through," replied Teren caustically. "How many of your men are left?"

Nim rose in his stirrups for a quick glance around but everywhere was chaos and his best guess was going to have to suffice.

"Maybe half, maybe more. We're riding around like banshees trying to confuse them, but soon they're going to realise just how few of us there are and then we'll be in trouble. You need to disengage the men and get away whilst there are still enough of my men to screen you."

Teren nodded his understanding. "Give us as long as you can and then save yourselves. I'll lead the men to the forest and then towards the foot of that mountain behind. Join us there."

Nim nodded and then suddenly nudged his horse forward barging past Teren and into two Narmidians who had been running up behind the Remadan. Nim's horse knocked one of the attackers to the ground but only sent the second one stumbling. Nim quickly hacked into the second man's shoulder sending up a spray of blood before reversing his sword and removing the head of the other Narmidian who had just about struggled to his feet again.

"Thanks," said Teren with genuine admiration of the man's skill. He hoped the fact that he was actually shaking like a leaf in a gale didn't show.

"Thank me by getting away from here now whilst some of us still sit atop our mounts," and with that Nim rode away immersing himself once again in the fight.

"Make for the trees. Make for the trees." Despite the roar of battle, Teren's voice carried across much of the battlefield where it was soon taken up by other officers.

Slowly, fight by fight, Teren's men began to disengage from the fighting and head for the forest. Some disengaged too soon or merely stopped fighting and turned to run and these were soon cut down by grateful Narmidians. Most, however, finished their own personal duel and then cautiously began to back away towards the trees and only when they were sure nobody was coming after them did they allow themselves the luxury of turning and running.

Teren was one of the last foot soldiers to leave the field. For him it was a matter of duty as well as honour and only when everybody who could be saved was on the move did he allow himself to back away. Still there were men he had to leave behind. As well as the badly wounded there were those who were ensconced in fights they weren't going to win, perhaps because they were outnumbered or cornered. Teren's pride screamed at him that he should go to their aid, but his head told him that would serve no purpose other than to end his own life.

Footsteps from behind made Teren turn and as he did so Brak came up alongside him. As if understanding the conflict in his friend's mind, Brak had come to escort Teren from the battlefield before he did something that they'd all regret.

"Come, Teren, we must go."

"But there's still some lads out there," complained Teren as Brak began to drag his friend away from the fighting.

"Yes and they are lost to us. If we had the men we could go to their aid, but we don't. All we can do is make sure that their sacrifice is not in vain by saving ourselves. Don't let their deaths count for nothing," urged Brak.

Teren's grip on his sword tightened as forty or so paces away from him he watched as one of his men was hacked mercilessly to the ground by four enemy soldiers. Even when he was down they continued to hack and chop at his flesh. Teren's blood burned like fire and the demanding cry of revenge reverberated in his ears.

Brak felt his friend's arm tense and tightened his own grip.

"It is too late, my friend. We will avenge them; just not today."

The small group of Narmidians had finally bored of hacking at the fallen soldier and now began to glance round, one or two of their gazes finally falling on Teren and Brak. One member of the group said something to his comrades and took a step towards Teren and Brak, but none of his comrades followed. The bolder of the Narmidians turned to look at his friends in disgust but evidently they didn't fancy taking on the big Remadan and his blood spattered friend, not when there were easier pickings lying on the battlefield. As his comrades turned and walked away, the leader of the group turned back to face Teren and Brak. He waved his sword in the air and started to shout something at them. He was only halfway through whatever threat or curse he was hurling in their direction when Nim galloped past him and removed his head.

Teren watched in satisfaction as the man's body remained upright for a few seconds and then toppled onto the dirt in front of him.

"Now can we go?" asked Brak.

"Aye, now we can go," replied Teren nodding at Nim as he raced past him, before turning and running towards the woods and safety.

Behind him he could hear the screams and the crying of the wounded as the Narmidians wandered around the battlefield looting and finishing off any survivors. Teren felt sick to the pit of his stomach. He hated leaving men behind especially those who were still standing and in the fight. Sometimes you had to leave the mortally wounded behind, but it was often a kindness to give them a quick and painless death, the last thing they saw being the face of a friend. He was still contemplating that when the cool air of the woods hit his face as they burst through the tree line.

Teren turned in time to see Nim and the other horsemen bear left rather than enter the trees. Teren had hoped that the woods would be sparse enough to allow Nim and his handful of men to enter with their horses, but too dense for the masses of Narmidians to follow. However, Nim had obviously decided that the trees were too thick and was now riding west to try and circumnavigate the woods and find another way to the mountain.

Teren watched as the Delarite led his men west and was shocked by how few of them remained. They had paid a high blood price indeed to allow Teren and the others to escape. The Delarite had acquitted himself well, as they all had and Teren would be sure to tell Yarik when he saw him.

Yarik!

Teren's thoughts turned to the big Delarite and wondered how he and his small band of riders were doing. Neither man had said as much but both knew that what Yarik was to attempt was virtually a suicide mission. Two hundred riders storming the strongest part of the Narmidian camp just before dawn, their aim purely to cause as much mayhem as possible before riding off and distracting the bulk of the enemy forces, couldn't be described as anything other than a suicide mission.

Despite the fact that Yarik's men would have had surprise on their side, they would have been outnumbered perhaps twenty-fold and however much confusion they managed to sow, it would not be enough. Timing would be everything. Stay too long and they would be swamped. Ride away too early and they may not have caused enough confusion and a pursuit could be organised quick enough to ride them down.

Despite his loathing of horse riding, Teren had wanted to be the one to lead the diversionary raid, but Brak, Yarik and some of the other leaders wouldn't hear of it; he was too vital to the resistance to risk losing. Teren had felt the same way about Yarik, knowing that if Yarik were to fall, he couldn't necessarily count on the continued support of the Delarites who made up a large proportion of the allied forces. Yarik, however, had insisted and eventually through fair means or threats, the others had come around to his way of thinking. Yarik was no fool. He knew that if he managed to succeed in his mission his standing amongst the men would only rise.

Ever the glory hunter, thought Teren smiling.

"Teren! Teren!"

"Uhm, what is it?" asked Teren suddenly feeling embarrassed. He had no idea how long Brak had been trying to draw his attention but evidently it had been some time judging by the confused and frustrated look upon the northerner's face.

"You all right?" asked Brak.

"Yes, I'm fine. I was just thinking about Yarik and wondering how he and his men were doing."

"Their fate is in the lap of the gods for now, but ours is not. We need to keep moving, Teren."

"Very well. Start to lead them to the foothills of the mountain," said Teren.

"Why me? What are you doing?" asked Brak confused.

"I shall remain here a while longer to make sure these Narmidian dogs don't follow."

Brak looked suspiciously at his friend. "Promise me you're not planning on doing anything stupid."

Teren laughed. "When have you ever known me do anything like that?" Brak just stared at his friend and widened his eyes. "Fair enough. I swear I will just tarry here a little longer and will follow once I'm satisfied none follow. Happy?"

"Happiness is an emotion that has forsaken these lands, but I am satisfied for now. Do not wait too long before you follow as this forest is easy to get lost in," said Brak.

"If I can't follow the trail of a couple of thousand men stomping their way through the undergrowth, I'm not fit to lead anyway and you'd be better off without me, but thank you for your concern. I will be right behind you. Now move them out."

Apparently satisfied with Teren's assurance, Brak nodded and turned. He gave a hand signal to the men around him and then slowly started to head through the trees towards the foot slopes of Mount Galok.

Teren watched them go for a few moments and then turned his attention back to the Narmidians in the distance. There was no sign of them mounting a pursuit and in all honesty Teren had not expected them to do so, at least not straight away. In fact he had just wanted a few moments alone. The men all looked to him for leadership but Teren was feeling more tired by the day, the burden of leadership weighing heavy on his old shoulders. He longed for the war to end and for the chance to go back to his cabin in the Lonely Mountains, but those days had gone he knew. The war had changed so many things. His wife who he had not spoken to for nine years was married to Starik Vesla the King of Narmidia and may no longer want to be rescued. His eldest daughter who had been captured by slavers was now living in a forest to the east with a band of outcasts, though she was happy and appeared to be in love with their leader, a young man called Col. Teren's youngest daughter was back in his home village of Lentor the last he heard and his son with whom he was just beginning to rebuild a relationship after so many years of estrangement, could be anywhere. He hadn't seen him for many months since their adventures in the east and the last thing he had told his son was to head west to safety. That sentiment no longer applied.

Teren suddenly felt very alone. He had friends he knew that. Brak was a good friend, a bond forged in the flames of slavery under the Salandori, as was the Delarite, Yarik, though publicly neither man would admit to it. Still he felt alone.

He gave one last glance in the direction of the Narmidians who still seemed to be looting the dead, then turned to follow Brak and the others and as he did so his mind turned to his other friends, Ro Aryk, former Captain of the Remadan Royal Bodyguard and Arlen Meric, the warrior monk from the small northern land of Silevia. He hoped they were faring better than he was.

Chapter 7

There it was again; the snap of a dry twig. There was no doubt in Eryn Rad's mind that he was being followed, in fact he had been sure of it for some time now. His friend Ro Aryk had taught him to track and how to know when you yourself were being tracked. What Eryn didn't know was who and how many were stalking him. If their intentions were friendly then they would surely have revealed themselves by now.

He nonchalantly loosened the sword in his scabbard and glanced around for somewhere to make his stand.

Another crunching sound this time off to his left, so unless his stalker was very fleet of foot, there were at least two of them. Eryn slowly began to ease his sword out of its scabbard desperately trying to control the tide of panic that was threatening to engulf him. He was good with a sword, his father, Ro and Arlen Meric had made sure of that, but was he good enough to face several men at once?

Above the sound of the blood pounding in his ears he almost missed it, but there it was, the sound of someone running up behind him, their steps careful and light but still audible to the trained ear. In one fluid movement Eryn released his sword and spun round, his left leg planted forward and his sword poised above his right shoulder.

The Narmidian was almost upon him and Eryn only just managed to bring his sword down in time to block the other man's downward slice. A fraction of a moment longer and he would have been dead. Two more swift strokes from his assailant were blocked before Eryn managed to get a strike in of his own which the other man easily parried before taking a step back.

The sound of more footsteps distracted Eryn and he risked a quick glance to his left where he saw another two men approaching with their swords drawn. Panic gave way to fear and started to overwhelm him. After everything he had gone through: the siege of Vangor and countless other battles was his life to end here in some unnamed forest in Breland?

Eryn leapt back a couple of paces just as another man who he had not seen coming at him from his right, sent his sword slicing through the air where Eryn had been just moments earlier.

Eryn considered running but doubted he'd get very far. He was younger than all of them but for all he knew they might have bows or worse still there might be more of them in front of him. Besides, how could he ever face his father again, the great Teren Rad if he had to tell him he ran away from a fight? With a roar of anger, Eryn hurled himself forward swinging his sword this way and that. It was not a disciplined attack and his father would be appalled, but Eryn didn't care. At that moment in time he was petrified and all reason had fled from his mind. All he could think about was escaping and if that meant throwing his sword around like a madman in an attempt to panic his attackers and weaken their resolve, so be it.

For a few glorious moments of hope Eryn thought that his plan was working as all four of his attackers were driven back by the ferocity and unpredictability of his attack, one of them even momentarily stumbling to the ground. After a few moments though they began to regain the upper hand taking it in turns to assault the young Remadan, while the effort of fighting off four opponents was clearly beginning to take a toll on Eryn. Unable to maintain a strong defensive posture and too tired to keep his sword working as feverishly as it had been, bit by bit Eryn was driven back.

First a sword tip grazed his face cutting him a thumb's width beneath his right eye and then another one sliced his left arm. Still Eryn fought bravely on, for there was no choice other than to submit to what he imagined would be a slow and painful death. Better to go out fighting and hopefully receive a quick killing blow. Mustering all his remaining strength, Eryn launched himself forward again in one last desperate assault, gambling everything. His attack caught them momentarily off guard and Eryn finally managed to wound one of his attacker's in the side before sweeping his sword in a low reverse arc where its blade eventually sunk into the soft unprotected flesh of another man's thigh. The warrior howled with pain and backed away from the fight but all that seemed to do was infuriate the remaining two Narmidians who launched their own furious attack. Eryn was totally spent and after weakly blocking and parrying three or four sword blows, his weapon was knocked from his grasp and he was sent tumbling to the ground. They were on him in a flash, one pinning him to the ground with a boot on his chest and a sword point at his throat, whilst the other stood next to him holding his sword with both hands ready to plunge down into Eryn's stomach.

Eryn closed his eyes and awaited death. He had put up a good fight, one his father would hopefully have been proud of, but ultimately it was futile. He tensed awaiting the killing blow. Images of his father, Lily, the girl he loved and of his sisters, flashed through his mind. He would see them again, but not on this world.

Somewhere close by somebody shouted one word in Narmidian and it was spoken as a command not a suggestion, though Eryn had no idea what it meant.

Eryn opened his eyes. The sword was still arrowed at his stomach and the eyes of the man holding it were wide and wild. The sword point was shaking as if the man was fighting desperately to control his rage and obey the order that somebody had issued.

Moments later there were more Narmidian words, spoken harshly and with authority. Somebody was definitely giving orders.

Eryn felt the other Narmidian take his foot off his chest and step back but the Narmidian holding the sword was obviously struggling to overcome the powerful urge to skewer Eryn on the end of his sword.

Eryn glanced to his right and watched as a Narmidian in a different coloured uniform to the other two, slid effortlessly from his horse before striding purposefully over to where Eryn lay. The two wounded Narmidians and the man who had previously had his foot on Eryn's chest, all bowed, but the fourth man holding the sword poised above Eryn, seemed oblivious to the man's presence.

A smart slap to his face from the back of the newcomer's

hand soon drew his attention. The man with the sword stumbled backwards a look of rage crossing his face and for the briefest of moments it looked like he was going to throw himself at the other man. Common sense then seemed to prevail and he too bowed. The newcomer, who Eryn assumed was an officer of high standing, stared at the other man for a while, perhaps deciding whether to further punish him. Then after a few moments he turned his attention to the prone body of Eryn.

Further orders were issued and then he swiftly mounted his horse before turning and resuming his journey. A small force of cavalry had also arrived in the clearing and as he was roughly hauled to his feet, Eryn could see there was also a large body of infantry waiting behind them. It seemed the whole Narmidian army had been close on his tail for some time.

The warrior who had initially attacked Eryn bound Eryn's hands with some rope tossed to him by one of the mounted men. Another rope was then tied around Eryn's neck before they all set off after the officer.

With the dense canopy of trees overhead it was difficult for Eryn to tell, but it felt like they had been walking for most of the day before the order finally came down the line to halt and rest. Before he could lower himself to the ground, a Narmidian soldier came up behind Eryn and kicked him viciously behind his left knee sending him sprawling to the ground much to the amusement of the watching soldiers.

Eryn struggled into a sitting position and glanced around him. His situation did not look good. He was surrounded by hundreds of enemy soldiers and had no idea where he was. Ever since deserting from the army to go looking for his father he had been heading northwest following what he hoped were his father's tracks and those of the men with him.

Eryn and his Remadan relief column had arrived too late to take part in the great battle to the east and all they had found was a field of death; thousands upon thousands of bodies. From a distance it had looked like the sky above the battlefield was heavy and dark, but to their horror it had turned out to be clouds of crows circling over a banquet of flesh.

The battlefield had been knee deep in dead from both armies and it had been clear that no side had won an outright victory. Eryn and his friends had found a mortally wounded man who had told Eryn that he believed his father and a handful of other men had managed to escape the battlefield and had headed northwest, though he couldn't be certain. When a search of the area in which his father and his friends had fought revealed no body, Eryn had taken heart that his father had indeed survived the carnage and had resolved to follow him. After confiding in his closest friends Eryn had reluctantly stolen away during the night, deserting his post. He wasn't proud of being a deserter and one day there might be a price to pay for his actions, but at that moment in time all he could think of doing was finding his father, a father whom he had lost for years and had only just begun to reconnect with.

No, he had many regrets, but deserting wasn't one of them.

Eryn suddenly became aware that someone was standing in front of him and he looked up to see a young Narmidian warrior of roughly the same age as himself. After staring at Eryn for a few moments he knelt down and placed a water flagon at Eryn's lips and Eryn gratefully tipped his head backwards to allow some of the lukewarm liquid to seep into his parched throat.

There was a guttural shout from his right, a flash of movement and suddenly Eryn felt the flagon knocked away from his mouth. The young warrior who had been holding it had been sent sprawling to the ground. Standing over them both was the warrior who had been poised to kill Eryn earlier in the day. He spat on Eryn and then shouted at the young warrior lying on the ground, though Eryn had no idea what he said. However, it was obvious that the older warrior was not happy at the kindness being visited upon him by the younger warrior.

For a moment or two it looked like the young warrior was preparing to launch himself at the other man as his hand sidled towards his dagger, but then he appeared to have second thoughts and averted his eyes. The older warrior laughed and said something to a group of his friends sitting nearby and they all laughed as well. There was discord among his captors Eryn noted and he began to consider ways in which he might exploit that to his advantage.

The older warrior turned his attention back to Eryn and slowly ran his finger across his throat in a clear demonstration of what he thought was going to happen to Eryn.

"You better hope that I don't ever get free of these bonds, Narmidian pig, or you'll be the first I kill," said Eryn with more confidence than he actually felt, but smiling at the same time.

Eryn wasn't sure whether the man understood his words but clearly he understood there was either a threat or a challenge and instantly responded with a tirade of his own insults before swinging a kick at Eryn's right leg.

"That all you got, you whoreson? Our women kick harder than you," said Eryn grinning. He had no idea whether this course of action was wise or not, but he clearly had the man rattled and he would take a win wherever he could get one.

The Narmidian kicked Eryn again and then went to strike him, but a shouted command stopped him in his tracks. Eryn looked up at his aggressor and sneered. He could see the rage in the man's eyes, the bloodlust and could see the battle going on inside him to control the fury and that just made Eryn grin even more.

Before he could goad the man further, however, the officer from earlier strode over and said something to the other man and he nodded and walked quietly back to his friends.

Eryn looked up and was immediately slapped across the face by the officer, drawing a trickle of blood from the corner of Eryn's mouth.

"I don't know what you hope to achieve, Remadan, by baiting my men, but it will not work. Your fate is certain; only the manner of your passing is yet to be decided," said the Narmidian officer in surprisingly good Common tongue.

"Nothing is written in stone, Narmidian," replied Eryn as he tried to wipe the corner of his mouth on his shoulder.

"That's good, Remadan, you keep that hope. You'll need it in the coming days. Nobody likes a deserter."

"I'm not a deserter," snapped Eryn.

"Really? You may not be wearing a uniform but you're a soldier, or at least you were until you deserted. Where's your unit? What Ligara are you from?"

"I got separated from my unit after the battle in the east. I was looking for them when your men stumbled across me. My uniform was soaked in Narmidian blood so I stole a change of clothes," lied Eryn.

"Do you know what we do with deserters in our army?" asked the officer.

"I told you I'm not a deserter," said Eryn.

"We put out their eyes and stake them upside down near an ants' nest. It makes for a very entertaining death."

"I would expect nothing more from filthy barbarians."

"Really! And how does the Remadan army deal with deserters? By hanging?" Eryn never replied. "Yes, I am sure it is by hanging. Perhaps when we are finished with you we will hand what's left of you over to your army and let them make you dance at the end of a rope. Ah, but I can't can I? There's no Remadan army left is there?" He laughed to himself and a few of the others sitting around nearby who also spoke the Common tongue, joined in.

"Remada will never be yours not whilst a single Remadan soldier draws breath," said Eryn.

"That is good, because soon there won't be any left drawing breath; they'll all be food for the carrion."

"From what I saw at the battlefield to the east there were just as many dead Narmidians as our side, maybe more."

"Perhaps, but we have an unlimited supply of soldiers from dozens of nations to the east just waiting to join the fight, whereas what remains of your pathetic army is holed up hiding behind the skirts of the northerners."

That was news to Eryn. If what this officer had inadvertently let slip was true, what remained of the fighting forces of the free nations of Arkadia was gathering in Breland on the northwest coast of Arkadia. If his father, Brak and the others had indeed survived, that is where they would have headed. He'd been close when he got captured, a day or two away from being reunited with his father and that just added to Eryn's feeling of bitterness.

"So is that where you are going now, to have your little army smashed by the northerners?" asked Eryn.

"We march to finish the war. Once Rad and his mongrels have been defeated, virtually the whole of Arkadia will be under our control and Remada, Delarite, Datia and all the others will be systematically wiped from the history records. These lands will again revert to the ancestral homelands they once were."

Eryn hoped that his face did not betray his feelings when his father's name had been mentioned. Whilst he had no doubt that they planned an unpleasant death for him he knew that if they were to learn that he was the son of their mortal enemy, the man who had denied them countless victories and sent so many of their warriors to the afterlife, his end would be that much more painful. Worse still, he feared that they might use him as a bargaining chip against his father.

At least he now knew that the Narmidians thought his father lived and was in Breland. He decided to test his theory and started to laugh.

A look of curiosity and then annoyance crossed the Narmidian officer's face.

"Why do you laugh, Remadan? Are you in that much of a hurry to join your countrymen in the afterlife?"

"I'm laughing because you're all so scared of Teren Rad. Even in death you fear he has risen up and leads the resistance still."

"Rad still draws breath," said the Narmidian.

"No he doesn't. I saw him fall during the battle in the east."

"Then you are a liar and a deserter. We checked the battlefield thoroughly for his carcass and then questioned several of your men. Those that claimed to have seen him during the battle all claim that he ran from the field of battle like a whipped dog, with his tail between his legs. He did not even have the courage or honour to die with his men. Still, we will root him out in Breland and then give him a coward's death."

Eryn's lower lip was trembling with rage and he found himself instinctively struggling with his bonds. He wanted nothing more in that moment than to get free and ram the

Narmidian's words forcefully back down his throat at the tip of a sword. His bonds were secure though; vengeance would have to wait. Still, at least he now knew for certain that his father had escaped the carnage in the east. Whether he was among those who had made it to Breland was another matter.

"So where are you taking me?" asked Eryn.

"For now you will travel with us deeper into Breland. How long you live depends on the level of cooperation you give us. You tell me things I need to hear and you get to live a while longer. If I decide that you have nothing of value to tell me or are lying, your end will be brutal and certain. Think on it," and with that he walked away saying something to the man who had been kicking Eryn as he passed him by. The man nodded at his officer and then glared with a look of pure hatred in Eryn's direction. Eryn blew him a kiss and laughed before closing his eyes and laying back to rest.

Chapter 8

The leaden sky was heavy with dark swollen clouds that threatened to turn the steady drizzle which had been falling for nearly an hour now, into something much worse. Ro Aryk pulled the hood of his cape over his head and peered over the battlements of the old tower. In the cobbled courtyard below, the latest batch of recruits to the New Order of Goresh, were being put through their paces by men hand chosen by Arlen Meric. Today it was sword practise.

In the months since they had arrived in Silevia and defeated Arlen's brother and the old Order, the two of them had brought about great changes in the day to day lives of ordinary Silevians, some of which were not welcomed by the people. Winning their trust was going to be a long hard road after decades of abuse by the old Order and their brutal enforcers, the Kaladri, but slowly Arlen was winning them over.

Schools were being built and children were returning to lessons for the first time in years. Land was being returned to its rightful owners and peace and order were being restored. The men training below would be the next generation of enforcers, though these would be fair and just unlike their predecessors. More importantly perhaps, these men were volunteers. Children would no longer be abducted and forced to join the Order. People were smiling again.

All of this was good news, Ro knew, yet still he felt unsettled. Something was gnawing away at the pit of his stomach; a feeling that something wasn't right. He had spent many hours over the last few weeks trying to work out what it was that vexed him so, but it always came down to the same thing: Arlen. His friend had changed. Nobody had crowned him king or elected him head of the Order, but everyone treated him as such. Worse still, Arlen was behaving as if he was the leader and he was enjoying it.

Ro had raised the matter with his friend on a couple of

occasions, but Arlen had merely waved his protests away. He was just filling in until his country and people got back on their feet, he would say. Then he'd hand power over to a Council. But every time a new target was achieved he would find some excuse not to relinquish power and would postpone the handover to some arbitrary date in the future.

It wasn't that Ro thought that his friend would make a bad leader, far from it in fact and Sulat only knew the man deserved some sort of recognition for what he had done for his country, for what he had lost, but it just didn't feel right.

"So what do you think of our latest recruits?" said the familiar voice behind him making Ro jump.

"They're raw but keen; they'll get there in the end," said Ro smiling when he turned to face Arlen.

"More and more turn up at the gates every day asking to join; we've no choice now but to be selective and turn some away."

"I didn't realise that you were still recruiting. Surely you've got enough to fill the ranks of the enforcers now?" asked Ro.

"We have, but now we're recruiting for the army," said Arlen proudly.

"The army? When did you decide that you were going to set up an army?"

"A couple of weeks ago I guess."

"You never mentioned it to me," said Ro suspiciously.

"Why would I? A king doesn't debate his plans with subordinates," replied Arlen bitterly.

"A king! Is that what you are now, Arlen? Do the people know or is this something you just woke up and decided one morning?"

"No, I'm not a king; it was a poor choice of words though there are those who have begun to suggest it."

"Yes, I have seen some of the sycophants who now surround you," said Ro unable to disguise the disgust in his voice.

"Well maybe they're right; maybe Silevia would benefit from strong leadership."

"It could get that through a Council of Elders or elected

representatives. I thought that was your dream for a new Silevia."

"Dreams rarely come true. Sometimes you have to compromise," replied Arlen.

An uneasy silence hung between them as both men leant over the battlements and watched the men below them training.

"So why are you building an army, Arlen? I thought that Silevia historically relied on its people to act as a militia?"

"That's true, but things change. I want Silevia to be strong and it can only be that if it has a strong right arm."

"And what will you use this strong right arm for?"

"For defence," replied Arlen earnestly. "If the Narmidians come calling here we want to be able to defend ourselves not have to roll over and lie at our new master's feet, as others have done."

Ro's thoughts turned to the war, hundreds of leagues to the south and west. News of the war had been hard to come by since they had entered Silevia although the odd trader and merchant would stop by from time to time with snippets of information. How reliable this information was and how exaggerated, he didn't know, but the consensus of opinion seemed to be that most of Arkadia was now in the grip of Vesla's Narmidians and what remained of the allied forces had retreated to the northwest, possibly Breland, one of the few nations so far left untouched by the war.

A couple of the travellers had talked of a great battle in Cardella that had left thousands dead on both sides. They said that had broken the back of the allied armies and only a few stragglers had got away and they had fled to the northwest pursued by Vesla's army. None seemed to give liberation much of a chance.

Ro wondered what had happened to his friends Teren Rad, Brak and Yarik of Delarite. They would have been at the battle in Cardella for certain, probably right at the forefront if Ro knew Teren. But had they survived it and where were they now? These thoughts did nothing but unsettle Ro further.

"You're thinking of the others aren't you?" said Arlen interrupting his friend's train of thought.

"Was it that obvious?"

"You always take on a worried look when you think of them."

"Is it any wonder? Wherever Teren goes, trouble follows," smiled Ro enjoying the easing in the tension between the two friends.

"They're big enough and ugly enough to look after themselves, Ro."

"I know, but I just feel as if I...we should be there fighting at their side."

"And we would, if we didn't have a massive job here."

"The old Order has gone, Arlen, the country's getting back on its feet and you've got some good men working for you. Why not leave them to finish what you've started and ride west with me tomorrow to find Teren and the others?" pleaded Ro.

"It sounds tempting, Ro, but you know I can't. My people need me. What I've started here is a long term job. If I left now I would risk losing everything I've worked for. What sort of message would that send out to my people?"

Ro turned away from his friend and glanced back down at where the men had been training with swords. Most were sat down in the shade now taking a drink, whilst others continued to move around trying to keep their muscles supple.

"I know," replied Ro, "but I had to ask."

"I'm glad you understand, my friend," replied Arlen clapping Ro on the shoulder.

"But soon, Arlen I must go, with or without you. This is your country. Mine lies to the south, overrun by Narmidians. Soon I must re-join the struggle to free her."

"Well, let's cross that bridge when we get to it shall we? In the meantime I must go; court is in session this afternoon and I have to sit in judgement on a number of disputes."

"You're a judge now?" asked Ro incredulously.

"Of course. Who else can do it?"

"Well who used to do it?"

"My brother and other members of the Order, but they're gone now of course, so it falls to me. Now if you'll excuse me," and with that Arlen turned and made his way down the stone steps towards the courtyard in which a vicious battle had been fought to overthrow the old Order just a few short months earlier.

***

Ro had remained on the battlements for a little while longer casually watching the men below going through sword practise, before curiosity got the better of him and he headed downstairs into the old conference chamber of the Order. The room was crowded with an orderly queue of people strung out along the middle of the hall and crowds of onlookers huddled together on either side. Sat up front on an ornately carved wooden chair, was Arlen. Whilst the chair couldn't be called a throne as such, the symbolism wasn't lost on Ro. Several of Arlen's new Order guards, smartly dressed in their black tunics and breeches and armed with a sword and a pike, stood either side of Arlen and at regular points along both sides of the hall. Two more stood guard just inside the double doors through which Ro had just walked.

Ro tried to blend in with the onlookers and worked his way up towards the front of the crowd positioned on the right hand side of the hall. He did not want Arlen to see him just yet and wanted to witness the proceedings from a position of anonymity, although the likelihood of that was reducing by the minute as people recognised him and moved out of his way.

"Next," called Arlen's voice.

Two men stepped forward. They were dressed like peasants or poor farmers and were clearly ill at ease in these surroundings as they both fidgeted nervously.

"Speak," commanded Arlen.

Both men began to talk at the same time drawing an exasperated look from Arlen.

"Silence!" he suddenly shouted raising his right hand. "You first then you," he added pointing at each of the two men in turn.

"Sire, this man has allowed his cattle to roam onto my land and graze freely, destroying one of my crops in the process. The loss of harvest will hit us hard," said the first man.

"Is this true?" Arlen asked the second man.

"It was not intentional, Sire. I did not realise that the fence was down. The legal ownership of that strip of land has been a point of contention between our families for generations anyway."

"You will divide the contested land in half and arrange for it to be partitioned accordingly," said Arlen. The second man seemed really pleased with the decision and began to thank Arlen profusely. "You will also give your neighbour one third of your herd to do as he pleases, by way of compensation for his lost harvest." The man's grin dropped away.

"But, Sire."

"Silence! That is my judgement. Make sure that you do not appear before me again regarding this matter. Next."

Before they could protest some more, two of Arlen's guards ushered the men down the hall and out of the doors, bickering as they went.

The judgement seemed fair to Ro watching on, even if he was a little concerned at the authoritarian tone Arlen had employed. Then again if the people were looking to him as a leader then perhaps he should behave as one. Maybe he had misjudged his friend.

The next two disputes called before the court concerned similar matters and Arlen had dealt with them in much the same way he had the first one Ro had witnessed. The case Arlen was currently presiding over concerned the theft of a loaf of bread and Ro had just decided that he had seen enough and was about to sidle out of the door, when what he heard stopped him in his tracks. He slowly turned and then began to gently work his way through the crowds again, positive that he must have misheard what Arlen had said.

"I'm sorry, my Lord, but my family were starving; I had no choice. Mercy please," cried the thief as he was dragged away by two of Arlen's guards.

"What judgement did Arlen just pass on that man?" Ro asked a man and woman standing in front of him.

They both turned to face him and smiled when they recognised Ro's face.

"*Lord* Arlen has decreed that the thief's right hand be cut off," replied the woman. Clearly she was totally supportive of

Arlen and everything he was doing and wanted him referred to by what she considered his rightful title.

"He's to lose his hand for stealing a loaf of bread?" asked Ro incredulously.

"A loaf, an apple, money, it's all the same thing; theft is theft and the only way they learn that it is wrong is to punish them severely. Lord Arlen recognises this and has acted accordingly," replied the man.

A woman had been hauled before Arlen now, running a gauntlet of abuse from the onlookers as she had been dragged before him. Ro listened in trepidation as the woman was accused of committing adultery with a traveller to the city who had moved on. The woman's husband and two other people had given evidence against her. Arlen's judgement was swift and brutal; she was to be taken to the town square and publicly flogged before being exiled from the city.

The woman sobbed as her sentence was announced and had to be helped from the hall by two more guards as her legs had given out with terror and could no longer bear her weight.

Ro stared up at his friend sat on his makeshift throne as if he were the lord or king that everybody seemed to refer to him as. Where had his friend gone? The Arlen Meric that he knew would never have ordered that a man's hand be sliced off or that a young woman should be publicly flogged.

"Are there any more?" Ro heard his friend say.

"Just one, Sire," replied one of the sycophants who now surrounded Arlen and appeared to be poisoning his mind with hate. "Mal Lukic is accused of murder. He was found covered in blood, was holding a knife and the body of Coric Mansur, a butcher, was found lying at his feet."

"That sounds a pretty clear cut case," replied Arlen yawning. "Bring him forward so I might hear what pathetic excuse he has to offer."

The sycophant whose name Ro didn't care to remember, beckoned with his fingers and two guards dragged a man whose hands and feet were manacled together, in front of Arlen.

Arlen raised his right hand slightly and one of the guards kicked the man behind his left knee sending him crashing to the ground. To the watching Ro the man looked like a poor wretch, incapable of ever murdering someone.

"Well, what have you got to say for yourself?" Arlen asked glaring down at the man.

"I didn't murder him," the man spluttered out.

A hard kick to his right side sent him sprawling to the floor.

"You will address Lord Arlen as lord or sire," said the sycophant indignantly.

"I didn't murder him...Sire," the man repeated hauling himself back to his knees.

"Despite the blood, despite the knife and despite the fact that the man's dead body was found at your feet, you are denying killing the butcher, Coric Mansur?" asked Arlen.

"No, Sire, I killed him, but it was in self-defence. We had an altercation in his shop earlier in the day and he came round my house later that evening armed with a knife. We argued some more and then he went for me with his knife. We wrestled and struggled for a while and I managed to grab hold of the knife before we both went tumbling to the ground. When I scrambled to my feet again he was lying dead with the knife buried in his chest."

The hum of conversation broke out around the hall as people digested the man's story and Arlen once again raised the fingers of his right hand.

"Silence! Lord Arlen demands silence," bellowed the sycophant.

"Stand up," Arlen said.

The man hauled himself to his feet. Arlen stared at the man for long anxious moments as the tension in the hall rose.

"Sire…"

Arlen put his fingers to his mouth in a signal for the man to fall silent.

"I knew Coric Mansur the butcher; he was a good man. More to the point he was a big man. There is no way a scrawny little weasel like you could have bested him in a fight. I could not imagine a bigger mismatch. Therefore I have to conclude that there was foul play and you attacked him unexpectedly, killing him with a knife which was in fact yours or perhaps stolen from the butcher's shop. Either way you are guilty of murder and it is the judgement of this court that you be stoned to death, the sentence to be carried out immediately."

The hall erupted into a cacophony of noise as people began animated conversations about the judgement and the sentence. Ro stood open mouthed staring at his friend, unable to believe what he had just heard. Around him he heard snippets of conversation and although there was the odd remark of dissent, most were apparently in support of Arlen's decision. The butcher it seemed was a popular man, that or his killer was a very unpopular one.

Ro could take no more and barged his way through the front ranks of the crowd until he was in view of most people in the hall. Some stopped their conversations curious as to what their lord's friend was doing whilst others ignored him or merely glanced in his direction.

Ro started to stride towards Arlen but immediately two of his guards rushed to intercept him and crossed their pikes in front of him barring his way. Ro glared at them trying to control his rising temper. Arlen, who had noticed his friend's appearance, signalled for the guards to let him pass and they immediately stood aside. However, instead of striding up to Arlen's side as his friend had expected, Ro merely took a couple of paces forward so that he was situated in the middle of the hall where most would be able to hear him.

"Ro, I did not see you enter," began Arlen. "I am glad that you could make it though."

"So am I, for I would not believe what has transpired here had I not witnessed it with my own eyes," replied Ro, his comment and tone drawing murmurs of discontent from all around.

The smile had also started to fade from Arlen's face as he grew suspicious of his friend's motives.

"And what is it exactly that you think has transpired here?" asked Arlen.

"For the most part, fair and just rulings as I would expect of the Arlen Meric I know and love as a brother. But your last three judgements have been...excessive."

"Excessive?" repeated Arlen.

"Yes, excessive and harsh."

"But they are guilty and need to be punished," said Arlen to a loud muttering of support from many in the hall.

"I agree. If they are guilty they should be punished, but not like this. Dismemberment, a flogging and a stoning; it's barbaric and unbecoming. I thought we fought to free the people from such tyranny and injustice?"

"These are my people, Ro, not yours. Allow me the courtesy of knowing what is best for them better than you."

More murmurings of agreement drifted from various places in the hall.

"If you go through with these punishments, Arlen, it makes you no better than your brother and his Kaladri thugs; it will make a mockery of what we fought for."

This time the mutterings were in opposition to what Ro had just said. One or two even called him an "outlander" and shouted that he should go home.

"Have a care, Ro. You are my friend, but every friendship has its boundaries. These people are guilty of the crimes of which they stood accused. It is my job to see that they are punished in a way that discourages others from treading the same path as them, brutal as it may seem."

Ro shook his head in disgust.

"What has happened to you, Arlen? Where is the man who fought beside me at Vangor and countless other battles? That Arlen Meric would never have been so cruel. You are not king here. What gives you the right to administer such cruelty in the name of justice?"

The mood of the crowd was turning distinctly hostile towards Ro and the space in the middle of the hall seemed to be shrinking as the people on either side began to slowly edge towards him.

"I think, Ro that it is time for you to leave. It seems that not everyone in here thinks as you do," said Arlen calmly.

The two guards who had previously blocked his way now came and stood in front of Ro again and the sound of heavy footsteps behind him told him that another couple had taken up position slightly to his rear.

Ro took a long calming breath. No good would come of further protestations on his part. He doubted that his friend would ever hurt him, but given what he had just witnessed he couldn't be sure. Without uttering another word he turned and marched out of the hall escorted by four guards who accompanied him a safe distance from the hall. Satisfied that he was unlikely to turn and head straight back in there, they eventually turned and headed in the opposite direction.

Chapter 9

After being escorted out of the meeting hall, Ro had sat down on a low wall to contemplate his next move. It had not been long before the sound of many animated voices drifted across the square and he looked up to see the three prisoners being led out by a number of armed guards. Behind them the crowd jostled and pushed their way out of the hall, eager not to miss anything.

The three prisoners were lined up in the centre of the square flanked by a number of guards, whilst the crowd gathered around them. Ro stood and climbed halfway up a staircase that led to the battlements so that he too could see everything. A few moments later Arlen came out of the hall flanked by four more guards and stood a few paces in front of the three terrified looking prisoners. Without any further delay, Arlen nodded at one of the guards whom Ro recognised as one of the officers and the thief was immediately dragged forward and made to kneel.

As the hushed crowd looked on, one of the guards tied a thin rope around the thief's right wrist and then took a couple of paces to his left, pulling the rope tight and thereby extending the man's arm. The thief was whimpering and continued to beg for mercy but Ro knew there would be none, not now; the proceedings were too far along even if his friend did suddenly have a change of heart.

The guard officer stepped forward and drew his sword and the crowd gasped in anticipation. He then rested the sword blade on the thief's wrist at the point where he intended to sever it. When he was good and ready he glanced over at Arlen who merely nodded and in a flash the sword was raised and then brought down in a powerful sweep that took the man's hand clean off. So swift and clean was the blow that it was only when the man saw his own hand lying on the ground beside him that he cried out in pain or perhaps shock. When he then looked at the bloody stump of his right arm which was pulsing blood, he began to wail piteously. Two of the guards then stepped forward and led him away, but only after one of them had grotesquely picked up the man's severed hand and given it to the thief to hold in his remaining hand.

Next the woman was led out and tied between two posts that had been hastily erected. One of the guards then tore open her dress to reveal the pale flesh of her back. The woman was sobbing uncontrollably and Ro noticed with a deal of satisfaction that not all of the crowd could watch, some looking away, some down at their feet. Some even tried to wander off unnoticed but any the guards saw trying to leave were ushered back into the crowd and forced to watch the spectacle.

A vicious looking whip with multiple leather strands was handed to the guard officer after he had wiped his sword clean and sheathed it. For a few desperate moments he stood there admiring it and ensuring that the strands were untangled. It all added to the woman's torment. Then he slowly pulled his arm back ready to deliver the initial stroke, but firstly looked to Arlen for approval.

The approval was not immediate and for a moment Ro dared to believe that despite the public outcry that might ensue, his friend was having a change of heart. Instead Arlen issued instructions for the woman's husband to step forward. To add insult to injury, the woman's husband was to inflict the flogging. The husband eventually stepped forward and after several prompts from the guard officer, finally took the whip into his hand. Then he stood staring at his wife's back for a few moments and Ro found himself wondering what level of torment the poor man was going through at that moment. Finally the man looked over at Arlen who smiling slightly, indicated with his hand that the man should commence the flogging and so he did, albeit with a deal of reluctance.

The first stroke was half hearted though the woman's scream in response wasn't. The second and third weren't much harder but eventually, urged on by the crowd and perhaps caught up in the moment, the man started to lash his wife harder and harder, flaying the skin from her back. When the twenty lashes had been applied, her back was nothing but a livid mess of torn flesh and bright red blood. The woman had mercifully passed out somewhere around the eleventh or twelfth lash.

Ro watched as the woman was cut down and her limp body dragged over to her husband who had collapsed onto his knees, either in exhaustion or shame. With tears streaming down his face, the man stood, tenderly picked up his wife's ravaged body and carried her away from her scene of degradation.

Ro had had enough. As the man condemned to be stoned to death was led to the posts to be tied up in the woman's place, Ro made his way down the staircase and towards the barn where he knew that his horse was stabled.

He was halfway to the stable when two guards intercepted him, one reaching out an arm and placing it on Ro's chest.

"Remove your hand or lose it," snapped Ro.

"Nobody leaves the square until punishment is complete, orders of Lord Arlen," replied one of the guards.

"I don't give two damns what Arlen Meric wants right now, so I suggest that you get out of my way."

"Don't make this a bigger problem than it needs to be," said the other guard, a stocky man with a bushy moustache.

"Trust me it won't be a problem to me," replied Ro.

Out of the corner of his eye Ro watched as the other guard's hand slipped almost imperceptibly towards his sword hilt.

"If your hand so much as grazes that sword hilt, you won't live to see another day. Now either let me pass or make your move, because I really haven't got the time or patience for this right now," said Ro fixing both men with a cold stare.

The two guards glanced at one another as if checking each other's resolve and for a moment Ro thought they were going to do the sensible thing and step aside. Then he saw it, the smallest of changes in expression from one man to the other. They had made up their mind that facing Arlen's wrath for not doing their duty was a far more daunting prospect than engaging the man in front of them, despite knowledge of Ro's prowess in a fight.

The first to move was the soldier on the right who swung a

right hook at Ro's head. Ro had anticipated it though and swayed back at exactly the right moment before leaning forward and smashing his forearm into the man's nose. There was a satisfying crack as bone shattered and the man reeled away, his face a bloody pulp. The other guard hesitated for a second and in that moment Ro was able to regain his balance and prepare himself so that when that man's punch was thrown he was able to deflect it with his left forearm before landing a pile driver of a punch into the man's midriff. It was a clean punch but did not have as much effect as Ro had been hoping as the man was protected to a certain degree by his thick leather breastplate.

The first guard was starting to recover his senses, anger at the damage done by Ro's blow superseding the pain he felt. Ro knew that he had to deal with both of them and quickly before others came to their assistance.

Behind him a great cheer went up in the square and without turning round Ro knew that the stoning had begun. It would not be long before the poor wretch was killed and then the crowd's attention would turn elsewhere.

Ro had let his mind wander and the second guard had sensed an opportunity and swung his left fist at Ro's head. Ro had seen it at the last moment and although he managed to swivel his head just in time, the fist still landed a glancing blow that rocked Ro on his feet.

Another cheer went up behind him but this time Ro didn't let it distract him and with a roar of anger he barrelled into the second guard shoulder first, sending him stumbling backwards and then immediately swung a huge right hook which connected squarely with the jaw of the first guard who was just about to re-join the fight. He went down hard and never got up again. Ro turned to face the remaining guard just as he was about to launch another attack of his own. Ro kicked him hard in the left knee and the man crumbled to the ground. He then delivered three fast and hard punches to the man's face, the third of which seemed to render him unconscious. The guard's body slumped to the ground next to his comrade who was groaning with the pain of his ruined face.

The sound of running feet behind him drew Ro's attention

and he spun round, his right hand instinctively reaching for his sword. Eight guards, four of whom carried vicious looking pikes, had formed a semi-circle behind him and at the command of their officer, those carrying pikes lowered the points so that they hovered merely a couple of hand lengths from Ro's chest.

"Hold," called the familiar voice. A few seconds later Arlen stepped through the clutch of guards. He looked firstly at his beaten guards and then at Ro. "You've got to stop damaging my men like this, Ro; it's becoming a habit."

"Perhaps if you taught them some better manners I wouldn't have to educate them."

Arlen laughed. "You sound more like Teren Rad every day."

"Maybe that's not such a bad thing. I thought that you'd forgotten about our friends out there," replied Ro waving his arm in the direction of the newly replaced town gates.

"No, I've not forgotten them. I've just been busy with matters of court."

"I know, I just witnessed two versions of your justice," said Ro bitterly.

"Only two? Then you missed the grand finale," said Arlen smiling.

"What I missed was a man being tied to a post and stoned to death by a mob."

"He was a murderer. There is only one way to punish a murderer."

"He killed someone, yes, but claims it was in self-defence; it needed investigating."

"What it needed was swift and decisive justice and that's what happened. Unless you disagree?" asked Arlen.

"You know that I do."

"Then we have a problem, don't we? I'm not sure you can continue to be my right hand if you truly feel that way."

"I agree. That is why I was heading to the stable to get my horse when these…gentlemen took exception. I think they see things my way now though."

"You were just going to leave without telling me?" A brief look of anger crossed Arlen's face.

"What was the point? You have long since stopped listening to me."

"Then go. Silevia thanks you for your services in the fight for freedom but perhaps it is for the best that now you leave. Silevia is for Silevians." A murmuring of agreement rose from the large crowd which had gathered behind Arlen and his guards.

"So be it. When you finally come to your senses you will find me to the west. I plan to track down Teren and the others and re-join the fight. The allies could always use another good man," said Ro.

"I've done my bit for the war and killed my share of Narmidians. My duty is here now, with my people. Fare well, Ro Aryk," and with that Arlen turned and strode away followed by his guards.

Some of the crowd hung back for a while as if waiting to see what Ro would do next, but when he eventually turned and headed towards the stables, the rest of them dispersed.

He had done his best to persuade Arlen to leave with him but it was not to be. Maybe in the future he would come to his senses and come looking for him, but for now he was on his own. He would do as he'd told Arlen and head west and try and join up with Teren and the others though in truth he didn't even know if they were still alive. All he could do was hope. Without it he was nothing. He would head west to Breland and hope to pick up their trail there. One thing was for certain; if Teren was still alive and he had more than a handful of men, then this war wasn't over. Not yet.

Chapter 10

Balok Vesla, last surviving son of Starik Vesla, the Narmidian King of Kings, smiled smugly as his horse paddled through the narrow river that marked the border between Datia and Lotar. Finally he had been given the opportunity to seize some personal glory. All of the victories so far had been credited to Starik even though he had been nowhere near the fighting, but now it was Balok's turn. He had been forced to beg his father for the chance to lead an expedition north and attack the supposedly mystical lands and although his father had eventually acquiesced, Balok would never forget the way his father had humiliated him in the process. Instead of readily agreeing and assigning him troops, his father had sought the advice of his most trusted generals who were consulted on the likelihood of Balok being successful given his lack of experience. Perhaps with one eye on the future, most of the younger ones had supported his mission, but the older more experienced commanders had dissented. In the end though Starik had agreed but only on the condition that General Livik, one of his father's most trusted advisors, accompanied him. Balok was not stupid, however, and knew that Livik had been sent not only to report back on their progress but also to assume command if Balok had not appeared up to the task.

Well he won't be doing much spying now, thought Balok as he recalled how the old general had tragically died in his sleep courtesy of some quietly administered poison, of course.

Balok's lack of experience was not the only reason that some of the king's advisors had cautioned against an invasion of the north. They like many of the rank and file troops believed that the people of Silevia and Lotar held magical powers and commanded demons and that is why they had never been conquered. Balok believed none of it. They were just people who bled red like the rest of the world.

It was unusual for his father to totally ignore his senior generals' advice, especially when they were for once so unanimous in their opinion that Balok was not ready to lead an expedition and that thought troubled him. Perhaps he did not give his father enough credit. Perhaps like him his father didn't believe any of this superstitious nonsense about magic and demons. Or perhaps he did. Perhaps he was counting on it being true. Balok's desire and ambition to acquire the throne was well known, as was his father's reluctance to step aside for the foreseeable future. Maybe his father had let him go north in the hope that he would meet his end or at least be so badly defeated and humiliated that his reputation would be so damaged that the people and lesser kings would never consent to him taking the throne.

That was most likely his father's reasoning behind letting him go he decided. Maybe Livik had been assigned to give bad advice that would have led to defeat. Balok would never know, but either way he was better off without his father's spy.

He would prove his father wrong. He would conquer all the northern lands and return to his father's court covered in glory. Then he would see whom the people and more importantly, the army, looked to for leadership.

"My Prince, our scouts return."

Balok looked to his side and saw his most trusted officer, General Xalit, staring at him. Then he nodded to their front where two riders were racing towards them. A few seconds later they reined in a few strides in front of the prince and made to dismount, but Balok signalled for them to remain where they were. After a nervous glance at one another, unsure how to react to this break in protocol, the older of the two bowed to the prince from his saddle.

"Report," said Balok.

"My Prince, we have ridden many leagues to the north and west and all we have seen is a number of small isolated villages, with peasants working in the fields."

"And what of the Lotari army?"

"We have not seen any sign of it, my Prince."

"Not a single soldier?"

"Not one, my Prince, not even a scout."

"They must know we are here surely?" said Balok turning

to General Xalit. "I know we have only just crossed into their country but word that a large host of riders is heading north towards them must surely have reached their ears by now."

General Xalit nodded and rose slightly in the saddle and slowly swivelled around looking at the distant mountains and the nearby hills.

"They know we're here, my Prince," he said confidently.

"You have seen them?" asked Balok.

"No, but I can feel their eyes upon us. Even now we are being watched."

"Then why do they not reveal themselves and give battle?"

"They are most probably watching and waiting for the most opportune moment. This is their country and they know the terrain. They know that they don't have the numbers or skill to defeat us in open battle so they are waiting till the terrain and circumstances suit them. Then they will nibble away at us piece by piece."

"How do you know this?" Balok demanded.

"Because it is what I would do."

Balok turned to his scouts. "Get fresh horses and another six riders. Work in groups of four, one going north and one west. Go as far as your horses will permit and send a rider back from each party at midday and then mid-afternoon. The last four riders are to return by sundown. The column will continue moving north. Do you understand?"

"Yes, my Prince," said the scout who had spoken earlier before bowing again and then riding away to carry out his orders.

"Tell the men to be vigilant, General. We will rest here for a short while and let the horses drink their fill in the river and then we will resume our journey north. If you are right then an attack, however small, could come at any time."

The general nodded and then slowly rode away to pass the orders on to lower ranked officers.

Balok glanced around at the nearby hills and had an overpowering sensation of being watched.

Let them watch and let them fear. My army is invincible. They can nibble away all they like, but it will make no difference, my men are as numerous as the stars in the sky.

Sooner or later we will trap them and then they will be crushed.

***

The first attack had come less than two hours later. They had been riding in extended order through a narrow gulley with a steep slope to their left. A few paces away from the edge of the slope had been a tree line. It was from here that the Lotari had suddenly emerged, overpowering the thin line of horsemen who Balok had sent up the slope to act as a screen. By the time that the commanders down in the gulley realised that their riders above were in trouble and hastily tried to arrange their men in defensive order, it was already too late. At first all Balok's men could hear was a gentle whirring noise and mere moments later, scores of *jemtak,* small metal throwing objects with spikes protruding, came raining down on the largely unprotected men and horses. Dozens of men and beast were hit. Those who were hit either in the face or neck were killed outright, the rest sustained nasty or incapacitating injuries. The *jemtak* was a weapon of panic rather than death.

After the initial onslaught had finished, Balok's generals ordered two hundred of their light cavalry to climb the slope and engage the enemy but by the time they breasted the summit the Lotari had melted away into the trees and all that remained were the bodies of their dead skirmishers.

"Well?" snapped Balok as one of his commanders reined in alongside of him.

"All of our skirmishers are dead, my Prince and sixteen more were killed in the column. Another eleven are badly wounded and won't be able to fight again."

"Our losses are but a grain of sand in the desert and I care not. What of the enemy?"

"There is a forest set just back from the top of the slope running down the other side of the hill, my Prince; the enemy had retreated into this by the time our cavalry reached the top. They picked their spot well," said the commander.

"And they will continue to do so, my Prince," added General Xalit. "We can expect them to hit us like that in a number of locations they will have identified."

"They think they can defeat us by repeatedly attacking and

inflicting fifty or so casualties each time? It will take them an eternity," said Balok dismissively.

"I think they are cleverer than that, my Prince. I believe their aim is to wear us down and erode our will to persist. They know they can never beat us in an open fight," replied the general.

"And you know this because this again is what you would do if you were in their position?" asked Balok.

"It is."

"Then what do you recommend, General?"

The general stroked his short black beard which was flecked with grey as he considered his prince's question.

"We need to deny them the opportunity to use the terrain to their advantage. We must find a way of forcing them to fight us on our terms on ground of our choosing, ground where our superior numbers will be a help not a hindrance."

"And how do we do that, General when we don't know this accursed country at all?"

"Whilst we send out more pathfinders to scout the lie of the land we must force their hand by doing something that their army commander cannot ignore."

"I'm listening," said Balok his interest piqued.

"We must deny them sustenance, shelter and aid from the villages."

"You're talking about occupying every village that we come across and leaving a garrison there."

"I'm talking about razing every village to the ground, burning crops and if necessary, putting the villagers to the sword. If their commander learns that we are wreaking such a terrible price on his people all the time that we can't find him, he must surely bring his army to battle to spare his people, even if he knows that he can't win," said the general.

"Because this is what you would do?" said Balok grinning with enthusiasm at the suggestion.

"No, my Prince. I would stay the course and continue to harass their army regardless of what atrocities the invader committed."

"You are a cold hearted man indeed, General Xalit," said Balok smiling.

"I prefer to call it determined, my Prince."

"And that is why we shall win, General, because you are prepared to do the unthinkable."

The general bowed slightly in recognition of the compliment and was about to say something further when a commotion further down the line could be heard. The prince's personal bodyguard immediately formed a tight circle around him and the general, raising their shields to make a wall through which no arrows or terrifying *jemtak* could penetrate.

"What now?" snapped Balok to no one in particular.

A few minutes later the sound of horses reining in just outside the ring of shields reached Balok's ears.

"My Prince," somebody called.

Balok signalled for the shield wall to release and slowly they disengaged, though they remained vigilant and ready to assume the formation again in an instant if necessary.

Balok looked round and his eyes finally settled on two captains from the Drakani regiment, excellent horse soldiers from a subject people who lived in a land to the east of Narmidia.

"What is it, Captain? What has happened?"

"The Lotari hit the very rear of the column, my Prince. They appeared from a gulley we didn't even know was there. They rode quickly up, hurled their weapons and then turned and ran."

"Casualties?" asked General Xalit.

"Unsure at this time, General, but no more than thirty I would estimate and most of them were drivers of the baggage train."

"And the enemy rode off unscathed again I take it?" asked Balok.

"Apart from one, my Prince. One of their horses went lame and threw its rider."

"We have him prisoner?" asked Balok eagerly.

"No, my Prince. One of my men gave chase and ran the man through."

"That is a shame. Give orders to all the men that where possible, we are to try and take a few of the enemy hostage. An interrogation might be very revealing," said Balok.

"I will, my Prince. And my man who killed the Lotari; you want me to kill him for not using his initiative?" asked the captain dreading the answer.

"No, he was doing what he is paid to do. Reward him with five gold Gracu."

"Yes, my Prince, thank you," and with that the two riders turned their mounts and galloped away.

"Very well, General Xalit, we will do this your way. I have already had enough of them gnawing away at us. Let's teach these people that if they continue to refuse to fight us in open battle, then their people will pay the price."

"As you command, my Prince. I will see that the wounded are loaded into the baggage train and then brief the other commanders."

"No, General. If a man is no longer able to fight, then he is of no use to me and will just be a drain on our food and water resources. Only those that can still wield a sword or spear come with us. Leave the wounded behind or dispose of them, whichever you see fit and then get us moving out of this accursed valley."

But even as Balok spoke the sound of fighting, shouting and the cries of pain, drifted down the column, this time from the front. It seemed that the Lotari had struck a third time, this time at the head of the column.

Balok could feel his anger rising. He was going to enjoy putting this people down.

Chapter 11

It had been with a heavy heart that Ro had saddled his horse and departed Silevia city. Although he and Arlen had only known each other for a little over two years, they had for Ro's part at least, grown to be close friends, both owing the other their life on more than one occasion. In fact the first time they met had been when Arlen had come to Ro's aid after he had been attacked by a party of Narmidian pathfinders right at the beginning of the invasion. The fact that in his opinion he still owed his friend, weighed heavily on Ro as he made his way due west at a steady pace.

Right up until the last moment he had held out the hope that Arlen would come to the stables and plead with him not to go or better still, come and saddle his own horse and ride west with him. Neither had happened though and as the Silevian capital shrank in the distance, Ro realised that for the first time in over two years he was on his own.

It was a warm afternoon and the sun, high in a cloudless azure sky, beat down on his face raising his spirits. He knew that if he continued due west he would soon come to the border between Silevia and Lotar, another of the small northern kingdoms. It had been many years since he had had reason to visit Lotar and he had nothing but fond memories of the place.

Except for the initial fight perhaps, he thought ruefully.

Several years earlier, whilst on a diplomatic mission for the old king of Remada back when he had been Captain of the Royal Bodyguard, he had been visiting Lotar when he suddenly came across a handful of beleaguered Lotari who were being attacked by bandits. Ro had intervened and with his help, the Lotari had defeated the bandits. Ro had not known it at the time but concealed within the wagons that the Lotari were protecting, was Princess Shala of Datia who was on her way to be married to Prince Zerut of Lotar. The commander of the convoy had insisted that Ro accompany him back to the capital where once the tale had been told to the prince and the king, Ro was treated as an honoured guest. Everything that Ro had been sent north to try and negotiate with the Lotari king was agreed upon which had delighted the Remadan king and raised Ro's own profile on his return to Remada.

More importantly still, at least to Ro, he had made a lifelong friend in Zerut, who was unstintingly grateful to Ro for saving the life of his betrothed. And Ro could understand why; Shala was the most beautiful woman he had ever seen and when she had stepped out of her carriage on that fateful day, she had all but taken his breath away.

Ro smiled at the memory of that first encounter and his hand instinctively dropped to the pouch he wore around his waist and tapped its contents reassuringly. Inside were a dozen *jemtak,* small metal throwing stars which in the right hands, particularly at close quarters, were deadly and terrifying. They had been a gift from the prince, one of many. The prince himself had spent many hours trying to teach Ro how best to use the weapon and although Ro could never claim to be as proficient in their use as even the lowliest Lotari warrior, he managed to get by. In fact he had used them to good effect on several occasions, not least of which was at the siege of Vangor a couple of years ago.

As his horse plodded on towards the west, Ro allowed his mind to recall some of the memories from that battle. It had been a terrible, bloody affair and many good friends had been lost but other friendships had been forged in blood. One of those friends was receding into the distance behind him but he hoped that he would eventually meet up with some of the others like Teren Rad and his son Eryn when he finally reached Breland or wherever the allied army was gathered.

Lost in his thoughts, Ro had ridden west for the rest of the afternoon his journey pleasant and uneventful. The sky was beginning to darken as dusk approached and Ro had been wondering where to stop for the night when he had almost stumbled into them. He had been aware that at some point he had crossed into Lotar from Silevia. There were no border guards or signs marking the transition from one kingdom to another, but the landscape and terrain had noticeably altered and Ro had been sure that he recognised the odd landmark.

Lost in contented memories Ro had almost blundered straight into the Narmidian riders. Judging by their numbers and the familiarity of their uniforms, Ro had guessed that they were scouts or pathfinders. They had crossed his path not fifty strides in front, but their attention had been rigidly fixed ahead of them and they had not noticed him. The ground between Ro and the pathfinders was littered with rocks and large thorny shrubs and Ro had quietly eased his horse behind a large boulder as he watched the riders' progress.

His horse whinnied gently and Ro patted its neck reassuringly and whispered some calming words in its ear. The riders cantered off to the north and Ro waited until they were out of earshot before moving out from his place of concealment.

Had the Narmidians launched an invasion of the north or was this merely a scouting party sent to reconnoitre the kingdom's defences? His head told him that he should turn south or double back and then turn south before resuming his journey west, but his heart and an overpowering curiosity told him differently. He had to find out whether the scouting party were a long range patrol or part of a larger force.

He didn't have long to wait to find out.

After continuing to ride due west for a little over two leagues, he had come across a grass covered hill with a gentle slope. The area looked vaguely familiar and if he was right, he recalled that the downward slope on the other side was extremely steep and not negotiable on horseback. However, the view from the top on a clear day was unrivalled and although dusk was now gathering if he was quick he would still be able to see for leagues. If the Narmidians had launched an invasion of Lotar and those men who had passed him by earlier were their pathfinders, then from atop the hill he would surely be able to see the Narmidian invasion force.

What he saw when he reached the summit took his breath away.

Stretched out almost for as far as the eye could see to the south, was a long column of men, both foot and mounted, snaking their way northwards as they crossed the River Aryx which marked the border between Datia and Lotar. Ro had never been particularly good at estimating numbers, but even he could tell that the Narmidian army stretched out before him numbered in the thousands. This was not a force built simply for the invasion of Lotar, this was an army sent to crush and occupy all of the northern kingdoms which had so far been left untouched by the war. Barring a miracle, even the combined forces of the north would not be enough to defeat the invader, not that there was much chance of the small northern kingdoms working together; mistrust and animosity had existed between some of them for generations and could not be easily overlooked, even for the greater good.

A shout from below alerted Ro to the fact that he had lingered too long as one of the skirmishers riding on the flanks of the main column had spotted him watching them from the top of the hill. However, with the steep side of the hill between them and him, the chance of them catching him were slight, but even as a group of riders detached from the main force to pursue him, another shout went up from somewhere in the column. Ro watched as seemingly out of nowhere, scores of Lotari warriors emerged from the treeline at the top of the hill opposite, overpowered the riders skirting the ridge and then rained dozens of *jemtak* down on the frightened men below.

As quick as they had appeared, the Lotari vanished so that by the time that a force of armed riders had scaled the hill opposite Ro, the Lotari had melted away into the trees leaving behind them the bodies of the dead skirmishers.

Not long after that the Lotari launched another attack, this time on the baggage train towards the rear of the Narmidian column. This attack like the one before it was not designed to cause mass casualties, but more to sow panic and fear into the enemy, proving that they could be attacked anytime anywhere. It was a classic Lotari tactic when faced by overwhelming odds Ro remembered from his time spent training with the Lotari army.

By the time that some light Narmidian cavalry had chased their attackers off and reported to their leader who had been sheltering beneath a wall of shields, shouts of alarm were already reaching them from the front of the column where yet another attack had just been launched.

Ro was fascinated and in awe of the speed and precision of the Lotari attacks. They had obviously been aware of the impending invasion and had been waiting for them with a prepared plan for harassing the enemy. It was a battle that they knew they could not win given the overwhelming size of the Narmidian army, but still they were determined to make a fight of it by harassing them at every opportunity.

The whinnying of a horse drew Ro's attention back to his immediate surroundings and he was alarmed when the first Narmidian horseman appeared over the ridge of the slope just to his left. He knew that some of the Narmidians, particularly those from the subject nations to Narmidia's south, were excellent horsemen, but he never imagined that they would manage to get up the steep slope in front of him, at least not that quickly.

He reached into the pouch at his waist and drew out a *jemtak* and hurled it at the rider just as he breasted the hill. It was a hasty and ill-considered throw and the weapon whizzed harmlessly by the man's head. Not relishing another one of the deadly stars being thrown at him the rider urged his tired horse on trying desperately to close the gap before Ro could throw again, but his horse was exhausted from the climb and didn't respond as fast as he hoped. Realising he was in trouble the rider looked up at Ro hoping that perhaps he had fled but he was still there and was pulling back his arm.

A split-second later the Narmidian rider toppled from his horse, a *jemtak* buried squarely in his forehead. Ro breathed a sigh of relief but the relief was short-lived as another rider then another and then two more, began to emerge over the brow of the hill. Whilst he calculated that he might be able to take down another couple if he concentrated and took his time, the other two would soon be on him and it would end badly.

Ro turned his horse deciding that on this occasion, fleeing was the best option and as he did so, he became aware of a line of riders strung out behind him. How they had got there without him hearing he did not know, nor did it matter, as there was now nowhere to escape. He reached for his sword but as he did so, a gentle whirring noise filled the air followed by a series of grunts and soft thuds. Ro swivelled in his saddle just in time to see all four Narmidian riders tumble to the ground, each with a *jemtak* buried in their head or neck.

Ro turned back to face his Lotari rescuers and express his gratitude but realised that he may have misread their intentions when a number of lance points were brought down level with his chest.

Ro eased his sword back into its scabbard and slowly raised both of his hands in a gesture of surrender. Four horsemen circled behind him, whilst all but one of the others formed a cordon around the sides and in front of him. The one remaining rider, who had not yet moved, now edged his horse nearer to Ro before speaking in the Common tongue.

"You will come with us. Do not attempt to escape or my men will not hesitate to run you through."

Ro glanced over his shoulder and looked at the grim countenance of the men sat behind him and didn't doubt it for a minute. He looked back at the man who had spoken and nodded. Satisfied, the Lotari officer turned his own horse and rode off signalling for the others to follow.

It had been some years since Ro had last been in Lotar and the fact that he had not been back to visit his old friend, Prince Zerut was one of his greatest regrets. That these men didn't recognise him was perhaps not surprising but what was of more concern to Ro was that because of the war perhaps he was no longer welcome in the kingdom. He would soon find out he reasoned.

He wasn't even sure whether Emperor Cyrix was still on the throne, whether his son Prince Zerut had succeeded him or someone altogether different was in charge. He suspected that his continued existence very much depended on that answer.

His escort led him due east for a while before turning northwest and then northeast. Ro imagined that the deviations were an attempt to lose any pursuers, but Ro doubted that the Narmidians would be giving chase to a small band of riders. Their objective was the conquest of the country and the destruction of the whole Lotari army and they would be most unlikely to deviate from that plan for the sake of killing a few warriors.

Twice Ro tried to strike up a conversation with his escort, once with the man to his left who just ignored him and continued to stare ahead with a stony expression and once with the leader who was riding a couple of horse lengths ahead of him. He immediately swivelled in his saddle and left Ro in no uncertain terms as to what would happen if he tried to talk again.

Left to his own thoughts, Ro began to ponder his predicament. The Lotari obviously knew that their country had been invaded by a large force and had already started to harry that enemy, though whether that was a pre-determined battle plan or just the reaction of a local border commander Ro didn't know. What was for certain, however, was that they knew who their enemy was otherwise they would surely have disposed of Ro just as easily as they did the men pursuing him. Nor had they taken his weapons away. Either they didn't think he posed much of a threat or were sure he wasn't an enemy and just wanted to verify that before letting him go about his business.

It took a little under two hours of fairly hard riding and a brief skirmish with a patrol of Narmidian pathfinders, before they arrived at Helot, the capital of Lotar. Despite his uncertain predicament Ro had enjoyed the ride, a ride that took them through some of the most beautiful countryside in the whole of Arkadia. Some parts of it Ro remembered others were completely new to him but when his eyes finally settled on Helot, the magical jewel of the north, a lump formed in his throat as a string of happy memories came flooding back. As his mind processed those memories and his eyes drank in the visage of the magnificent white towers and marble temples, Ro couldn't think of one plausible reason why he hadn't returned to Helot. But he was fooling no one he knew, least of all himself; the reason he had not returned was Sula, the woman he had fallen hopelessly in love with all those years ago and had been forced to leave behind when he was summoned back to Remada. She had told him to choose between his country and her and although it had been a gut wrenching decision which he had agonised over during several nights, the call to duty had finally won. But only just.

Sula had been angry and disappointed. When Ro had left she had not even come to say goodbye and although Prince Zerut had offered to send some men to find her when he saw the pain in his friend's eyes, Ro had politely declined. He had made his choice and so had she. They would both have to live with them.

Now as he was led slowly down the slope towards the magnificent white gates to the city, Ro found himself wondering whether he'd made the right decision.

Chapter 12

Teren nodded to himself satisfied that his gut instincts had once again been right. After watching them for a few minutes from the safety of the tree line, Teren was now confident that the Narmidians were not going to pursue them into the forest, at least not yet. He glanced at the body strewn battlefield one last time before turning to follow Brak and the others, his heart heavy with the weight of responsibility and loss.

They travelled for some time deeper into the seemingly unending forest before Brak finally gave the signal for them to swing southwest which he assured them would lead in a parallel course to the coast. Brak had drawn Yarik a rudimentary map of the surrounding area and had pointed out where they were to try and rendezvous, several leagues to the southwest at the farthest edge of the forest. The hard part for Teren and his men was getting safely through the Narmidian lines but he had anticipated that once they made it to the forest they would be relatively safe. Yarik on the other hand had ridden southeast with his men in an attempt to cause a diversion and enable Teren and the bulk of the army, to slip away relatively unscathed. After bursting through the Narmidian camp the plan had been for Yarik and his two hundred men to ride several leagues to the south before heading due west and meeting up with Teren's force. Every league that they had to cover was through occupied territory and was fraught with danger. There was also a very good chance that they would be pursued by the Narmidians meaning that they could potentially have enemy soldiers on all sides. It was essentially a suicide mission and Teren knew it. So did Yarik, but despite his lifelong aversion to horses he had insisted that he be the one to lead the breakout.

Ever the glory hunter, thought Teren shaking his head.

"Do you think he made it?" asked Brak as he dropped back a little to walk alongside his friend who was beginning to look his years.

"Who?" asked Teren.

"You know full well who I'm talking about; Yarik, the man you've been worrying about these last hours."

"Worrying? I'm not worrying. If I was worried that would imply that I care and I don't," replied Teren.

"Of course you don't, that's why you tried endlessly to talk him out of going because you knew there was little chance of survival. As did he, by the way."

Teren snorted with derision. "The only reason I tried to talk him out of it was because I was worried that he'd make a mess of it and get everyone killed within the first five minutes. Besides, you know that oaf doesn't even know which way round to sit on a horse let alone ride one."

"True, but I still know you worry about him as you do all your men," grinned Brak. He enjoyed baiting the surly Remadan almost as much as he did the big Delarite.

"Well you're wrong. I wouldn't miss any of you if you went and got your ugly backsides skewered on a Narmidian lance."

The two men walked in companionable silence for a few moments and Teren hoped that his friend had dropped the subject as he truly was worried about Yarik and the others. With every passing minute he wished that he'd knocked the Delarite out and led the diversionary force himself.

"So do you?" asked Brak.

"Do I what?"

"Do you think Yarik's dead?"

"It was a fool's mission into hostile territory against an overwhelmingly strong enemy led by a reckless glory hunter, Brak. No, I think the big oaf's still alive; it's the others I worry for. The only harm that's likely to come to that fool of a Delarite is if he falls off his horse." When Brak didn't reply Teren glanced across at his friend. "Don't worry, Brak, he'll be back. Besides it's like you said; he knew what he was getting into."

"I suppose."

"They're all brave lads that have gone with him and most of them were his men. You can be sure of a couple of things though."

"And what are they?" asked Brak.

"They won't die cheaply."

"You said a couple of things. What's the other?"

"That if the fool does survive we'll never hear the end of it, Sulat help us."

Brak started to laugh. "On that at least I fear you are right."

Both men were suddenly distracted by the sound of someone running through the undergrowth towards them and they both instinctively reached for their weapons until they recognised the face of one of their scouts.

"What is it, Orton?" asked Teren as the man came to a stop, puffing and panting in front of him.

"Men ahead, Teren."

"Narmidians? How in Kaden did they get ahead of us?" he asked looking at Brak.

Brak was shaking his head.

"No, not Narmidians, our men," said Orton.

"What do you mean our men? I sent no other men other than yourself and the other scouts ahead of us. You been at the mushrooms again, Orton?"

Orton gave Teren a funny look. "You know I haven't touched those since we left Salandor," he replied indignantly.

"Perhaps, but maybe not by choice, eh?" said Teren. The other man shrugged. "So who are they?"

"Deserters," Brak said for the other man.

Teren looked from Brak to Orton. "Is that true?"

"It is. I even recognise one or two of them."

"I hate deserters," snarled Teren. "I think we should teach them a lesson." Teren made to move forward but Brak put a restraining hand on his chest.

"Easy, Teren. These were our men, some of whom have been with us since Salandor."

"Yes and then they deserted."

"Only because nothing was happening. They've sat with us in that camp for months and nothing has happened."

"There were reasons for that, Brak you know that as well as I do. We needed to build more strength and were waiting on a decision of support from your people."

"I do know that, Teren, but perhaps they didn't. I don't

think we were as honest and open with the men as perhaps we should have been. They've all got families somewhere in Arkadia, Teren, or at least they used to. They followed us... you because you were a beacon of hope, a chance to avenge their people and free their families, but perhaps when we sat here inactive for so long they lost faith. We can't blame them for that."

"So what are you saying that we should just welcome them back into the fold as if nothing has happened?" asked Teren incredulously.

"Yes, I am. We still need every man we can get. Besides, they didn't run very far did they? What does that tell you?" asked Brak.

"That the cowards decided to skulk in here for the rest of the war whilst their brothers in arms fought and died for them," replied Teren harshly.

"No, it tells you that they still want to be part of the fight but lack leadership and direction. They've been waiting here for you to make your move. They'll rally to your flag if you ask them to, Teren, I'm sure of it."

Teren stared at his friend for a few long moments turning his words over in his mind until eventually he seemed to come to a decision.

"How many of them are there, Orton?"

"Perhaps fifty."

Teren raised an eyebrow in surprise. Whilst that was a drop in the ocean compared to the Narmidian horde, fifty good veterans would be a welcome addition to his force.

"This forest is vast, Teren; they might not be the only ones," added Brak as if reading his friend's mind. "Kill these and there's no way the others will join us again. Worse still, they might turn on us and that could lead to infighting between all the different nationalities that follow us. We are a loose alliance of brothers after all."

Teren looked at the two men in front of him and nodded. Brak was a Brelander, Orton a Lydian, whilst he himself was a Remadan. Brak was right. One wrong move here could break apart everything they had been fighting for all these months.

"Very well, then let's go and be reunited with our brothers," said Teren waving the men behind him forward.

Teren and Brak followed Orton through the dense undergrowth for about eight hundred paces until they came to a clearing of about twenty paces by thirty. On Teren's orders, the rest of the men had followed quietly behind them and had stopped roughly two hundred paces from the clearing. Despite his misgivings Teren was pleased to see the deserters standing in the clearing facing them with their weapons drawn when Teren and the others emerged from the trees. He was also aware of at least four men with bows in the nearby trees watching their every move.

"Teren!" said one of the deserters when he recognised the Remadan. His own lookouts had warned him that a small group were approaching the camp. "You're a sight for sore eyes."

For a moment or two Teren could not recall the man's name. He was not one of the originals from the Salandori slave camp but had joined his men on the journey west after the siege of Vangor. He was a good man as far as Teren could remember and he was surprised to see him there with the deserters. Then the man's name suddenly came to him.

"Coric."

"You finally decided to leave the camp?" asked Coric.

"Let's just say that their hospitality has left a little to be desired of late," replied Teren. "No offence, Brak."

"None taken," smiled the northerner.

"And the others?" asked Coric.

"Nobody stayed. Those that aren't with me are dead."

"You mean the whole army is behind you in the forest?" Coric looked startled.

"Aye, what's left of it."

Coric glanced to his left at the lookout who had reported that Teren and a handful of men were approaching and wondered how the man had missed the other couple of thousand soldiers. The lookout looked sheepish and then shrugged.

Teren grinned picking up on the unspoken communication.

"The rest of the lads are a way back. Far enough that your

lookouts wouldn't have spotted them, yet close enough to come running in the event of trouble."

"And is there going to be any…trouble I mean?" asked Coric nervously. Teren's loathing for deserters was well known.

Teren fixed the man with a hard stare and deliberately left it a few long lingering seconds before replying.

"No, not for my part at least."

"Nor mine," replied Coric looking mightily relieved. "So you fought your way through the Narmidian lines?"

"We did and it would have been that much easier if our numbers hadn't been eroded these last weeks." The barb wasn't lost on Coric.

"Few of us really wanted to leave, Teren, but the men were becoming restless. An idle soldier is a poor soldier and idle soldiers tend to start missing home that much more. I regret the manner of my leaving but not the fact that I left, especially if it was the catalyst to force the breakout."

The man's arrogance staggered Teren.

"You still should have come to me with your concerns. There would have been a better way of handling this," said Teren.

"Perhaps. So what happens now?"

"Now we head south and then east back to our homes," said the man standing to Coric's right. He was a small, wiry man dressed in a tatty Cardellan infantry uniform. Teren had seen him before around the camp but had never been interested enough to learn the man's name.

"The fighting is to the north, son," said Teren eyeing the man suspiciously.

"Well we don't want any part of your war now, Rad; we've done our share of killing and fighting. All we want to do is go home to our families," said the Cardellan, though he was clearly not sure of himself and kept glancing around nervously as if seeking support.

"And you think the Narmidians are going to let you do that do you? You think that they're going to let you go wandering around the countryside unmolested? Fools! If they see you, they'll kill you."

"That's your opinion, old man, not ours." Some of the men gathered behind Coric and the Cardellan were muttering their agreement. Others nodded but most just stood there silently watching the exchange.

"I promise you all that the Narmidians are Kaden bent on nothing short of the total conquest of Arkadia and if they have to kill every man able to wield a sword in the process, they will. If you leave here in ones and twos heading to your homes, you're going to be picked off with ease. It is only through strength and unity that we will prevail," replied Teren.

"Prevail? All you've led us to is defeat after defeat. We've had enough of your grand speeches and false promises, Remadan. If you want to stay and have your own private war with the Narmidians be my guest, but the rest of us are going home," said the Cardellan.

"Watch your mouth, Rylak. Do I need to remind you that this is Teren Rad of Remada, one of the greatest warriors ever seen in Arkadia? He was killing the enemy whilst you were still crawling on all fours. You will treat him with the respect he deserves otherwise you will answer to me," said Coric, his face turning red.

"I do not answer to you, Coric any more than I do this fool. None of us do. We only followed you here because you said you had a plan but what was it in the end; to run to the trees and hide? We should have left here days ago but your courage failed you and here we've remained."

"Do you think your homes are even there anymore? You saw enough destruction on the march west to know that's unlikely. Only by sticking together and fighting this enemy shoulder to shoulder do we have the chance to free our lands and our people," said Teren trying desperately to keep his own temper under control. If it had just been this one man he would have cut his throat by now but he was fighting for the support and loyalty of around fifty men and killing the weasel in front of him would not get the job done, however satisfying it might be.

"More lies. You won't be happy to you've killed us all, old man. Go back to whatever hole you crawled out of and leave us be we are sick of taking orders from Remadan whoresons."

Brak winced as the Cardellan uttered those last words and a deathly silence fell across the clearing as most waited to see what would happen next, though Brak was pretty sure he already knew. So too did some of the men standing around Rylak who instinctively started to back away, distancing themselves from his words as well as his body.

Teren was staring at the Cardellan and smiling, though Brak could see that the smile did not reach his eyes. He had been surprised yet pleased that Teren had not reacted to some of the man's earlier insults but knew this time Rylak had gone too far. It was not going to end well for him. Brak braced himself for what was coming next but before Teren made his expected move, there was a hiss as a sword was withdrawn from a scabbard and then a soft grunt.

Rylak looked down, his eyes wide with shock when he saw the point of a sword protruding from his stomach. Slowly it was withdrawn only to be replaced by an ever widening circle of red. With a questioning look to his left where Coric was standing holding a bloody sword, Rylak collapsed silently to his knees and then face down onto the forest floor. Coric leant forward and wiped his sword clean on the back of Rylak's tunic before once again sheathing it.

"Well I didn't see that coming," Teren muttered to himself as he looked at Coric.

"That man's been a thorn in my side since the day I met him and needed to learn how to show respect. I did warn him," said Coric.

"It's true, he did," said Teren turning and grinning at Brak.

The other men who had fled the camp with Coric were all milling around unsure what to do and looking to each other to take a lead. Teren was reminded of a flock of sheep who discover a wolf amongst them and know that they should run, but don't know where. Coric glanced about him and then turned to face Teren.

"I think you should say something."

"Me? You're the one who just gutted their mate."

"Rylak was nobody's mate, trust me. Now speak before you lose them," urged Coric quietly.

Teren looked at Brak who just nodded his agreement and then sighed.

"Brothers! You all know me and I know some of you. We are all soldiers here. I understand why you fled the camp and I know that I've made some mistakes whilst I've been leading you, but coming here wasn't one of them. Breland was…is the last major nation still unconquered by the Narmidians and was an obvious rallying point for men prepared to carry on fighting; men like you. What we couldn't have known was that one man's personal ambition was so great that he was prepared to sacrifice thousands of men's lives and possibly the security of his own nation, to achieve it. So we have been forced to leave and find ourselves skulking in a forest. But we are still alive and we are still in this fight and whilst one free Arkadian still draws breath and is prepared to stand up and say 'no', then Arkadia will never be truly conquered. I am prepared to be that man, but who will stand by my side?"

Brak immediately took a step closer to Teren as did Orton. A few seconds later Coric walked over to his side until one by one, they all came and stood behind him. He wasn't sure where it had begun, but somewhere somebody started to chant Teren's name, a lone voice that was soon joined by others until all around him had joined in. The sound of fifty men chanting Teren's name drifted through the trees to the bulk of Teren's army until eventually the trees reverberated to the sound of nearly three thousand voices roaring his name, sending clouds of crows scurrying into the early morning sky.

Teren looked at Brak and winked. Once more the great man had worked his magic and despite their predicament Brak had a feeling that this was some sort of turning point.

Chapter 13

Ro and his escort slowly made their way down to the gates of Helot picking their way through the crowds of people going about their daily business. If the people knew about the invasion of their country by the eastern hordes, they were unfazed and seemed content to go about their daily routines as usual. The Lotari were a disciplined people, raised by a strict code from the moment they could walk and taught to obey their betters without question. There was no panic here, no unseemly scramble to reach sanctuary inside the city gates as Ro had witnessed at both Tahara, the capital of Lydia and at Vangor. If and when the time came, Ro could imagine these people putting down their wares and tools in an orderly fashion and then strolling into the city in neat columns of two.

Ro turned his thoughts from the people to the city itself as they passed through the majestic white gates with their ornate carvings. He had forgotten how beautiful they were and what an artistic and gifted people the Lotari were. It was a shame that like their neighbours the Silevians, they were very insular and whilst they didn't refuse travellers access to their country, neither did they encourage it, fearing an influx of settlers would dilute their proud heritage and alter their way of life, a way of life that had existed for thousands of years.

The courtyard inside the city gates was exactly as Ro remembered it and he had no doubt that it had been like that for decades. Activity inside the city was a little more animated with clusters of imperial soldiers either drilling or carrying bundles of weapons to various locations. There were fewer civilians inside the city gates than outside and most of those paid little heed to Ro and his escort despite the rarity of a southern visitor.

The escort led Ro through the square and up a series of narrow cobbled streets, with tightly packed three storey stone buildings on either side. The ground floor of the majority of these buildings was occupied by shops and traders, whilst the first and second storeys were peoples' homes.

They took another left turn and then a right until eventually they emerged onto a wider road leading up a gentle slope, which Ro remembered led to the imperial residence. The houses on either side of this road were larger and less in number, their size and location testament to the owner's standing in the Lotari hierarchy. There were no shops or traders here.

The small party of riders made their way up the slope towards the magnificent looking imperial residence and when they were no further than fifty paces away, the gates slowly swung open and a score of immaculately dressed imperial guards hurried out and formed two perfect lines either side of the gates. The officer in charge of the escort spoke briefly with the guard commander, the latter of whom glanced at Ro and then nodded.

The officer in charge of the escort then said something to his men and they obediently swung their horses round and headed back down the slope and into the city. Then the officer turned to Ro and spoke in the Common tongue.

"Follow me." He then sedately walked his horse through the gates and into the courtyard of the imperial residence. Ro obediently followed and was aware of the guardsmen falling in behind him and then the sound of the gates being shut and secured.

A few seconds later two men who were not dressed in military uniform, came rushing forward seemingly out of nowhere and took the reins of both horses. The officer of the escort climbed down from his horse and signalled for Ro to do the same. Once he had dismounted the horses were led away and the majority of the guards marched briskly away leaving just six in close attendance.

In front of Ro were a flight of about a dozen marble steps leading up to two more intricately carved doors, which were flanked on either side by pristine looking pillars. The doors of the building suddenly swung open and two huge men in armour polished so brightly that when the sun caught it, the glare made Ro squint, strode purposefully out and glared down at Ro and his companion. These were the Emperor's personal guards, men trained in the use of just about every type of weapon imaginable and men who were trained to fear nothing and endure everything.

Without waiting to be told, Ro dropped to his knees and kept his eyes down knowing that the emperor and his wife would be right behind them and that to show disrespect was usually terminal.

Everything had gone silent and Ro imagined that everyone except the men on guard duty, were doing the same as him in that moment.

A young man's voice spoke in Lotari and although Ro had a rudimentary grasp of the language the words were spoken so quickly that he was unable to discern any of them. Another man slightly to his left and front replied and Ro guessed that this was the officer of the escort who was probably making a report and informing the emperor about his captive.

There was another brief exchange and Ro heard the officer get nimbly to his feet.

"Raise your head, but do not look at his imperial majesty; keep your eyes down at all times," he said to Ro in the Common tongue.

Ro did as he was ordered and knelt upright, keeping his eyes firmly cast down. He had no idea whether the old emperor would recognise him and whether if he did, he would even care.

Long seconds passed without anybody speaking and Ro became aware of gentle footsteps approaching him from the front. The desire to look up was overpowering and it took all of his will power to control, especially when he considered that whoever was approaching him might be about to run a knife across his throat. He calmed himself with the thought that surely they wouldn't have brought him all this way to do something they could easily have done where they found him.

Whoever it was stopped two or three paces in front of Ro and Ro found himself staring at a pair of well-manicured feet in exquisitely crafted sandals. The skin on the feet and legs looked young and healthy and not in keeping with how he imagined the old emperor would look.

"Ro? Ro Aryk is that you?" said the voice in perfect Common tongue.

"Yes...your majesty," replied Ro unsure whether he had been given permission to look up.

"I can't believe it, it is you, Ro. You're back after all these years." Then almost as an afterthought he added, "Stand, Ro, please get to your feet, you never have to bow to me."

Ro did as he was commanded and slowly stood up and raised his head. Standing before him and beaming was not Emperor Cyrix, but Prince Zerut. The younger man stepped forward and enthusiastically hugged Ro.

"Prince Zerut," said Ro when the other man eventually released him.

"Not quite, my friend. It is Emperor Zerut now. My father died a couple of months ago."

"I'm so sorry," replied Ro. "I had no idea. No one did."

"And that is how we wanted it. If the world had learned that my father was dead, the Narmidians might have felt that the time was right to attack us and we were not ready."

"How did your father die?"

"Peacefully in his sleep though he had been ill for a long time and had been in a coma for some time prior to his death."

"I mourn with you, Emperor Zerut. Your father was a good man."

"Thank you, my friend. He was."

"Now, I'm sure your captain has just told you, but the Narmidians have attacked; they are inside your borders."

"Yes, he has, but much has changed in the last few months. Whilst my father lay sick in his bed I assumed command of our armed forces. This time has been well spent in rearming and recruiting. The eastern men will pay a heavy toll in blood for every minute they spend on Lotari land, of that I can assure you," said the emperor confidently, but Ro found himself wondering whether his friend realised how strong his enemy really was.

"I know that to be true as I have already witnessed the ability of your men to approach an enemy unseen, launch an attack and then melt away before the enemy can respond. In fact I owe my life to your captain and his men," said Ro.

105

"Truly? Then I shall see that the captain and his men are well-rewarded." The emperor said something too quickly for Ro to understand and the officer of the escort bowed to his emperor and smiled, obviously delighted at what he had just been told. He then turned to face Ro and bowed again before backing away half a dozen paces and then turning and striding purposefully away.

"Come, Ro, we have much to discuss and I would hear of your adventures since last we spoke. First, however, you must be tired and thirsty from your journey. I will have my servants show you to your room and have them bring you food and wine. Then we will talk."

"You are most kind, majesty," replied Ro.

The emperor turned and started to make his way back up the steps and at the signal from one of his two giant bodyguards, Ro followed him, the guards falling in behind. At the top of the steps waited Shala, the new empress. She too was delighted to see Ro, but protocol demanded that she do nothing more than smile at her old friend and guest. Ro bowed and smiled warmly back and after Shala took her husband's arm, Ro followed them into the imperial palace.

Ro was shown to a palatial room, lavishly furnished and ornately decorated. A series of servants had brought him a wide variety of food, some of which he recognised and some he didn't and as much wine as he required. After eating and drinking his fill he was shown to a private bath where he was able to soak away the grime and dirt of his journey. It also gave him the opportunity to consider everything that had happened in recent days including his departure from Silevia and the bitter parting from his friend, Arlen Meric.

After bathing, Ro dressed in the clean tunic and breeches he was left by one of the servants whilst his own clothes were taken away to be laundered by servants. His weapons, cloak and shield were all neatly stacked in the corner of the room. He hoped that his mare was also receiving such loving attention in whatever stables they had taken her to.

Once dressed he lay back on the sumptuous bed and momentarily closed his eyes, waking several hours later to find that the sky outside had darkened. Embarrassed and worried that the emperor might be annoyed by his disrespect he hurried to the door and flung it open, startling the servant who was stationed outside. When Ro asked them to take him to see the emperor immediately, the servant who spoke excellent Common tongue explained that the emperor had come to see Ro several hours earlier and found him asleep. He had then left specific instructions for Ro not to be woken but to be brought before the emperor when he finally awoke. Relieved, but still somewhat embarrassed that the emperor had come looking for him, he gestured for the servant to lead the way whilst he adjusted his clothing and smoothed down his hair.

Ro followed the servant down a series of corridors all of which were decorated with fine artwork, pottery or tapestries. Eventually they came to the throne room doors and after bowing, the servant opened the doors and beckoned for Ro to enter, the two guards seemingly expecting him as they moved quickly out of his way.

Ro entered the room and immediately all eyes turned to the newcomer. Emperor Zerut was discussing something with one of his aides whilst a civilian waited patiently on his knees for the emperor to make a decision about whatever issue the man had brought before him.

The emperor looked up at the sound of the doors opening and his face immediately broke into a giant grin. Seemingly not wanting to be distracted any longer the emperor said something to the man kneeling in front of him and then dismissed him with a wave of his hand, his eyes now fixed on Ro. Whatever the emperor had said to the civilian was welcome news as the man was positively beaming as he excitedly backed away from the throne and towards the doors.

The emperor beckoned for Ro to approach and Ro marched smartly up the centre of the room coming to a halt a respectful distance from the bottom of the steps leading up to the emperor's throne. Then he started to kneel.

"Stop! I told you before there is no need for that, my friend. Ro Aryk kneels to no man in my kingdom," said the emperor.

"Once more you honour me, your majesty," said Ro smiling. Then he turned and looked at the woman sitting next to the emperor. "Empress Shala; you look as radiant and beautiful as ever. Time is no enemy of yours it would seem."

"Thank you, Ro. I see that the years have not robbed you of your charm," replied the empress.

Ro smiled warmly and bowed.

"My servants have treated you well I trust?" asked the emperor.

"I have been very well treated, your majesty, thank you and I apologise for being indisposed when you came to see me earlier."

"Think nothing of it. A man snoring that loudly must have been in dire need of sleep." The emperor and everyone else in the hall who spoke the Common tongue laughed.

"So it would seem, but I am refreshed now and at your service."

"Good. I look forward to hearing of all your adventures now you are rested but first I must sadly deal with an urgent matter. Colonel Ulikath who you have already met," the emperor gestured towards the soldier standing to his right whom Ro recognised as the captain of the party that had saved him earlier, "has already made his report whilst you slept, but others have returned with equally disturbing reports which I must hear. I would welcome your input if you would join us?"

"Again I would be honoured, your majesty."

"Excellent, then let's get on with it." The emperor and empress stood and immediately everybody except the soldiers who had to remain vigilant at all times, bowed, including Ro. The emperor then turned and headed for a chamber room directly behind the throne, followed by some of his senior aides and some military commanders. The empress smiled at Ro and then headed in a different direction attended by four hand maidens. Unsure of the protocol as to when he should follow, Ro looked nervously around and found Colonel Ulikath gesturing with his arm for Ro to follow. Ro nodded his thanks and did as bade and the colonel followed behind him.

"Congratulations on your promotion, Colonel," Ro whispered to Ulikath.

"Thank you. The emperor honours me for the small matter of saving you."

"It wasn't a small matter to me," said Ro smiling as they entered the chamber room.

The council chamber was less ornately decorated than the throne room, with one wall depicting a battle scene from a long ago war and the wall opposite containing a mural of a Lotari warrior fighting a two headed dragon.

Everyone waited for the emperor to be seated at the head of the table and then everybody else sat in order of seniority, the most senior with pride of place next to the emperor. Ro sat right at the other end of the table next to Colonel Ulikath.

The table in front of them was not so much a table as a panorama of the country of Lotar. With every city, town, river, hill and forest marked on it, it was a work of art and Ro found himself staring at it in awe. The skill and craftsmanship of the Lotari people was something to behold indeed.

"Gentlemen, it seems we find ourselves in dark times. You are all aware of Colonel Ulikath's report earlier this afternoon, when he told us of his clashes with the forces of King Vesla, which have crossed into our territory over the River Aryx," began the emperor, letting his gaze wander round the faces of those gathered around his table. "Well, since then I have received no fewer than eight further reports regarding Narmidian incursions. Some have come from soldiers but some have been from civilians and whilst the latter might be more prone to exaggeration, I think we can safely conclude that this is no punitive strike by Vesla, but a full blooded invasion. I had hoped that we would be able to sit out this war as we have so many before, protected by our traditional neutrality and the mysticism that surrounds our country, but it would appear not to be the case this time. This time we are going to have to fight for our cherished freedom and fight hard.

"So far we have only been involved in small engagements, the likes of which Colonel Ulikath and his men performed this morning, harrying the enemy and then retreating before they can retaliate. Whilst this tactic is laudable and will frustrate the enemy, it will not defeat him. We need a plan, gentlemen."

That, Ro realised, was the cue for his aides and generals to speak up.

An officer began to speak in Lotari and the emperor immediately raised a hand to stop him.

"In the Common tongue please, General, for the benefit of our Remadan friend."

The officer nodded before resuming in the Common tongue. "Your majesty, perhaps the tactic employed by Colonel Ulikath this morning will not defeat the enemy but maybe it will be enough to persuade him to abandon the invasion. If we continue to harry his columns, nibble away at his men and supplies without giving battle, perhaps he will decide that the cost is too high and will withdraw." Several sat around the table nodded, although Ro noted that Colonel Ulikath himself did not seem to agree or perhaps thought it was not his place to comment where his superiors were involved.

"Perhaps, but at what cost?" asked another general.

"We don't have the men to fight the Narmidians in a pitched battle; they are as numerous as blades of grass," added another.

"I don't think you give our men enough credit, General. I would back any one of our men against five Narmidians," replied another officer.

"And it still won't be enough," snapped one of the emperor's civilian aides. "We have it on good authority that they outnumber the imperial forces almost twenty to one."

"Why don't we withdraw to our cities and wait them out? If their forces are as numerous as you say then their supplies will run out long before ours do even with an influx of people," said another aide.

"Because there is no way we can get all of our people inside the cities. Even if there was room for them, which there isn't, there wouldn't be enough time," replied the first aide.

"His imperial majesty's army does not cower behind the walls from any army," said the senior general indignantly.

"Surely his imperial majesty's forces do whatever the emperor commands, General?" the aide bit back.

"Of course," replied the general embarrassed. "I apologise, your majesty."

"Not necessary, General. You are right. My army will not

cower behind walls and neither will the emperor. How can I sit safely in my palace whilst my people are being butchered? Already we are receiving reports that farms and villages are being razed to the ground and everyone…everyone, put to the sword. No, I will not hide. I want a better plan than that, gentlemen."

The room fell silent for a few long moments and everyone's gaze dropped to the panoramic map in front of them. Finally the chief aide looked up and fixed his gaze on Ro.

"And what are our southern neighbours doing about this scourge from the east may I ask?"

"Fighting, losing and dying mostly. I have personally fought in many battles and skirmishes against these men. They are not invincible, they are just too numerous. Had the nations of Arkadia woken to the danger earlier and united, we could have stopped the invasion in Delarite or Lydia perhaps, but the Delarite invasion of Remada weakened the two strongest armies in Arkadia and made us vulnerable. Only now are we united but united in defeat," replied Ro.

"No one fights on?" asked the emperor.

"Every army that I'm aware of has been routed, your majesty. But still men resist. What strength is left in the free men of Arkadia now follow my friend Teren Rad." A murmur of recognition of the name rippled around the table, but Ro could not tell whether it was friendly or not. "I have not seen him for many months, but the information I have suggests that what fighting men are left in Arkadia have fled with him to Breland to seek sanctuary."

"So the great Teren Rad has run from the fight and now hides behind the skirts of those northern barbarians?" asked one of the aides.

"I am a guest here, sir and will not disrespect the hospitality your emperor and people have shown me, but would in the same breath thank you not to insult my friend again. If what I hear is true and Teren has travelled to the north to seek refuge, it will only be temporary. He will have a plan; he always does. Whilst he rests there you can be sure that he will be doing his damnedest to persuade the northerners to join the fight, whilst all the time men will be flocking to his banner from every corner of Arkadia."

"I hope you are right, Master Aryk," replied the aide. He looked up and caught the look in his emperor's eyes. "And I apologise for my insult to your friend, which I wholeheartedly withdraw."

"Apology accepted," said Ro nodding.

"So what do you think we should do, Ro? How would you fight them if you were me?" asked the emperor. All eyes turned to look at the Remadan.

Ro took a deep breath and then puffed out his cheeks as he considered the emperor's question.

"For now I'd task some of my best riders under a competent commander, to keep harrying the enemy whenever and wherever possible. Their columns are long and their supply lines even longer. It will be a while before Vesla can bring his forces to bear and overwhelm you. Use that time to consolidate and mobilise whatever forces you have and construct a plan. This is your country and you all know the terrain better than any of the Narmidians even if they have sent scouts ahead of them. You need to choose the place of battle. You need to choose somewhere where his numbers won't count for much: a narrow pass, a steep hill flanked by woods, anywhere like that. You need to nullify his numbers. It also needs to be somewhere where the skills of your men can be put to good use; somewhere where your *jemtak* can be hurled to their maximum distance."

The emperor was nodding, as were most of the people round the table. After a few seconds the emperor glanced down at the map below him studying it thoughtfully.

"Perhaps here, at Myaki Pass?" said the emperor looking round at his men for support.

"I don't believe I know the place, your majesty," said Ro.

"It is a narrow pass through the Volantir Mountains. On one side is a dense wood and on the other is a rocky and barren slope. At the northern end of the pass is a gentle grassy slope. The pass itself at its narrowest point is no more than…twenty strides wide. It would provide a narrow front in which to engage the enemy, whilst our infantry could be raining *jemtak* and javelins down from either side. I would hold our heavy cavalry in reserve with me at the top of the final slope to either crush any breakthrough or as a screen should we be routed." Now everyone was nodding. The plan was taking shape. "Have the servants bring food and wine here; we have much to discuss and plan," and as the servants scurried away to carry out the emperor's orders, Ro and his hosts huddled round the map and began to plan for war.

Chapter 14

Their journey through the woods was slow and sometimes arduous but after some four hours of walking Brak finally announced that they were nearing their arranged rendezvous point with Yarik and his men, assuming that they'd survived. As they'd made their way through the forest, they'd come across several more bands of deserters. Some were perhaps only two or three in number but others were more substantial, numbering a score or even more. In the overall scheme of things they weren't going to tip the balance in the allies' favour Teren knew, but it did the men's morale good to see some of their old comrades coming back into the fold. Only a few declined Teren's offer to re-join the allied army.

"How do we know that the Narmidians haven't just skirted around the edge of the forest and aren't waiting outside with several thousand arrows and spears to say hello?" asked Coric.

"We don't," replied Teren.

"And…" encouraged Coric.

"And we'll deal with it if we find that to be the case," said Teren much to Coric's frustration.

"The forest is vast, Coric and the Narmidians do not know the lay of the land; it is therefore highly unlikely that they would be waiting at the right point for us to emerge," said Brak, worried that Teren's dismissiveness might encourage a whole new spate of desertions.

"But not impossible?"

"No, just very unlikely. Chances are they haven't even organised a pursuit yet. They've got Yarik's men giving them the run around and a small matter of a couple of thousand angry northerners in the town to worry about first. Besides, if we did find them waiting outside for us we will be forewarned and surprise will be on our side. They won't know exactly where we'll be emerging from."

"All sounds a bit risky to me," said Coric.

"Nothing in this world is risk free, my friend. Besides,

what were you going to do; just sit in the forest for the rest of your life?" asked Teren.

"No, of course not, but it would have been a darn sight easier to sneak past those whoresons with only a handful of men at my back rather than three thousand."

"Aye, it would, but it wouldn't be as much fun now would it?" said Teren grinning.

After a few seconds of saying nothing, Coric broke into a wide grin of his own. "I guess not."

Brak raised his arm in the air and like a chain reaction, the entire column which was stretched out for hundreds of paces behind him and Teren, ground to a halt.

"What is it, lad?" asked Teren.

"This is the spot."

"Are you sure? You haven't been here for a long time remember. One tree looks pretty much like another if you ask me."

"This is the spot, trust me."

"So be it. You want to scout ahead with some of the lads?" asked Teren.

Brak nodded and then turned and pointed at half a dozen men stood behind him including Coric. "You men follow me. We're going to spread out along the forest edge up ahead and check the horizon. Work in pairs and report back here in a few minutes. Understood?" They all nodded. "Good, let's go."

Teren watched them go and then turned to the men behind him and told them to pass the word down the column to fall out and rest for a few minutes. Satisfied that his orders were being obeyed, Teren looked round for somewhere to sit and rest his aching knees and settled on a fallen log lying about a dozen paces away.

With Yarik away and Brak off scouting, his other trusted lieutenants were positioned throughout the column and at the rear, so no one else nearby felt comfortable enough to come and join Teren on the log. He was glad as he needed time to think and clear his head. He had not foreseen their early departure from the Brelandic camp and had hoped that in time he would march out at the head of a vast army made up of his men and the northerners. Brak's brother's scheming and the unexpected murder of his father had put pay to that and now he found himself at the head of his own men running away from two adversaries with his tail between his legs. Worse still he was forced to skulk in the trees and gratefully accept the allegiance of men who had deserted his camp under the cover of darkness. It did not sit well with him.

This part of his plan had gone well, or at least as well as he could have hoped. He had managed to get approximately three thousand men away from the enemy and into the relative safety of the trees. Two hundred more were somewhere off to the east, though whether they still drew breath or were now food for the carrion birds, he had no idea.

Unfortunately this was as far as his improvised plan went. The proposed rendezvous with Yarik and his men was the end to it. He couldn't go north, back to where they came from, at least not yet. He couldn't go east where they'd travelled from as all that land was now under Narmidian control and nor could he go west as all that lay that way was the ocean. That only left south. To the south lay the vast open fields and plains of Angorra. The Angorrans were an agricultural people and the country was lightly populated. If your dream was to own a homestead or a large farm and work the land, then Angorra was the perfect place. Nothing but green pastures and crop bearing land for as far as the eye could see.

When the Narmidians had invaded the west the Angorran government, such that it was, had immediately surrendered much to the contempt of other western nations, but in truth they wouldn't have been able to do much. With no standing army and just a light militia they would have been nothing more than target practise for Vesla's battle hardened troops.

No, it was to the south they would go. If Teren read the situation right, Vesla would have realised that the Angorrans were no threat and would only have left a small garrison in the country, one that would be no trouble to Teren and his men. They would head to Angorra, rearm and formulate a new plan. Then they would strike back.

Teren rested his sword against the log and arched his back in an attempt to relieve the ache that had been slowly building up there, wincing as it gave a satisfying click. He was about to repeat the process when the sound of someone approaching through the undergrowth drew his attention and his hand instinctively reached for the hilt of his sword. He relaxed and laid his sword down again when he recognised Brak returning from his scouting mission.

"What news, Brak?"

"The immediate area is clear, but Fila reckons he saw a large group of horsemen travelling due west. I didn't see them but then that man has got devilishly good eyesight. I've left him there with another man with orders to report back immediately if the horsemen reappear or anything else changes."

Teren nodded his approval. "Good. Get something to drink and then rest."

"How long are we going to wait here for Yarik, Teren?" asked Brak.

"As long as it takes."

"Every hour we tarry here is another hour the Narmidians have to figure out where we're hiding and come after us."

"I know, but we've got to wait for Yarik. At least for now. He will come."

"I hope you're right."

"So do I, lad, so do I."

Teren allowed the men to rest until he estimated the sun had reached its highest point in the sky before finally giving the order for them to gather their equipment and prepare to move out. Due to the distance the column was spread out inside the forest it took some time for the order to trickle down the line and Teren waited what he hoped was long enough for the order to reach the last man before he moved off. The last thing he wanted to do having bolstered his numbers with former deserters was to inadvertently leave some men behind. He was just about to raise his hand and give the signal to move when Fila, one of the two lookouts posted by Brak, came scurrying through the undergrowth towards him.

"Problem?" asked Teren.

"Horsemen, approaching from the west," replied Fila.

"Narmidians?"

"Too far to tell."

"How many?" asked Brak who had joined Teren and Fila.

"Difficult to guess at this distance but I'd estimate about two to three hundred."

"Too big to be a patrol, too small to be a pursuit force," said Teren.

"Not long after you left us, Brak, a second band of horsemen rode west in roughly the same direction as the first ones I told you about," said Fila.

"What happened to them?" asked Teren.

"I've no idea."

"They can't have merged with the first party as the numbers just don't add up," said Brak.

"Yarik?" suggested Teren.

"That would make sense. The first group of riders we saw was Yarik and the party behind him was Narmidians pursuing him," agreed Brak.

"So why did he ride west and not turn towards us for help?" asked Fila.

"Because he didn't want to give our position away in case a larger force of Narmidians were pursuing him further back," replied Teren.

"That just leaves one question then," said Brak. "Which party is riding towards us now: Yarik's or the Narmidians?"

"Well we're not going to find out waiting here. Tomask?" A middle aged man with a scar running across his left cheek courtesy of a Narmidian sword came scurrying over to Teren. "We've incoming riders. Take your archers and position yourselves just inside the treeline, Fila will show you where. We don't know yet whether they're friend or foe so make sure your men don't shoot until you're certain. I don't want that oaf of a Delarite taking one in the backside and coming in here like a bear with a sore head, understood?"

The man nodded and then whistled a signal and immediately around a hundred men came to join him. Teren had deliberately made sure that the bulk of his archers were positioned near the front of the column so that he could deploy them quickly in such an event. The others were at the rear of the column ready to provide covering fire had the Narmidians pursued them into the forest.

"What about the rest of us?" asked Brak.

"We'll form up as best we can amongst these trees ready to engage the enemy if Tomask's men can't finish the job. If they are Narmidians it's important that none of them get away to make a report."

Brak nodded and strode over to a small group of men stood chatting a few paces away. A few moments later they all scurried off to prepare the men and in no time at all everyone was in position. Satisfied that everything was as it should be, Teren signalled for Brak to follow him and then made his way through the trees and undergrowth to the forest edge, where Tomask and his men were knelt in line with arrows nocked.

Teren nodded approvingly and then took another step towards the treeline careful not to step in front of any of the archers' firing view. His eyes, like the rest of his aching body, were starting to fail him and try as he might he couldn't make out the riders bearing down on them at pace. He tried rubbing his eyes, peering, anything to improve his vision, but the fact remained that he wasn't going to be able to make out who was coming until they were virtually on top of them. In hindsight he realised, he was not the ideal man to be there giving the order whether to fire or not and he breathed a silent breath of relief when Brak stepped up alongside him.

Teren glanced to his right and saw the anxious look in some of the archers' faces.

"Steady, lads, just a few moments more."

The riders were less than four hundred strides now. Teren flexed his fingers before wrapping them around his sword hilt. Three hundred strides.

"Can you make them out, Brak?" asked Teren.

Two hundred and fifty strides.

"Brak?"

"Wait," replied Brak.

Two hundred strides.

"Brak, for the love of Sulat, who are they?" Teren could almost feel the anxious tension emanating from some of the archers and feared an arrow might be loosed by mistake at any moment.

One hundred and fifty strides.

"Brak!" Teren almost screamed the word.

"It's Yarik," said Brak relieved.

"You sure?" asked Teren.

"I'm sure."

"Stand down, stand down," Teren shouted and one by one the archers lowered their weapons and released the tension from their bow strings. By the time that the last man had lowered his bow, the first riders had reined in a few paces from the forest edge.

Teren and Brak stepped out of the cool shade and into the warm midday sunshine just as Yarik lowered himself tenderly from his horse.

"Still alive then, big man?" said Teren holding out his right arm.

"Despite the best efforts of several Narmidian dogs, I yet draw breath, Remadan. You'll not get rid of me so easily," said Yarik clasping Teren's arm in the warrior's traditional greeting.

"I guess next time I'll have to pay them more," said Teren grinning.

"I guess you will," replied the big Delarite grinning back. He released Teren's arm and turned to clasp Brak's. "You still with us as well, young Prince?"

"So it would seem, Yarik. It is good to have you back."

By now all of the men had reined in and sat atop their horses drawing breath, their horses white with sweat. Teren looked around and winced. There were a lot fewer men here than he sent out with Yarik. Worse still, the force with Yarik also contained the remnants of the cavalry under Sergeant Nim who had covered their escape from the Brelandic camp. Obviously at some point they had run into Yarik's men and joined them.

"You must have much to tell, but first what of the riders we saw following you?"

"They won't be going home again, any of them. They chased us several leagues west of here until I eventually found a spot we could use to our advantage. We then set a trap and ambushed them. There were no survivors. Then we rested for a while before heading back here," said Yarik.

"You're a sight for sore eyes, that's for sure, all of you are," said Teren raising his voice so all the riders could hear him. "Welcome back, lads." Teren turned to look for Tomask. "Tomask, send men back to give orders for the army to advance. It's time for us to leave the safety of the trees. Your horses look spent," he then said turning back to face the Delarite.

"They could use a rest, we all could, but we'll walk them for a while. I for one am in no hurry to resume the saddle any time soon."

Teren and Brak both laughed at the Delarite's obvious discomfort.

"Okay, as soon as the men are clear of the trees, we'll move out," said Teren.

"Were you pursued?" asked Yarik.

"No, once we broke through their lines we were able to make the trees unmolested. None followed. Some madman was apparently attacking their camp with a couple of hundred horsemen; it distracted them somewhat."

"Sounds like whoever led them was a great warrior and will have songs sung about him for centuries to come," said Yarik smiling.

"That's if his ego doesn't kill him first," replied Teren.

All three men started to laugh as behind them, hundreds and hundreds of soldiers began to emerge from the trees.

"So where are we heading now, Remadan?" asked Yarik.

"South."

"South! There's nothing south but those cowardly goat herders in Angorra."

"Exactly. Wide open space, probably garrisoned by a small force which we can quickly overwhelm. It will give us the ideal place to plan our next move and regroup. Besides, there's nowhere else to go," said Teren.

"I've been thinking about that," said Brak.

"Oh," said Teren.

"And I agree with you about north and east, but what about if we went northeast, to the northern kingdoms?"

"You mean towards Lotar and Silevia?" asked Teren.

"Yes. The last we heard they were still free. Perhaps we

121

will receive a warmer welcome there than we did from my own people."

Teren and Yarik looked at one another as they considered the proposal.

"The northern peoples are hostile to all outsiders; we will receive no cheer there," said Yarik eventually.

"I don't think they're hostile to outsiders, they're just not keen on them," replied Brak.

"They are hostile towards Delarites," said Yarik dismissively.

"That's because you Delarites normally turn up by the thousand carrying weapons and shields."

Yarik snorted in derision.

"Besides, didn't Ro and Arlen return to Silevia?" asked Brak.

"They did, but that was many months ago and we have heard nothing since," replied Teren.

"Maybe they have convinced the Silevians to join the war. At the very least they would surely be able to persuade them to provide us sanctuary."

"I don't know, Brak, with our backs to the sea we'll be trapped if the Narmidians come."

"Or you could look at it the other way and say that the sea would provide us with the means of escape if things went badly."

"We'd need an awful lot of ships to move three thousand men. What do you think, Yarik?"

"To the south there are vast open plains and a small number of enemy and the chance to rest and regroup. To get to Silevia we have got to travel through hundreds of leagues of enemy occupied territory with the prospect of having to fight for our lives every single day and an uncertain welcome when we get there. The choice is easy. When do we leave for the north?" said Yarik grinning.

Teren nodded. "And they call me mad. Silevia and the northern kingdoms it is then. Give the order to move out, Brak."

Moments later, three thousand men all that remained of the free peoples of Arkadia started to march east. Teren and the others had decided that to avoid the Narmidians surrounding the southern border of Breland, they would march due east for about a hundred leagues and then turn north east. By their calculations and with the guidance of some of the men who knew the territory, they would arrive at the northern kingdoms within two weeks assuming they didn't run into a sizeable portion of Vesla's army in the meantime.

Chapter 15

Ro watched as the first row of Lotari warriors stepped forward out of the trees and effortlessly hurled their *jemtak* at the enemy. By the time the cry of warning went up from one of the riders on the flank of the Narmidian column, it was already too late. The small metal stars slammed into the largely unprotected Narmidian soldiers. The Lotari were always careful to launch their attack at the light infantry who wore no armour and only carried wicker shields, therefore rendering the most casualties. As soon as they had hurled their weapons, the Lotari line melted back into the trees as a second wave took their place and repeated the process. The second barrage of *jemtak* usually rendered fewer casualties, but the fear and panic they caused were almost as effective.

A Lotari officer gave the order for the second wave to retreat into the woods and as the Narmidians slowly began to advance on them with better armoured troops leading the way, a wave of Lotari emerged from the woods on the opposite side of the track and hurled their *jemtak* into the unprotected backs of the light infantry who were sheltering behind their armoured comrades.

Confusion reigned as the light infantry ran around desperately trying to find cover from the deadly metal stars which were raining down on them. When the second wave of *jemtak* started to fall, discipline broke and they started running in all directions ignoring the shouts and threats of their officers. Disturbed by the confusion and pandemonium behind them, the armoured troops who had begun advancing on the Lotari position to the right, started to falter, some even stopping and turning round. Ro saw his chance.

"Now Borati, now is your time," shouted Ro and after drawing his sword he charged towards the mass of Narmidian soldiers milling round in confusion.

Two hundred of Lotar's finest cavalry regiment, the Borati, smashed into the Narmidians on their light ponies, slicing and hacking with their curved swords. Dozens fell under their onslaught with minimal casualties on the Lotari side. As soon as the men who had been put under temporary command of Ro cleared the column and made it to the woods opposite, Colonel Ulikath emerged out of the trees with a similar force of men, repeating the tactic they had employed with the *jemtak*. This time though some of the Narmidians, particularly the heavy infantry, had anticipated the second wave and whilst they were in no shape to fight back or launch a counterattack, they were in a position to better defend themselves.

Ro watched from the safety of the treeline opposite as Colonel Ulikath's men smashed through the Narmidian line and made for the trees opposite. The ground between the two woods was littered with the dead and dying. Whilst the casualties they had inflicted on Vesla's forces were in reality, but a drop in the ocean, they would be eroding the morale of his men with their constant attacks. This was the sixth such ambush Ro had been involved in and he knew that Colonel Ulikath had launched a couple on his own. Soon it would be time for the main battle. Emperor Zerut was already at the chosen site gathering as many forces about him as he could muster. He was also preparing the ground. Traps were being dug; deep ditches with spikes in the bottom and oil pits which could be set alight at a moment's notice.

Still Ro was not convinced that it would be enough.

Colonel Ulikath and his men had by now escaped into the trees opposite, so Ro turned his horse and disappeared into the trees behind him. He would now ride for the emperor's position by one direction and Colonel Ulikath would approach it from another. It was time to join the main force. The enemy would soon be at the site the emperor had chosen to make his stand.

***

Balok Vesla was in a rage as reports of the latest attack on the rear of his column reached him later that evening. This was the seventh or eighth attack that he could remember and whilst his losses were insignificant they were a source of great irritation. They were also beginning to sap at the courage of his men and even some of his officers. He could see it in the eyes of some of the men around the table before him now.

"Well, what happened this time?" asked Balok without even a hint of genuine interest.

"They hit us from both sides with two volleys of those metal stars before launching a cavalry attack from either side," replied General Xalit.

"And why were we not prepared for this eventuality?" asked Balok. "It's not as if this is the first time they've attacked us is it?"

"No, my Prince it isn't. But every time they attack they employ a different tactic or alternate the sequence of their assaults. It is hard to prepare for such attacks effectively. That is the beauty of them."

"Are you offering me an excuse, General? Because if you are I'm sure I can find someone to replace you who might actually be up to the job," asked Balok.

"No, my Prince. I was merely trying to point out that it is hard to protect against these attacks whilst we are strung out in such a long column and moving as fast as you are insisting we go. If your majesty would just halt the column and allow me to take a thousand of our finest lancers I will personally ride these dogs down."

"I know you would, General. However, our losses are minimal, so we must keep our eye on the main prize."

"We are marching on Helot?"

"No, our scouts tell us that Emperor Zerut has left the city and is mustering his forces here, just outside the town of Qui'tang," said the prince pointing at a map on the table before him.

"What is this?" asked the general pointing at something on the map. The map was not very detailed as few Narmidians had ever been to Lotar and fewer still had ever returned.

"It is called the Myaki Pass," replied one of the lesser generals.

"And this?" asked General Xalit.

"We don't know," replied the other general apologetically.

General Xalit frowned.

"What is it, General?" asked Balok unable to mask the irritation in his voice.

"Your majesty, we must try and ascertain the lie of the land before we commit to battle there."

"Why?"

"Because we don't know what to expect. It will be difficult to formulate a battle plan without knowing the lie of the land. All of the advantage will be with the enemy. If we have to travel through this Myaki Pass to reach Qui'tang, we must make every effort to know the terrain. A pass is an ideal place to spring an ambush."

"We do not need to know the lie of the land, General. Lotar is a tiny land with a puny force. Wherever this fool plans to make his stand, it will be his last."

General Xalit glanced round the table for support from the other officers, most of whom would agree with him. None were prepared to meet his eyes, however. Evidently he was on his own. He had to choose his next words carefully as they could be his last.

"You are right, your majesty, of course; the Lotari do only possess a small force. However, a small force sensibly positioned can wreak havoc on a much larger force. I just feel that it would be prudent to scout the terrain first."

Prince Balok stared at the general for a few moments and for a while, General Xalit felt that his life was hanging in the balance.

"For your information, General, I have already sent a number of pathfinders ahead, but none have yet returned, though some of their horses have."

"That only strengthens my concerns then, your majesty. Clearly the Lotari are very keen not to let us learn what we will be riding into," said General Xalit feeling somewhat vindicated.

"Perhaps, but it alters nothing. Whatever they have waiting for us it will not be enough. We will overwhelm them with sheer strength of numbers." The look in the prince's eyes said that the topic was no longer up for discussion and the general bit back anything further he was going to say. "Now go and rest, gentlemen, we have a busy day tomorrow. By my estimates we should arrive at Myaki Pass around noon. By sunset, I will be the ruler of Lotar." The prince raised his glass of wine and saluted the men around him and they obediently followed suit.

General Xalit was not only concerned about the terrain they would find themselves fighting in, but also the state of the men themselves. They had been marching at pace for days now and had managed to get very little sleep, the Lotari launching small punitive raids at various times during the night as well as day. It would be a very weary and demoralised army that arrived at the Myaki Pass the following day. He just hoped that it would be enough.

***

"You wanted to see me, your majesty?" said Ro as he approached the emperor's makeshift desk inside his palatial tent.

"Ah, Ro, come and take a seat please." Ro sat down on the cushions arrayed on the floor to the right of the desk having first waited for the emperor to sit. Three generals and Colonel Ulikath were also inside the tent and joined them. "You are well, my friend?"

"I'm fine, your majesty, thank you."

"Excellent. Our scouts report that Vesla's army is just outside the southern entrance to the pass and will be upon us by noon at the latest. That means that if he launches his attack immediately, as well as the obvious advantages that the terrain give us we will also be fighting with our backs to the sun, which is going to make it very uncomfortable for them. Are our men all correctly disposed General Livar?"

A burly general with a long thin beard and grey hair nodded in response.

"They are all positioned as agreed, your majesty."

"How many men did we manage to muster in the end, your majesty?" asked Ro.

The emperor looked over at General Livar.

"Just short of six thousand, your majesty."

"And how many do you estimate that we are up against, Ro?" asked the emperor.

Ro pursed his lips as he considered the question carefully before he answered.

"Perhaps as many as twenty thousand, your majesty, of

which seven to eight thousand are cavalry. Would you agree Colonel Ulikath?"

"At least twenty thousand, yes. Many, however, are unarmoured light infantry drawn from Narmidia's client kingdoms; they will not stand long. It will be dealing with the household cavalry and the Diehards, which will be the problem."

"Diehards?" asked Ro.

"They are the Narmidian royal family's private bodyguard corps. They are skilled fighters who show no fear," said General Livar.

"We also found something interesting out this morning, your majesty," said the colonel drawing curious looks from around the table.

"And what is that, Colonel?" asked the emperor.

"It is not Starik Vesla who leads the men, but his son Balok. Vesla is still far to the west chasing the remnants of the free armies."

"So the cub seeks to make a name for himself by conquering my country and perhaps usurping his father in the process. Interesting. I fear, however, he is going to be disappointed."

The officers around the table started to chuckle at the emperor's joke.

"Did you send word to Silevia like I suggested, your majesty?" asked Ro.

"The Lotari emperor does not grovel on bended knee for the help of those fat farmers," snapped General Livar indignantly.

"And I wasn't for one moment suggesting that he should, General, but the fact remains that we are six thousand against twenty. Odds of nearly four to one. If Vesla's son is successful here, he will in all likelihood turn his attention to Silevia and then Tula and the other small nations. Better to unite and fight the common enemy now."

"Lotar does not need anybody's help, we are strong."

Ro glanced round the tent, his eyes finally falling on a quiver of arrows lying against a chest towards the rear of the tent.

"May I, your majesty?" asked Ro.

"You may, but whatever you are doing make it swift, as we have much to discuss," replied the emperor curious to see what his friend intended on doing.

Ro nodded his thanks and walked over to the quiver, picked it up and brought it back down to where he had been sitting. He handed a single arrow to General Livar who looked puzzled by the southerner's actions.

"You say you are strong, General, very well. Pretend that you are Balok Vesla and that the arrow in your hand is Lotar and try and snap it."

The general looked perplexed but convinced that he was about to humiliate the young upstart from the south who had just appeared on the scene and ingratiated himself with the emperor, he decided to indulge him. He snapped the arrow with ease and looked smugly around at the other officers who were all smiling their support.

"See, strong," said the general. "Arrow broken."

"Very good, General. Now imagine these are Lotar, Silevia, Tula, Carlir and others and try and snap them," said Ro handing him a bunch of around fifteen arrows.

The general took them reluctantly sensing perhaps that he had fallen into a trap and tried to snap them. Three times he tried, growing increasingly red in the face with exertion before Ro leaned over and took them back from him. The general looked bitterly at Ro and Ro hoped that he hadn't made an enemy in trying to make his point.

"Forgive me, General, I was not trying to embarrass you, I was just trying to illustrate a point. One arrow, one country on its own is perhaps defeatable, but when several nations stand together they are stronger and harder to beat. That is why I suggested sending emissaries to Silevia and the other nations."

The general's face was ashen with humiliation but then he started to grin as if he'd found fault in Ro's plan.

"That is all well and good, Captain Aryk, apart from one thing and that is that your notion of unity did not save your southern and western nations." He smiled smugly.

"Firstly, General, I thank you for the courtesy but since I was dismissed by the King of Remada I no longer carry a formal rank. Secondly, there was no unified force when the Narmidians attacked. Remada and Lydia were already at war with Delarite and Cardella and the speed of the Narmidian invasion took everybody by surprise. By the time that the various nations started to talk alliances, the major battles were already lost. Nevertheless I stand by what I said a few moments ago. If Lotar, Silevia, Tula and the other smaller nations stand together, there is a better chance of defeating the enemy."

"Your point is well made, Ro and I thank you for it," said the emperor smiling. "I have already sent emissaries to all of our neighbours calling for assistance, but whether they will respond is another matter. You must therefore forgive General Livar; he is a passionate man who believes that Lotar is invincible based on the fact that Lotar has not been defeated for a thousand years."

"There is nothing to forgive, your majesty," said Ro bowing slightly, though he chose not to point out that Lotar had been involved in perhaps two wars in the whole of that time, whereas other parts of the continent seemed to be perpetually at war.

"We will have to assume that no help is coming and try and defeat them ourselves," continued the emperor. "Is there anything else?"

"The point I just made about unity, your majesty; it works both ways."

"Explain."

"We know that Vesla's army is made up of troops from a myriad of nations. Some are allies of the king but most are from client kingdoms and provinces. They probably don't want to be here and that might be something we can exploit. He is bound to use such men as bait and to throw them into the first couple of attacks. Their morale will not be high after our raids and their loyalty to this prince may not be strong. If we can rout them so badly in their first couple of assaults, we may be able to get them to panic and perhaps break."

The emperor was nodding. "What do my officers think?"

Most were nodding their agreement, even General Livar.

"Your majesty, based on what I witnessed when we were

harassing Vesla's column, I would say that Capt…Master Aryk is correct," said Colonel Ulikath.

"Then it is agreed. We will stick to the existing battle plan, but we must be prepared to adapt; the plan must be fluid. If a situation arises whereby I think that his forces are ready to bolt, I will give the signal to go on the offensive. If that happens you must press home the attack like wild men because if our gamble fails, we are lost and so is Lotar." The men all solemnly nodded their agreement. "Excellent. Then I suggest that you all return to your men and make final preparations as it will not be long before the enemy makes an appearance. Courage and good fortune, gentlemen."

"Courage and good fortune," they all echoed.

Ro was the last to leave but before he did, the emperor called over to him.

"Ro, why are you still here? This is not your fight."

"It's been my fight for over two years now, your majesty. If I wasn't fighting here I would be fighting somewhere else. Better to fight with friends at my side."

"Thank you, my friend, I am pleased you are with us at this time," said the emperor embracing Ro before turning and leaving his tent flanked by two of his bodyguards.

Chapter 16

The officer leading the Narmidian column raised his right hand and slowly the long line of men came to a halt. The officer signalled to one of his soldiers and the man led Eryn's horse over to the officer's side. They had stopped on a low ridge a few leagues away from what Eryn assumed was the Northern Sea, or what the sailors called the Cold Sea. In the distance, nestling right next to the crashing waves, was a large town or city. About a league away from the town and the ridge upon which he now stood was row upon row of tents. Thousands of men and horses milled about between them.

"Now do you believe that you are doomed, Remadan?" said the officer grinning. "This is just a part of my king's army. What hope can possibly remain for you?"

Eryn desperately wanted to say something clever to unsettle the man's arrogance but the truth was the sheer size of the Narmidian army spread out before him had taken his breath away. It was true, what hope remained against such an army? He screwed his eyes up against the midday sun and peered towards what he now assumed was the capital of Breland in the distance. What were the northerners doing? Were they preparing to fight? If they were, there was no sign of it. And what of his father, where was he and his men?

Then he saw it; a smaller camp of tents, situated just outside the town walls. Compared to the magnitude of the Narmidian camp it was nothing, but it was there, consisting of several hundred tents. But something was wrong. Unless everyone from his father's army had retreated into the Brelandic town or was hiding inside their tents, the camp was deserted. A feeling of dread began to gnaw away in the pit of Eryn's stomach.

"Come, Remadan, I think I will present you to my king as a gift and let him decide the manner of your passing," said the officer signalling for the men to follow him as he slowly began to pick his way down the slope towards the larger camp.

A short while later, Eryn was escorted by the officer and four guards to the largest of all the tents in the Narmidian camp, which Eryn assumed belonged to Vesla. After a brief pause outside, he was roughly shoved through the tent flaps and marched towards the centre of the tent where a man and woman were sat on ornate chairs flanked by two of the biggest men Eryn had seen. When he was about ten paces away from the couple, one of the men escorting him kicked him behind his right knee and Eryn collapsed to his knees.

"And what do we have here?" said the man sitting in the chair whom Eryn now assumed to be Starik Vesla, self-proclaimed King of Kings and the tyrant of the east.

Eryn raised his head to look directly at the couple sitting on the makeshift thrones but immediately received a blow to his back from one of his escort.

"Keep your eyes down unless instructed."

"My King, this is a Remadan deserter we picked up on the march west; I thought he might amuse you," replied the officer who had captured Eryn.

"Did you now? And why is that, Captain? Many captives have passed through my hands...briefly."

"Apologies, my King, but this one has spirit. He still believes that the Remadans have a chance of defeating you. I thought you might enjoy convincing him otherwise."

"Does he now. Lift his head," ordered the king and one of the men flanking Eryn grabbed his hair and yanked his head upwards so that he was facing the king.

Eryn stared briefly at the king, but it was to the woman at his side that his attention was drawn. She was beautiful for an older woman, of that there was no doubt with her flame red hair, but that wasn't it. There was something else. It was then that Eryn noticed that the woman was looking at him strangely. He couldn't work out quite what her expression was, but if he had to guess he would have described it as surprise. They briefly locked eyes.

"It seems you are right, Captain," said Vesla glancing from Eryn to his wife and then back at the boy. "See how even now he disrespects me by not looking at me and instead gazes longingly at my beautiful queen? I shall enjoy breaking this one. You have done well, Captain." He glanced again at his queen but she had wisely already averted her eyes. "But first I wish to hear of your journey west; how goes the subjugation of the conquered lands?"

"For the most part they are quiet, my King, which is why I have brought you two thousand reinforcements as they were no longer required in the east. There are isolated pockets of resistance here and there, but they are dealt with ruthlessly and swiftly."

"That is good. And what of my son? Has he launched his invasion of the north?"

"Yes, my King. He set off north with twenty thousand men at the same time as I departed for the west."

"Twenty thousand?" said Vesla incredulously.

"Yes, my King. The reinforcements from Skythia and Numatra arrived and he immediately assumed command of them and amalgamated them into his army."

"That is more than enough men to conquer Arkadia let alone the northern kingdoms." This last comment was more like a spoken thought than a reply. Vesla turned to his queen. "I suspect my son has eyes on more than just the northern kingdoms, my dear. Perhaps he even seeks to usurp me."

"Surely not, my love. He is your son after all," replied the queen.

"You have lived amongst us for many years now, my dear yet still you do not fully understand our ways. My father killed his father to assume the throne and I considered murdering my father before he was killed in battle opening the way for me. My son is gathering an army around him and is seeking easy glory and riches by conquering the north. Once his men are bloodied I suspect he will make his move on me."

Eryn had been listening to the exchange with interest. If there was discord between father and son and the chance that they might start fighting one another, that was excellent news for the nations of Arkadia and might be something they could exploit to their advantage. Strangely though it was not that titbit of information that held his interest the most. Instead he was still captivated by the woman sitting at Vesla's side. As soon as he had clapped eyes on her Eryn had suspected that she wasn't Narmidian, not with her red hair and fair complexion. Now Vesla had confirmed that she had not always lived among his people and that only served to make Eryn more curious. Whenever he dared, Eryn would steal a quick glance towards the queen and more often than not he would catch her staring back at him. Once he had even thought that she was smiling at him, but it had been fleeting and his concentration had been broken by the sharp blow he sustained to his lower back when one of the guards caught him looking.

"What do you wish me to do, my King?" asked the captain. "Should I march north and watch your son?"

"No, let him have his battles in the north. Perhaps they will not go as well as he thinks despite his numerical advantage. Maybe the Lotari or Silevians will take care of him for me."

"And if they don't, my King?"

"Then we'll deal with him in due time."

"What of the reinforcements he has taken, my King? Those men were needed here I thought."

"They were, particularly the Skythian archers, but it seems we'll have to do without them, at least for now. Besides, the Arkadians are on the run again and these northern barbarians are falling over themselves to appease me. With nothing but cowards to face I should have more than enough men at my disposal. You are dismissed, Captain."

"What of the prisoner, my King?"

Vesla cast his cold gaze down at Eryn who once again tried to meet it only to receive a vicious kick to his ribs for the trouble.

"It seems this one has trouble with the concept of respect, so I will teach him the error of his ways. Bind him to that post and then go."

The captain bowed and then nodded at the men who had escorted Eryn into the royal tent. He was forcefully dragged to his feet and then had his arms tied behind a sturdy post holding up a part of the tent. After checking that the bindings were secure, the captain ushered his men out of the tent, closing the flap behind him.

"You don't really think Balok is planning to overthrow you do you, my King?" asked the queen when the men departed.

"I have no doubt of it. Why else would he take so many men? He knew those reinforcements were for the war in the west and he has deliberately deprived me of them. I should have drowned the deceitful runt at birth."

"So what will you do?" asked the queen stealing a quick glance in Eryn's direction.

Vesla stroked his neatly trimmed black beard as he considered the question.

"I shall cow these northern barbarians into acquiescence and run down Rad and his men. Then I shall march north and claim the northern kingdoms and insist that my son swears allegiance to myself in front of the other kings and nobles."

"And if he doesn't?"

"Then I shall have him put to death and any of a similar mind. Now come, I have a meeting with the new king of Breland and I wish you at my side. I'm hoping that your beauty will beguile him into siding with us or laying down his arms," and with that Vesla strode out of the tent followed by his two bodyguards. After a few seconds delay, the queen followed, briefly smiling at Eryn as she passed.

Eryn watched her walk out, more confused than ever. There was something about the queen that he couldn't figure out and something about him seemed to pique her interest. He had also learned of the potential animosity between the Narmidian king and his son and that was information that would be useful to his father.

At least I know he's definitely alive now.

A million thoughts were running through Eryn's mind each jostling for prominence. First, however, he had to focus on escape. He tried wriggling his hands to see if there was any give in his bonds but whoever had tied him up had made a good job of it. Already his wrists were beginning to chafe and feel sore. He glanced around at the floor to see if there was anything nearby he could possibly retrieve with his feet and perhaps use to weaken his bonds but there was nothing. He tried again to work his hands loose but the rope just burned into his skin and he could feel blood trickling down the back of his hands. He was just considering giving it one last go when the sound of someone entering the tent drew his attention. He quickly slumped and hung his head trying to give an air of defeatism. Maybe whoever had come in would come too close and he'd be able to overpower them.

Whoever it was they were alone he realised as he could only hear one set of footsteps and they were deliberately light as if trying not to make any noise at all.

Good, he thought, *the smaller they are the better my chances of overpowering them.*

With his head still hanging down Eryn could just about see their feet and he estimated that they had stopped perhaps a couple of paces in front of him. Close enough to speak quietly but too far for him to stand a chance of attacking them. Most interestingly the feet belonged to a woman and he imagined that someone had sent a slave girl in with water and food, though why they'd do that for a condemned man he had no idea. The more he stared at her feet though the more he became convinced that whoever it was, they weren't a slave. He could smell the sweet scent of perfume emanating from their body and the woman's feet were immaculately clean, with painted nails. He slowly began to raise his head and was surprised to find the queen standing before him and smiling warmly. Up close she was even more beautiful.

"Eryn? It is you isn't it?" she asked, the smile never leaving her face.

He had not told them his name for to do so would only further endanger his own life and weaken the position of his father should they decide to use him as a bargaining chip. So how did this woman know his name?

"My time is short and my bodyguards or husband will soon come back looking for me so if it is you, as I'm sure it is, please tell me," said the queen. She was either an extremely good actress or she was genuinely worried by the prospect of someone catching her alone with the prisoner, judging by the way she kept nervously looking over her shoulder at the tent entrance.

"My name is Eryn, yes. How do you know this and what does it mean to you?" asked Eryn suspiciously, although in truth his interest had been piqued.

The queen smiled some more, stepped closer and gently

reached out her right hand placing her palm tenderly on his left cheek.

"Don't you recognise me, Eryn?" She stared into his eyes for a few moments and watched as firstly recognition and then disbelief flashed across his face.

"Mother?" he finally said.

The queen smiled some more and then the first tear slowly began to meander down her cheek and she started to nod before throwing her arms around his neck and kissing him on the forehead.

"Yes. I knew it was you the minute I saw you. It may have been many years since I last saw you but a mother never forgets her son."

"You're Vesla's wife?" said Eryn incredulously.

"Yes, but I am your mother first and foremost."

"But father; he has spent years looking for you, he will…"

"There is no time now, Eryn," she said stepping behind him and cutting his bonds. "The guards will be here soon. My handmaiden has brought a horse to the rear of the tent. There should be a sword with it as well if she had time. Your father has fled to the west; go now and ride hard and if the gods are willing you will catch up with him."

"But you're coming with me," said Eryn.

"I can't. Not yet." She looked over her shoulder as if she'd heard something. "Now please go, Eryn and tell your father… tell him… I still love him, but not to look for me any longer."

"I'm not leaving without you," protested Eryn.

This time he too heard a noise outside and they both quickly glanced at the tent flap.

"Please, Eryn, go now, or what I have done will have been for nothing," pleaded his mother.

"But…"

Before he could finish the sentence the tent flap opened and a member of the king's guard stepped through.

"Eryn, go!" shouted his mother and from beneath her cloak she produced a short sword and turned to square off against the guard who had drawn his own sword.

The ring of steel upon steel reverberated through the tent and outside Eryn could hear some people shouting. He watched his mother briefly, impressed by the way she handled her sword and then turned and used the knife she had given him to cut his way out of the rear of the tent. Before he stepped through he glanced one last time at the mother he had not seen for nearly nine years. She was facing off against two guards now, but one of them had been wounded in the side and was bleeding heavily. Then with tears streaming down his face he stepped through the hole he had cut in the canvas. He had half-expected to be confronted by a number of armed men, but instead all that was waiting for him was a young woman holding the reins of a powerful looking horse.

He immediately grabbed the reins and swung himself into the saddle and once he was settled the handmaiden reached up and handed him a sword on a belt which he slung over his shoulder. Nodding his thanks, Eryn quickly glanced round trying to ascertain his bearings and once he had figured out which way was west, he kicked his horse in the flanks and rode hard stopping for nothing.

Few if any of the soldiers realised what was going on and by the time that some of them finally tried to react, he was already through them, the giant horse barging them out of the way or a well-placed kick from Eryn knocking them over. One or two tried to hit him with arrows, but in the midst of their own camp it was a foolhardy practice and their efforts were more likely to result in the death of their own men.

Before he knew it he was approaching the western boundary of the Narmidian camp and potential freedom, but before him stood two sentries who were alert to potential danger. One was holding a javelin, the other a torch and a short sword. The man with the javelin took aim at the rider hurtling towards them and threw, but his throw was rushed and sailed harmlessly past Eryn's right shoulder. He immediately reached for his sword but knew that at the speed the rider was travelling it wouldn't be clear of its scabbard before he arrived and instead stepped back out of Eryn's path.

The second sentry, however, did not move and swung his sword as Eryn passed, but Eryn had anticipated the swing and easily parried it before riding on past them. The swordsman ran over to where his own javelin was leaning against a post, picked it up and hurled it after Eryn who was fast disappearing into the darkness. The javelin landed in a prickly bush not two paces from where Eryn had been mere moments before.

Eryn knew that the Narmidians would mount some sort of pursuit, but by the time that they got themselves organised and with the benefit of a moonless night, he figured he could safely put enough distance between himself and the camp.

His mother had said that his father had marched west, which Vesla had also confirmed, but Eryn had no idea where. Would they head to the coast and try and embark for somewhere away from the invading army? Perhaps he would lead his men to one of the island nations and seek sanctuary whilst he rebuilt his forces. Or would he march west for a while and then turn south for the vast open plains of Angorra? That seemed a more likely plan to Eryn. Even if he had a couple of thousand men with him, finding his father would still be like looking for a needle in a haystack and all the while he would have to keep looking over his shoulder for any men Vesla sent after him.

Perhaps they wouldn't bother. He was after all, only a deserter. Unless his mother tells them who he is; then Vesla would send men after him for sure. His thoughts turned to his mother. To have her back in his life after so long just to have her snatched away so brutally was cruel. It was just like his reunion with his father all over again.

What would Vesla do to his mother when he found out that she had helped him to escape? Eryn reined in his horse and turned in the saddle to look back the way he had come. Should he go back? That made no sense. Even if he got past the sentries again, if his mother wasn't already dead she'd be surrounded by guards by now and what use would he be? His mother's sacrifice would also have been in vain. Yet leaving her behind that way made him feel sick.

Realising that there really wasn't anything he could do, he turned back around and started off west. He had much to tell his father when he next saw him and he was more determined than ever that they would meet again.

***

Starik Vesla stormed into his royal tent, the slaves only just

141

managing to raise the flaps in time, drawing a withering look from the king. Inside his tent he found his queen kneeling on the ground flanked by four of his royal house guards. Another was on the floor, evidently dead. He looked from his wife to the body and then back again to his wife.

"It seems my sword master has taught you well, Surita," said Vesla smiling, though the smile did not reach his eyes.

"A little too well perhaps," she replied.

Vesla studied her for a moment. She looked a little dishevelled but appeared unhurt.

"Maybe. So who was he, this young Remadan deserter for whom you have thrown away everything?" He had moved so that he was standing directly in front of her.

"He was just that; a deserter." Her answer sounded unconvincing even to her.

"I think not. Why would the Queen of Narmidia, with everything to lose and nothing to gain, risk everything for a deserter? It doesn't make sense. No, my dear, you are going to have to do better than that. So I'll ask you again, who was he?"

"He was just a deserter, nothing more, but he was the son of someone from my home village of Lentor. I thought I recognised him when he was first brought before us, but I went back to check and ask him his name."

Vesla stared into his wife's eyes trying to weigh the truth in her words and eventually nodded his acceptance. A few moments later, as previously arranged with one of his senior cavalry officers, the officer came bustling into the royal tent, saluted the king and then whispered something into his ear. The king smiled and nodded again, playing along with the pre-arranged charade. Then he turned to face his wife again who was watching the exchange intently.

"Well, whoever he is, he's now been caught. My men rode him down a few leagues from the camp. We'll torture the truth out of him soon enough. Perhaps you'd care to watch?" A thousand thoughts entered the queen's mind and her face betrayed every emotion she was feeling. "You look a little pale, my Queen. All this for the son of somebody you have not seen in nearly a decade?"

The queen stared at her husband for a few long moments and then prostrated herself on the rugged floor.

"Please, my King... husband... I beg you, do not torture him."

"And why would I not want to? The boy means nothing to me."

"Because...because the boy is my son," she eventually revealed without lifting her head.

Vesla stared at the prostrate form of his wife; he had not expected that. He clenched and opened his fists repeatedly as a blind fury threatened to consume him.

"Your son? You mean to tell me that you just helped Teren Rad's son to escape?" His voice was quivering and Surita could tell that he was on the verge of one of his legendary temper outbursts.

"Yes," was all she said in response.

With a roar of rage he kicked her hard in the left side of her ribs and she cried out in pain and rolled onto her back holding her side.

"I could have used him to draw Rad out and force him to surrender. Without Rad the resistance is nothing. This could have all been over and now thanks to you I have to waste valuable time and resources pursuing the scum and his band of mongrels all over western Arkadia." His face was red with rage and before he could move out of the way, a slave holding a tray of wine goblets was punched fully in the face, the cracking of his nose audible enough for those standing nearby to hear.

"I'm sorry, husband, but he is my son. I could not turn my back on him."

Vesla fixed her with an icy stare but then seemed to get his temper under control. He walked over to where she sat cradling her side and gently raised her to her feet, before drawing her into an embrace.

"I understand, my dear, of course I do. However, I cannot forgive such a betrayal."

Surita's eyes widened in pain as something sharp was slowly pushed into her back. She tried to cry out but he held her close to his chest and only withdrew the dagger when it had plunged its full length into her body. When he felt her body go limp, Vesla eased it to the ground but when he looked down he was surprised that she was still alive. It wouldn't be for long though. He turned to the officer who had come in to execute the pre-arranged ruse.

"Is there any sign of him?"

"We have a number of patrols out looking for him, my King, but the night is dark and it's almost impossible to track him."

"I don't care. Find him or you'll be joining my wife in the afterlife."

"Yes, my King," replied the officer swallowing hard, before saluting and striding out of the royal tent.

Just before everything went dark, Surita thought she heard the king ask whether they had found Eryn yet. He had tricked her. Of course he had. He was no fool and trusted nobody. She should have anticipated that. Still, Eryn had made it out of the camp and for now was free. If Teren had taught him a fraction of what he knew the boy would be fine.

Vesla looked down to taunt his wife one last time, but the light in her eyes had disappeared. He was surprised to find that in her last moments she appeared to have been smiling.

Chapter 17

"They are almost upon us, Colonel," said the Lotari sergeant after he reined in his horse in front of Ulikath and Ro.

"Very well. How many of his army has he brought?" asked the colonel.

"All of them, sir."

Colonel Ulikath and Ro exchanged a look. "Thank you, Sergeant, you may assume your position, and may Sulat watch over you," replied the colonel.

"May he watch over us all, sir."

The colonel nodded and the sergeant turned his horse and rode away to join his squadron.

The king had deployed his men as the council of war had discussed some days earlier; Ro and Colonel Ulikath commanded a force of five hundred horsemen on the grassy slope of the Myaki Pass whilst General Livar commanded a smaller force atop the gravelly slope on the other side. The bulk of the army was commanded by the emperor and was drawn up on the gentle slope at the end of the pass which led up to the town of Qui'tang.

Colonel Ulikath leaned back in his saddle and once again glanced around at his men before checking his own equipment for what Ro thought must be the tenth time. Nerves, it seemed, troubled even the bravest of soldiers in time of conflict.

"Relax, Colonel, your men are fine and so's your equipment," said Ro reassuringly.

Embarrassed, the colonel stopped his fidgeting and looked back down the pass. At first he couldn't see anything except for the lush green grass and the small brook that ran the length of the valley floor. Then a flicker of movement caught his eye and then another. He leant forward in his saddle and shielded his eyes against the sun. Then he could see them. The entrance to the pass was fast filling with columns of men.

"We have company, Aryk," he said gesturing with his head.

Ro watched the men funnel into the pass row upon row and hoped that his anxiety didn't show.

"Good, I was getting bored."

Colonel Ulikath looked at Ro strangely, still not quite understanding the nuances of the southerner's humour.

A few of the men behind them started to mutter to one another as the size of the force taking the field against them was slowly revealed.

Ro turned and looked in the men's faces. Some looked worried, others implacable. He had no idea how good Lotari discipline was as they had not fought in a major battle for many decades but Ro knew from experience that it only took one man to panic, to lose his nerve and it could spread like an infection. He had seen lines of brave men break and run before when confronted by a force much smaller than the one filling the valley below them.

"I think you'd better say something, Colonel and steady your men's nerves," said Ro.

Colonel Ulikath looked round at his men and nodded. Then he slowly turned his horse and began to speak to them, slowly riding up and down the front line so that all might hear. He spoke in the strange Lotari language and although he could not speak it, Ro did know a few words. Whilst the speech didn't appear to be as rousing as the ones Ro had heard Teren give, it seemed to do the trick and the men automatically straightened their lines and began to cheer.

Colonel Ulikath turned his horse round and sidled back alongside Ro as the cheering continued.

"How was that?" asked the colonel.

"From what I could tell, not bad, my friend, not bad at all."

"Thank you."

"And if they didn't know we were here already, they do now thanks to the cheering," added Ro wryly.

Colonel Ulikath smiled. "Ah, they knew we were here, trust me."

They both looked back down at the valley beneath them which now seemed to be teeming with men dressed in different coloured uniforms. Ro recognised some of the regiments having fought them at one stage or another over the last two years, but some were new to him. The same was apparently true of Colonel Ulikath.

"Who are those men in white tops and black leggings?" asked the colonel.

"Skythians," replied Ro.

"Skythians! Where is their country?"

"Far to the east. It is a client kingdom of the great king," replied Ro.

"Client kingdom?" queried the colonel.

"A conquered nation who now fights for the Narmidian king," explained Ro.

"They are a long way from home then."

"They say they are the best archers in the world," said Ro.

"Really? I look forward to putting that to the test."

Ro was about to say something along the lines of he hoped they didn't have to find out when a horn blew somewhere towards the end of the valley.

"Archers ready!" shouted Colonel Ulikath and a hundred men with bows came forward and knelt in a long line in front of the horsemen. "Draw." The archers nocked an arrow and pointed their bows high into the sky, the strings drawn all the way back for maximum power. A few moments later there were three sharp blasts on a horn. "Fire."

The archers in front of Ro loosed their arrows at exactly the same moment a similar number did on the opposite hill top. Ro watched the arrows arc into the sky and then drop with almost uncanny precision on top of the middle section of the enemy column. The screams of the men who were hit filled the air as panic rifled through the enemy ranks. Before the first wave of arrows had even landed the archers were already nocking their second arrow.

"Fire," shouted Colonel Ulikath and the second volley of arrows streamed into the midday sky before plummeting towards their targets. This time the Narmidians were better prepared and a shield wall and roof had been erected over the column. It was clear to Ro's trained eye that this was not a familiar move for these soldiers and inevitably gaps in the structure were left. Just as inevitably some of the Lotari arrows found their way through these gaps to pierce enemy flesh.

The minute the Lotari arrows struck their shields, however, bigger gaps in their shield structure opened and out of these suddenly poured hundreds of arrows. The order to raise shields was only half out of his mouth when the volley landed around Ro, killing and maiming dozens of men and horses. Many of the Lotari archers had been hit and when Colonel Ulikath gave the order for the archers to return fire a third time, only two thirds as many arrows shot into the sky. As soon as they had fired their arrows, the Skythians had retreated back behind their comrades so that the latest volley of Lotari arrows skittered harmlessly off the shields.

Instantly the gaps in their shield formation opened again and another storm of arrows descended on the Lotari. Most had managed to seek cover behind a shield but not all and with such a multitude of arrows falling from the sky, there was nowhere to go. Casualties among the Lotari were again high.

"We've got to attack now, Colonel before they murder us," Ro shouted to the other officer. "We can't win an archery contest. The Skythians are too good."

The colonel nodded his agreement and then shouted some orders in his own language. The archers immediately retired back through the slightly depleted ranks of horsemen whilst the riders readied their weapons.

"Good luck, Colonel, I'll see you on the other side," said Ro.

Not understanding the comment the colonel merely nodded and gave the order to charge. A few moments later another shower of arrows landed where the riders had been massed, killing some of those who had not been quick enough to move. Had the order to charge not been given at that precise moment, however, the casualty toll would have been much higher.

Ro and Colonel Ulikath led the charge down the slope. Ro had drawn his sword and was pointing it towards the enemy whilst Colonel Ulikath and his men lowered their lances. Below them the Skythian archers were again peering through the gaps in the shield wall their weapons pointing at the fast approaching riders. Ro expected the deadly arrows to strike home at any moment but the Skythian commander was obviously waiting until the Lotari were right on top of them, knowing that his men would wreak a terrible toll from such short range. Whilst the benefits of such a tactic were obvious it was also very risky because by the time that they had released their arrows any survivors from the charge would be upon them and would smash into their lines. Ro just hoped that he would be there to witness it.

Above the roar of his men and the thunder of hooves tearing up the soft grass, Ro did not hear the Skythian commander give the order to fire, but the cries of pain around him told him as much. Ro felt an arrow whistle past his left ear, another grazed his left forearm, drawing blood but not stopping him and a third ricocheted of his helmet.

Then he was amongst them. His horse, which had been in many battles, smashed into the front row of Narmidian soldiers, scattering them and trampling them underfoot.

Ro had no idea how many of the Lotari made it through the storm of arrows but he couldn't worry about that now. All that mattered was getting amongst the Narmidian column and causing as much mayhem as possible.

The Narmidians had organised themselves better since the first attacks after they crossed the Lotari border and now marched with their heavy and better armoured infantry on the flanks, which gave them better protection. It also meant that it restricted their ability to manoeuvre once their formation was penetrated, as their heavy shields were unwieldy and difficult to move in dense formations.

Inside this ring of steel were the lightly armoured infantry, the slingers and the Skythian archers and it was in the midst of these that Ro and some of his comrades now found themselves.

Ro sliced down with his sword slashing a warrior across the face before reversing his swing and opening the throat of a Skythian bowman. As soon as his sword struck he pushed on penetrating deeper into the enemy column. A large Narmidian with a lance thrust his weapon up at Ro, but Ro managed to lean back in his saddle just in time to avoid it. He immediately chopped down with his sword, severing the man's right arm just above the elbow. He howled with pain and fell away as Ro moved on.

To his right a Skythian bowman was taking aim at him but before he could fire the arrow his head was separated from his shoulders by a sword swing from Colonel Ulikath. He nodded at Ro and then pushed on.

Somebody grabbed Ro's cloak and he could feel himself being pulled backwards from his horse towards certain death, but as if sensing the danger his horse reared up scaring his assailant into letting go. Ro turned to confront the man but as he did so a *jemtak* took the Narmidian in the left eye and he collapsed to the ground.

Two light infantry armed with swords and wicker shields appeared either side of Ro's horse, the one on the right launching his attack first. His swing was predictable and Ro easily blocked it before fending the other man off temporarily with his foot. This time they both came at him together and it took all of Ro's skill to fend them both off, swinging first left and then right to either block or launch an attack of his own. After several such exchanges the Narmidian on the right over extended himself opening up his torso as an easy target. Ro did not miss his opportunity and thrust his sword deep into the man's chest. The warrior to his left also sensed an opportunity and raced forward, but again just at the vital moment Ro's horse reared up knocking the man to the ground winding him. Moments later his head was crushed like a melon as the horse's front hoof stamped down on it.

There was carnage everywhere. Even from his position atop his mare, Ro could not tell how the battle was going.

An arrow suddenly whisked past his face, but he had no idea where it had come from. Another lightly armoured swordsman ran screaming towards him. Ro parried his first stroke, then his second before surprising his attacker with a sharp thrust that caught the man in the groin. Screaming with pain he collapsed to the ground. Ro turned just as another arrow was fired at his head. The arrow head grazed his left cheek drawing blood before continuing its flight and striking somebody behind Ro, though whether they were friend or foe he did not know.

Ro had seen where that arrow had come from and whilst the bowman was busily nocking another arrow, he raced towards him, knocking several men over in the process, one of whom was trampled mercilessly by Ro's horse. The bowman was just raising his bow again for another shot when Ro's sword hammered down into his unprotected head opening up a sizeable gash. Blood and brains sprayed everywhere as Ro struggled to pull his sword free.

He was just turning looking for a new target when in the distance the unmistakeable sound of a Lotari horn sounded twice. It was the signal to withdraw. Ro pulled his horse round to comply but had to react quickly as a Narmidian heavy infantryman slashed at him with his sword. Ro blocked the swipe with his own sword, but the power of the man's stroke sent pain reverberating up his arm and into his shoulder. He tried to slash down at his attacker but the Narmidian managed to bring his heavy shield up and deflect the blow. Ro struck down twice more hoping that the man's arm did not have the strength to hold his heavy shield up for any length of time, but the soldier was strong and Ro's blows amounted to nothing. After trying one last downward slash which was again easily blocked by the Narmidian, Ro stuck out a foot and pushed down with all his strength onto the shield and shoved the man away. He stumbled backwards a couple of paces, regained his balance and then lowered his shield slightly so that he could look at Ro over the rim. The man was grinning, obviously confident that he could better the Remadan horseman.

Ro readied himself for another assault but the Narmidian suddenly stopped a look of sheer surprise on his face before collapsing face down with a lance buried in his back. Behind him on his horse sat Colonel Ulikath.

"We have to go, Aryk."

"I know," shouted Ro as he back swiped a Narmidian he saw running towards him from the corner of his eye. His sword slashed the man through the neck and he dropped instantly.

"Withdraw! Withdraw!" shouted Ro and Colonel Ulikath echoed his order but in his own language.

Moments later scores of Lotari horsemen tried to disengage themselves from the fight though some were so deep within the enemy column that it was going to prove impossible.

Ro kicked his horse into a gallop no longer bothering to swing his sword at any of the men around him. Now was all about retreating and regrouping and the best way to do that was at speed. As he made his way towards the foot of the slope he was aware of riders either side of him, but he couldn't tell how many. The next few seconds would be crucial and if the commander left with the archers and light infantry at the top of the slope got their timing wrong, Ro and his fellow riders were going to be slaughtered.

Even as he and the others began to climb the slope back up to their starting position he could hear Narmidian officers bellowing at their men. He didn't need to speak Narmidian or Skythian to know that they were trying to ready their archers. With their backs to the enemy and riding up a slope, they couldn't have made an easier target. Ro briefly closed his eyes and offered a silent prayer to Sulat.

He was halfway up the slope when they suddenly appeared. Every archer and man able to hurl a *jemtak* had formed two lines at the crest of the hill; those armed with *jemtaks* formed the front line and archers who would shoot up and over their comrades, formed the back row. Moments later a mass of arrows and *jemtak* filled the sky over Ro. He rode hard for the crest of the hill shouting and encouraging those around him to do likewise. As they reached the top, gaps in the lines appeared allowing the riders to pass through whilst a storm of projectiles continued to hurtle down on the enemy.

It was only when Ro dismounted and came running to the front line did he realise that the Lotari archers and *jemtak* throwers had timed their attack to perfection and few if any Skythian archers had been able to fire at Ro and the other retreating riders for fear of being hit themselves.

Ro slapped the commander of the archers on the shoulder and grinned. No words were necessary; the man knew that he had probably just saved Ro's life and those of the other riders.

At the bottom of the hill, the Narmidians were once again sheltering behind the long shields of their heavy infantry though the ground was littered with those not quick enough to make shelter.

Colonel Ulikath rode alongside Ro and dismounted.

"Well fought, Colonel," said Ro smiling, "and thank you for saving my life not once, but twice."

"Three times actually! You weren't even aware of the first time," grinned the colonel. "And you're welcome."

"Then I am truly in your debt," said Ro bowing slightly.

"Think nothing of it."

"How many did we lose?"

"I haven't had time for a proper count, but I would estimate that we lost perhaps forty per cent of our strength. Most of those were lost in the initial charge."

Ro winced; forty per cent was a heavy price to pay.

Below them the Narmidians were slowly getting the column back into marching order, but even as they did so, General Livar's men suddenly appeared on top of the steep rocky slope on the other side of the valley and began to hurl scores of *jemtak* down onto the enemy. The Narmidians were quicker to react this time and a shield wall of sorts was quickly erected meaning that there were far fewer casualties.

"Should we continue to attack them with our archers as well?" Colonel Ulikath asked.

Ro thought about it for a moment then shook his head.

"No, we'd just be wasting our arrows. Let them advance unhindered up the valley for now; there'll be other opportunities before this day is over."

When he realised that his missile onslaught was having little effect, General Livar also ordered his men to stop throwing and then withdrew out of sight.

Chapter 18

"How many?" asked Teren.

"Hard to say.Maybe four or five thousand; all mounted," replied the scout, a Datian, whose tracking and evasion skills were second to none in Teren's army.

"And how long before they're upon us?"

The Datian frowned and massaged his aching neck before replying.

"Sunset tomorrow if they really push it, otherwise mid-morning the following day."

Brak let out a long whistle. "So he outnumbers us by almost two to one and has the advantage that all of his men are mounted. It doesn't sound good does it?"

"We've faced worse," said Yarik.

"I know we have, just about every day. Don't you wish that for once we could go into a battle with some sort of advantage?" he replied grinning.

"And where would the fun be in that?" asked Teren. "Thanks, Dagor, go and get yourself something to eat and drink and then try and get your head down for a few hours; I'm going to need your skills a lot again tomorrow I should think."

The Datian nodded and then turned and left the small group of leaders gathered round the fire.

"So what do you want to do, Teren?" asked Brak.

Teren took a deep breath and puffed out his cheeks before slowly expunging the air.

"Seems to me that we have two choices. We can either continue to march east and hope that they disengage and return to Vesla, which seems a bit unlikely in the extreme, or we can stand and fight, though the odds on us winning must be slim."

"Strikes me that if we do keep moving east we run two risks," said Brak.

"Go on," urged Teren.

"Firstly, for all we know Vesla might have sent another

force on a parallel course to our north meaning that at some stage we could get caught in a vice and secondly, sooner or later they are going to catch us up and in all likelihood we're going to be strung out in column. Their cavalry will annihilate us."

"Sounds to me that we have no choice but to stand and fight," said Teren.

"Would have been my choice anyway," growled Yarik.

"Then it's settled, we'll turn and fight these whoresons following us," said Teren.

"We just need to find somewhere to make our stand then," said Yarik.

"I know a place," said Brak thoughtfully, "not more than a few hours march from here. We could be there by midday tomorrow."

"That won't give us long to prepare the ground," said Teren stroking his beard.

"Who cares? We'll meet them man-to-man the old fashioned way. My money's on those Narmidian dogs running before we do," said Yarik.

"I guess time will tell. Go to your officers, my friends and tell them the plan. Double the watch tonight just in case, but make it only three hour shifts so that everyone gets at least a few hours' sleep. We have a forced march to make in the morning and we need to arrive with enough energy to fight and win a battle," said Teren.

Brak, Yarik and the other commanders all nodded and then filed away from Teren's fire leaving the Remadan alone with his thoughts. For the first time in a long while he found himself thinking about his family scattered to the four corners of Arkadia. His wife, the Queen of Narmidia was probably still with her new husband camped outside Breland, his youngest daughter whom he had not seen for over two years was Sulat only knew where, hopefully being cared for by former neighbours from his home village of Lentor. His eldest daughter Keira, whom he had briefly run into some time ago, was last seen living in a forest with a gang of bandits. No, that wasn't right, he corrected himself. She had called them displaced persons, who had nowhere else to go, refugees from the war. Their leader was a boy named Cal, no, Col, he again corrected. He was a nice enough lad. He hoped that he was still looking out for his daughter. They seemed to care for one another. Then of course there was Eryn, his son. A son he had been estranged from, but then became reconciled with during the war in the east. The lad had been hostile towards him at first which was only to be expected but then he had started to thaw. He had also proved himself to be a brave lad and had fought well at Vangor and elsewhere. The last he had heard of him was over a year ago when he, Ro Aryk and Arlen Meric had sent the boy home from Salandor with the girl he had rescued. He had no idea where the boy was now, he realised with great sadness. He didn't even know if he was still alive.

***

Teren woke with a start. He didn't remember laying down for the night but obviously at some point after the others had left, he had simply fallen asleep. Sometime during the night, someone had come and covered him with an old blanket.

He was still muttering to himself and feeling embarrassed when Brak approached him a few minutes later with a hot broth to drink.

"Why didn't you wake me for my turn on watch?" snapped Teren.

"And a good morning to you as well," replied Brak holding out the bowl containing the broth for Teren to take.

Teren took it from him and muttered his thanks. "Well?"

"Teren, there are over two thousand men in this camp, most if not all of whom are younger than you and by quite some distance incidentally. Why would I wake you to take a turn when I have all of them to choose from? You're the leader and don't need to worry about such things."

"They need to see that I'm right there suffering with them, Brak. It's the only way I'll keep their respect."

Brak laughed. "There isn't a man in this camp who doesn't respect you and you sure as Kaden don't need to stand watch for three hours in the cold night air to earn it. You've gained their respect by leading them and saving their lives on more occasions than I care to remember. They're not going to leave just because you didn't take your turn on watch."

Teren took a long sip of his broth and enjoyed the warmth as it slipped down his throat. His body ached, it always did first thing in the morning, particularly when he'd been forced to sleep on the cold ground in the open air.

"They've left me before," said Teren bitterly recalling the deserters from Breland.

"Some of them and only then because they felt we'd lingered too long. A bored soldier is a poor soldier; I've heard you say that enough times. Besides, they mostly all came back to you when they had the chance."

He was right they had, Teren had to concede. He took another long sip of his broth.

"You still should have woken me."

"If you didn't need the sleep, you would have woken of your own volition, so just accept it and move on."

"Where's the ugly Delarite?" asked Teren as he drained the last of his broth.

"Still snoring over there where he's been all night. You won't hear him moaning to me that I should have woken him up and put him on watch," said Brak.

"And what are they doing?" asked Teren pointing to a small group of men who appeared to be having a good natured argument about something a few paces away from where Yarik slept.

"They're arguing about who's going to be the one to wake the Delarite. He doesn't take being woken up from a deep slumber particularly well, especially if he's got some ale inside him."

"And has he?"

"Oh, yes."

"This should be interesting then."

They both looked over to where one man was being pushed forward by his comrades, the debate as to who had to wake Yarik up, having apparently been settled.

The man edged his way closer to Yarik until he was finally standing next to his slumbering form. He glanced back at his friends for encouragement and they all urged him on with jeers and arm gesticulations. The man swallowed nervously and reached out with his right foot and gently tapped the Delarite in the side. There was no response. He again reached out with his foot and tapped him a little bit harder this time. Yarik made a series of growling noises and suddenly rolled over onto his back making the man jump with fright much to the amusement of those watching. Still Yarik didn't wake. The soldier placed his foot on Yarik's side again and rolled him backwards and forwards. For a moment it didn't look like it had the desired effect but then Yarik's eyes shot open. Before the soldier could react Yarik grabbed the man's foot with his right hand and shoved him backwards sending him flying through the air and crashing to the ground with a thump. The soldier lay winded for a few seconds and in that time Yarik had leapt to his feet and was now in the process of lifting the man off the ground by the scruff of his tunic.

Above the sound of everyone laughing Teren could just about make out the sound of the man desperately trying to apologise right up until the moment that Yarik lifted him above his head and dumped him back first into the small stream that skirted the southern tip of their camp.

"And they say bears have sore heads," said Brak.

"Guess they've never met a Delarite then," replied Teren.

"At least not our one."

By the time that Yarik had walked over to where his two friends were watching, he too was smiling.

"That's what you get for sending a Remadan to do a man's work," said Yarik gruffly.

"If you're quite finished playing with your friends, we've a battle to fight," said Teren not rising to the bait.

"There is news?" asked Yarik.

"No, but we know they can't be far behind now. We'll break camp shortly and head to Brak's location, so if you want to get something to eat or feel the need to give any more of my men baths, now is the time to do it."

Yarik laughed as he stomped off, those in his path quickly moving out of his way.

"Well I don't know what he does to the enemy but he sure as Kaden scares me," said Brak.

"Let's hope that's enough when the time comes," said Teren as he too walked off to prepare for the journey east.

Behind him, a soaking wet and cold Remadan soldier clambered out of the stream to the sound of men laughing.

***

They arrived at the spot where Brak recommended they made their stand late morning having made good time on the march. Twice their scouts had ridden back and informed Teren that they had seen Narmidian pathfinders, but as yet there was no sign of the enemy vanguard.

The men were tired but generally in good spirits despite having being asked to carry long branches they had found or cut down when they had passed through a small wood. Still they didn't need too much cajoling to set to work. Their plan was simple. The ground on which they had chosen to make their stand was a short, but steep grassy slope that stretched for hundreds of paces in either direction meaning that to flank them, the Narmidians would have to climb the slope giving the defenders enough time to manoeuvre. In the direction from which they had come and from which the Narmidians would also arrive, was nothing but open rolling plains affording the defenders plenty of time to see the enemy approaching. Behind the allies and over the crest of the slope, the terrain was much the same, with vast open plains for as far as the eye could see and just a forest in the distance which would be too far to reach if things went badly. The enemy cavalry would ride them down with impunity.

The allies would make their stand here and they would either win or they'd die, it was that simple.

"You weren't joking about this place," said Teren to Brak as he glanced around. "There's no hiding or running away from here."

"We stand or we fall," said Brak matter-of-factly.

"I wouldn't have it any other way," added Yarik.

"No I don't suppose you would," said Teren grinning. "How go the preparations?"

"Once the men found out why they'd been asked to carry those branches, they settled down and got to work. We may not have as many ready as we'd have liked but we should have enough," replied Brak.

"How many javelins have we got?"

"I would guess that we've got enough for every man not lifting the poles to have one each."

"Two would have been better," said Teren ruefully.

"And three better still, but we'll have to make do with the one."

"What about archers, Yarik?" asked Teren.

"Two hundred maybe. Of those, I would say only about a hundred and fifty are trained bowmen. The rest are just men who've picked a bow and quiver up along the way."

"So long as they know in which direction to aim the thing I don't care. I'm hoping that they're going to come onto us in such dense formations that even the worst archers couldn't fail to hit their target."

"Did you hear that, Yarik? There's hope for you yet," said Brak.

Yarik snorted with derision. "Bows are for little people with little courage. I shall be leading the charge with my axe."

"Well just make sure that you don't lead it too soon. Timing will be everything this afternoon," replied Teren.

"You think there'll be here this afternoon for sure then?" asked Brak.

"If not sooner," replied Teren pointing at something behind his two friends.

They both turned in time to see two riders racing towards them.

"Our scouts?" asked Brak.

"Looks that way and they seem to be in a bit of a hurry I'd say."

The two men reined in just in front of Teren and his friends.

"General Rad… they're…almost…" began one of the two scouts, a young lad who had been out on a number of scouting missions with Rad's more trusted scouts and was now deemed ready to work on his own.

"Slow down, son and get your breath," urged Teren. "Here, have a drink." He passed the young boy a water skin and he drank greedily.

"Thank you, General."

"Now make your report, lad and leave nothing out. Accuracy and detail are everything."

"Sorry, sir," said the young lad forcing himself upright in the saddle and pulling himself together. "The Narmidians are no more than an hour behind us, General."

Teren and his friends exchanged a brief look of concern.

"Have they split their forces at all?" asked Brak.

"No, sir."

"Did they see you?" asked Teren.

"Yes. A small party of their horsemen gave chase but they gave up after a while."

"Anything else?" asked Teren.

"They're riding hard as if they're desperate to catch us up," replied the young scout thoughtfully.

"Interesting. Their commander will have two choices then when he finally gets here. Either he gives his men and horses enough time to recover before attacking, in which case he risks us taking advantage of the pause to slip away, or he throws his already tired forces into an attack uphill with all the risks that carries."

"He probably doesn't know we're positioned up a hill," said Brak.

"He will do soon," said Yarik nodding towards something behind the two riders.

Brak and Teren followed his gesture but Teren couldn't see anything.

"What is it? I can't see anything," said Teren.

"Riders, in the distance," said Brak pointing.

"Narmidians?"

"Pathfinders I should think. Seems like they didn't give up the chase after all but were merely trailing these two lads to see where they led."

Teren was squinting, peering and shielding his eyes as he searched the horizon in the direction in which Brak had indicated, but he still couldn't see them. His eyesight was steadily getting worse though he had no intention of admitting that to the others.

"Ah! I see them," he finally said staring off into the

distance. "Let them go and report back; it won't make any difference to what we do."

Brak and Yarik looked at one another but said nothing. The riders had ridden off a few moments ago and were no longer in sight.

"Very well," said Brak. "I doubt the main force is very far behind them. I will go and check how the staves are coming along."

"Make sure the men have enough time to grab something to eat, Brak. I don't want the men fighting on an empty stomach if we can help it."

Brak nodded and waved his agreement as he walked briskly away towards where many of the men were busy whittling away at the long branches or digging small holes in the hard ground.

"So who went and made you general?" Yarik asked Teren.

"What?" replied Teren distractedly.

"The scout; he called you general. You been and promoted yourself?"

"No, no I haven't, but it does have a nice ring to it don't you think?" said Teren grinning.

"Well don't expect me to call you general," growled the Delarite.

"Really? You'll hurt my feelings," said Teren as he walked off smirking. Behind him he could hear the big Delarite moaning and muttering to himself.

Chapter 19

The battle was not going well. Despite the continued harrying of the Narmidian forces from either flank by the Lotari bowmen and *jemtak* throwers, they were having little effect on the Narmidian forces which had reorganised on the march. A large force of heavily armoured infantry now formed the vanguard of their army and had already engaged the first rank of Emperor Zerut's men stationed on the hill. Behind the heavy infantry Prince Balok had stationed a vast number of light infantry ready to pour forward and exploit any breaches in the Lotari defence. Just behind them Skythian archers were firing high into the sky so that their arrows dropped over the first couple of ranks of Lotari soldiers causing disruption in their reserve ranks. Other Skythians continued to guard the attacking force's flanks exchanging a hail of projectiles with both Ro's men and those of General Livar whose troops simultaneously moved along the valley ridges parallel to the Narmidian force. The Skythians were far superior in their craft and were reaping a terrible toll on both of the Lotari flanking forces although the *jemtak* continued to cause terror within their ranks.

Ro and Colonel Ulikath watched the fight on the slope to their right unfold and it was already clear to Ro's trained eye that the soldiers in the emperor's front rank were no match for their adversaries despite the advantage of holding the higher ground. Even as he watched from somewhere near the emperor a horn sounded and the remaining soldiers of the front rank began to withdraw under a covering volley of *jemtak,* whilst the second rank slowly advanced to take their place. The manoeuvre was smooth and disciplined but already the Lotari were ceding ground to the attackers. It did not bode well.

Colonel Ulikath standing to Ro's right shouted something in Lotari and the men standing nearby stepped forward and hurled their *jemtak* at the Narmidians below. The Narmidians were prepared, however, and on command hundreds of shields went up to form a wall against them. Here and there one of the projectiles found a way through where the soldiers had not been fastidious in their wall building, but generally the majority of the *jemtak* lodged harmlessly into the shields.

Ro glanced back to the hill to his right. Already the second rank of Lotari was hard pressed by the Narmidian heavy infantry. The emperor's men were fighting bravely and in a disciplined fashion as he'd expect, but they were losing.

Again the horn sounded and again the Lotari repeated the earlier manoeuvre and the second rank withdrew under a volley of *jemtak* to be replaced by fresh troops. More ground had been yielded in carrying out this move but the bit of the slope that the Narmidians now moved up to occupy was slightly steeper and the fresh Lotari troops were not only holding their ground but also seemed to be pushing their attackers back.

Hope briefly flared in Ro's heart but it was quickly extinguished as a Narmidian officer realised what was happening and ordered more Skythian archers to the front. Their arrows filled the sky as they looped up and over their own troops and down onto the Lotari warriors who dropped by the score. Many Narmidians fell too due to their proximity to the Lotari, but better armoured than their enemy, their casualties were far fewer. The Narmidian prince could also afford the luxury of the casualties whereas the Lotari couldn't. They would lose a war of attrition.

Their numbers decimated, the Lotari faltered and lost cohesion and the Narmidians seized their opportunity. With a great roar, the mass of light infantry which had been held back by the Narmidian prince surged forward past their comrades seeking to exploit the confusion in the Lotari ranks. None of the Lotari ran but they were quickly overwhelmed by sheer numbers.

Ro watched in despair. The Narmidians had committed at least half of their forces to the attack an attack which looked like it was going to succeed unless something changed. The Lotari emperor was sat upon his horse at the top of the slope surrounded by his personal bodyguard. In front of them were massed the heavy infantry, the fighting elite of the Lotari army. In front of them were the men who had been hurling the *jemtak* and providing cover to the men as they changed formations. In front of them were the remnants of the three ranks of light infantry already committed to the battle and the fourth rank which was now engaged with their counterparts from the Narmidian army.

The men around Ro stepped forward again and once more hurled their *jemtak* into the air and down onto the enemy below and once again most failed to find a target due to the swift shield wall the Narmidians erected.

"Aryk, that was the last of our *jemtak*," said Colonel Ulikath.

"So be it." Ro looked from the colonel back to the fight happening on the slope to his right. The emperor's generals were urging the remnants of the first three attacks forward to support their beleaguered comrades in an effort to stop the massed Narmidian light infantry breaking through. Those who had been throwing the *jemtak* were also pressing forward with swords, having also apparently run out of their favoured weapon. Behind them the emperor's elite infantry were altering formation ready to join the battle. "Time for us to join the fun I think, Colonel. Have the cavalry formed up on me will you? The infantry to follow as closely behind as possible."

The colonel nodded and immediately barked orders out in his own language as around him, a long line of men took shape.

The slope to his right was awash with colour as men from numerous different regiments and nationalities clashed. There were no longer any neat ranks of men facing each other down; now it was a huge melee of intermingled men. Still the emperor's men fought bravely, but it was obvious to Ro that moment by moment, the Narmidians were gaining the upper hand through sheer weight of numbers. Ro glanced over to the other side of the valley and was pleased to see that General Livar too was planning on committing all of his men to the attack, they too presumably having run out of arrows and *jemtak*. Their descent down the gravelly slope would be more perilous and would take longer putting them at greater risk from the Skythian archers, but he had no choice. It would have taken too long to ride and march his forces off the slope and round to join his emperor. Ro hoped that the pitiful force of men he had left with him would be enough to draw the attention of the majority of Skythians away from General Livar's men.

Ro turned to face Colonel Ulikath. "Translate for me please." The colonel nodded and Ro pulled his horse in front of the line of anxious looking Lotari soldiers. "Lotari warriors, we ride to glory. Ride hard and ride fast. Hit them in the flank like we did earlier. Fight as you have never fought before and make your emperor who is watching from over there, proud," shouted Ro leaving enough time after every few words for Colonel Ulikath to translate. Then he drew his sword and roared.

The Lotari started shouting and waving their weapons in the air and Colonel Ulikath glanced over at Ro and nodded his approval.

"Colonel, if you'd be as kind as to give the order."

The colonel smiled and offered his hand to Ro who took the proffered hand and shook it warmly.

Then the colonel turned to his men and drawing his own sword gave the order for them to charge. Moments later, scores of Lotari riders backed up by slingers turned infantry, thundered down the slope towards the enemy's right flank.

As with their initial attack, Skythian archers were sent forward to confront the attackers, but unlike the first attacks, this time they were being attacked on both flanks at the same time and had to split their forces accordingly. Already weakened by the fact that approximately half their number had been sent forward to support the assault on the emperor's hill, the number of archers facing Ro and his men was considerably fewer and their effect less devastating.

Still men dropped but it wasn't enough to break Ro's charge and because there were fewer archers, instead of being ordered to retreat inside the column after firing their first shot, this time the Skythians were encouraged to fire twice to make up for the numbers. With a vengeful force of sword wielding enemy bearing down on them, the archers' second shots were panicked and hurried, and most missed their mark. More importantly it left them exposed and outside of the shield wall.

Ro's men tore into the unarmoured and defenceless Skythians, hacking and slicing with impunity. Unable to bring their bows to bear at close range, most of the Skythians turned and ran presenting the vengeful Lotari with easy targets. For a couple of hundred heartbeats, Ro and his men were on their own, but eventually General Livar's men made it down the treacherous gravelly side of the valley and joined the fight. Now battling on three fronts the Narmidians initially gave ground under the vicious onslaught but then an officer who stood at least two hands taller than any of the men around him, appeared from further up the column and began to bully, harass and berate his men into standing their ground.

Ro thrust his sword into the exposed back of a fleeing Skythian and then pulled it free and back swiped a light infantry man approaching him from his right. As soon as he dealt with the man in front of him another two or three would appear to take his place. Ro had no doubt that it was the same all over. Wherever he looked he would find hard pressed Lotari fighting against overwhelming numbers and it would only get worse as more Narmidians arrived from the rear of their huge column.

Without warning, Ro's horse suddenly lost its footing and went crashing to the ground, crushing a Narmidian warrior beneath it. Ro just managed to free his feet from the stirrups in time to prevent himself from also being crushed under his horse's weight. He hit the ground hard, momentarily winded and then rolled clear, slowly getting to his feet. He ducked just in time as a wild swing from a terrified looking young Narmidian nearly removed his head and then stepped forward and drove his blade into the boy's groin. The warrior screamed, dropped his sword and collapsed to the ground but another warrior had already stepped forward to take his place. A *jemtak* hurled by some unseen ally, caught the man in the throat and he too dropped to the ground clutching at his wound as dark red arterial blood began spurting out through his fingers.

Something hit Ro's shield and deflected away and he turned just as a Narmidian was bringing his sword down towards Ro's shoulder. Ro raised his shield just in time to absorb the blow, but before he could recover the man sliced down twice more, the shield taking the full impact on both occasions. Ro tried to back away and give himself room to manoeuvre but his foot slipped on something and he collapsed to the ground still holding his shield aloft as yet another blow thundered into it.

The meagre contents of Ro's stomach almost resurfaced when he realised that he had slipped and was now lying in the entrails of the young boy he had gutted a few moments earlier. Another blow lashed into his shield and Ro's arm began to burn with the exertion of holding his shield aloft. Another blow or maybe two and he'd have to drop it. Then he'd be finished. He desperately tried to back away through the slimy entrails but he couldn't get enough purchase to move or get up. Another powerful blow struck his shield and Ro cried out with the pain as his shield finally dropped bringing some much needed relief to his arm muscles. His attacker, a brute of a man a head taller than Ro with arms like tree trunks, stepped forward with a murderous look in his eye. Ro raised his sword in a last ditch effort to avoid death but just as the Narmidian raised his sword to deliver the killing blow, the man's abdomen was suddenly pierced by a javelin that had either been thrown or thrust through him from behind. The Narmidian dropped his sword and collapsed to his knees and then the ground, ending up face first in his comrade's intestines.

The Lotari officer standing behind him nodded at Ro and then begun to pull his javelin free but as he did so, a Narmidian slashed him across his back before his gaze fell on Ro. This time Ro managed to scramble to his feet but was unsteady and did well to deflect the Narmidian's first thrust, before swinging his left fist into the side of the man's head. The Narmidian stumbled backwards but didn't fall and although he still had the presence of mind to raise his sword, he did not do it with enough conviction to block Ro's counter thrust and Ro's blade pierced him in his chest.

In the distance Ro heard the sound of a couple of horns blowing, three short blasts and then a long one. It was the signal for the emperor's elite troops to enter the battle. Now everyone was committed. There could be no escape. They would either emerge victorious or they would die; there was no third alternative.

Colonel Ulikath suddenly appeared next to Ro covered in blood though whether it was his or other people's Ro couldn't tell.

"General Livar has fallen. There are just too many of them. We need to rally the men and make our way towards the emperor's position. If I am to die here today I want it to be in defence of my emperor," said the colonel.

"That's not going to be easy, Colonel," said Ro as he rolled his wrist and disarmed another Narmidian before running him through.

"It never is. Still we must try."

"Very well. On your command," said Ro.

Colonel Ulikath shouted at the top of his voice for the men to try and disengage and make their way to the slope where the emperor and his elite troops were hopefully pushing down into the Narmidian vanguard. Slowly men tried to disengage and rally to where Ro and the colonel stood, but some were so far within the Narmidian lines that there was no way they could hope to make it out. All that was left to them was to fight ruthlessly and die with honour. One or two less disciplined Lotari turned and tried to run to the rally point but they were soon cut down. It was a pitifully small force of no more than a hundred men that eventually stood around Ro and the colonel.

"Well this ought to be interesting," said Ro.

His humour was clearly lost on the colonel who merely glanced at his southern ally with a strange expression.

After bullying and cajoling their men into a circle, they began to slowly try and work their way through the throng of enemy soldiers towards the emperor, but after some initial progress, their advance ground to a halt. Bit by bit the circle of men was whittled down and every time one of them was killed the circle was forced to contract. Twice Ro tried to disengage from the fight and see where they were in relation to the emperor's men, but the teeming mass of soldiers fighting in front of him restricted his view. They could have been two hundred paces or a handful of paces away; he couldn't tell. Nor he realised, did it really matter. They were losing, of that there was no doubt. Their tactics had been good but it was always a forlorn hope that such a small force could triumph in the face of such an overwhelming foe.

The man to Ro's immediate right suddenly collapsed to the ground, clutching at a spear that was protruding from his abdomen and two Narmidians immediately tried to exploit the breach in the circle's defences. Ro quickly stepped forward and slashed one of them across the neck before stooping low and stabbing the other one in the groin as his sword sliced harmlessly through the air at head height.

More Narmidians immediately stepped forward to take their place and Ro shouted for the men around him to draw tighter together. When his order wasn't immediately translated by Colonel Ulikath, Ro glanced round for him but couldn't see him. He could have been too busy fighting to help or he could be dead, there was no way for Ro to know.

A man several places to Ro's left suddenly went down and then another to the man's right and although the men's comrades immediately tried to close ranks, Ro could tell it was already too late and he watched helplessly as Narmidians flooded into the breach. Now he was just as likely to die from a sword in the back as he was one in the front. Panic began to sweep through the Lotari around Ro and discipline finally broke down. Now instead of facing the enemy with a uniform line, men broke away into personal duels whilst others tried to flee. Still the Narmidians pressed forward, with an unstoppable and seemingly inexhaustible supply of men.

His life span could now probably be measured in moments he realised and Ro merely began to wave his sword wildly around, cutting and slicing, every stroke seeming to make contact with an enemy soldier. But there was always more to take their place. He was tiring fast and soon they would overpower him, but he would not die cheaply. If only the emperor's Northern Army had managed to get there in time, then things might have been different.

Ro stabbed forward with his sword at a large Narmidian with a long black moustache, but he easily managed to sway out of its way, but Ro immediately followed up with a swipe of his shield which caught the man in the jaw, sending blood and teeth flying through the air. The man dropped to the ground unconscious but three more men immediately piled into his place, hacking and chopping at Ro. Most of the blows Ro managed to hold off with his shield, but he was spent and no longer had the strength to lift it. He parried two more swings and then tried to back away but his feet once again slipped on the blood and gore beneath him and he fell backwards, landing heavily on the body of a dead Lotari warrior.

Eager to finish him off the first Narmidian raced forward with his sword raised above his head, but he had thrown caution aside and thought Ro beaten until he ran stomach first onto his sword. The Narmidian dropped his sword behind his back and slowly collapsed to the ground, his lifeless body coming to rest on Ro's legs. His two comrades stepped cautiously forward but realising that Ro's sword was now irretrievably buried in their dead comrade's body, they prepared for the kill.

The look of triumph on both their faces turned to one of shock as their bodies suddenly shuddered before dropping to the ground with several arrows lodged in their backs. One of them landed heavily on top of Ro and the other dead Narmidian and Ro let out a cry of pain as he was once again winded. Unable to do anything else Ro lay back and watched the battle as best he could, fascinated that so many Narmidians were suddenly dropping with arrows in their backs. The only explanation was that the emperor's Northern Army had flanked them and then come up behind the enemy to attack their rear.

A series of blasts on a horn carried over the tumult of battle though what command they were transmitting he had no idea. He couldn't be sure but to him it hadn't sounded like a Lotari horn. He decided that in all likelihood the Narmidians were sounding the retreat having been caught off guard by the arrival of the Lotari Northern Army. From his position on the ground he could not see much, but what he could see filled Ro with hope. The Narmidians were indeed trying to disengage but unable to retreat the way they had come their only option was to press forward into where the emperor and his elite troops were making their last stand.

Ro tried to heave himself free from the bodies on top of him, worried that some passing Narmidian might spot him lying there helplessly and take their anger out on him. He pushed and heaved but could not shift the pile of bodies lying on top of him which had been added to by another Lotari warrior who had taken an arrow in the back.

Suddenly a figure loomed over Ro, silhouetted by the sun and apparently staring down at him. All around him Ro could hear the sound of men running past him, but his focus was on the man standing over him about to end his life. It was an ignominious way to die Ro decided, flat on his back and helpless. The very least he wanted was to die with his sword in his hand looking his enemy in the eye. Instead he was prostrate, weapon less and unable to even make out the man's face.

"Well get on with it you whoreson," snapped Ro, determined to wound the man with his tongue if not his sword. "Am I still too much of a threat to you, you gutless worm?"

"Now is that any way to greet an old friend I wonder?" said the strangely familiar voice above him.

Ro stared at the silhouetted shape unable to comprehend if his ears were hearing right. "Arlen?"

"Who else would come and pull your backside out of a mess like this?"

"Arlen is that really you?" asked Ro incredulously.

The figure leaned forward so that Ro could see. Arlen Meric, Priest of the Golden Tree of Silevia and most recently ruler of the country, smiled down at him.

"Aye, it's me. Were you expecting someone else because if you were I can always come back?"

"You'll do. Do you mind?" asked Ro gesturing for Arlen to help pull him free of his prison of bodies.

Arlen looked at the predicament Ro was in and slowly shook his head.

172

"I'm gone for a couple of minutes and look at the mess you manage to get yourself in. What were you doing down there anyway; making friends?"

"Your timing may have improved, monk, but your humour has not."

Arlen laughed and clasping Ro's proffered hand pulled his friend free. Ro cried out as his back, which had been arched over a dead body, slowly straightened itself.

"Thank you," said Ro as he glanced round for his sword before pulling it out of the dead Narmidian's body. He wiped the blade clean on the man's tunic.

"You're welcome," replied Arlen.

"Now do you mind telling me what you're doing here?" asked Ro once he had glanced round to make sure there were no Narmidians likely to run up and attack them. All he could see though were Silevians pursuing the Narmidians to the north. "I thought it was the emperor's Northern Army that came to our assistance."

"Oh, they're here as well. They're supporting the emperor's forces from the north whilst we flanked the Narmidians so we could attack them from the south in a pincer movement. Just as well we did judging by the state I found you in."

"But how did you know?" asked Ro.

"The emperor's herald. He told us what was going on in Lotar and the emperor's call for assistance."

"But they never returned. We didn't know if they had even got through to you. We never saw them again. The emperor thought that he stood alone."

"Nor will you see them again; we found them hanging from a tree on our way here, but sadly for the Narmidians the message was already delivered."

"Still, we were not sure you'd come. Lotar and Silevia have not always seen eye to eye," said Ro.

"No, they haven't and that is something that is going to change. I'm hoping that my appearance here with my entire army will convince the emperor of that fact," said Arlen earnestly.

Ro grinned and hugged his friend.

"By all the gods it is good to see you again, Arlen."

"And I you," said Arlen hugging him back. "I am sorry for…"

Ro felt Arlen's body judder before the monk's hold on Ro's back lessened.

"Arlen, are you…"

Arlen slowly collapsed to the ground, a black arrow buried deep between his shoulder blades.

Ro looked up from his friend just as a large Silevian with a bushy beard cleaved the head of an already wounded Narmidian holding a bow, clean off his shoulders. The man had either been feigning death or had been laying wounded waiting for his chance. Around Ro men were calling for a healer, but as Ro cradled his friend in his arms, the blood seeping through his fingers, Ro knew that it was already too late; the arrow had been fired from almost point blank range and had pierced a vital organ. His friend had but moments to live.

"Stay with me, Arlen, a healer is on his way. You're going to be fine," said Ro.

Arlen looked up at his friend but found he was unable to focus, the darkness of death already closing in the peripheral of his vision.

"You are a fine warrior and a good friend, but a terrible liar, Ro Aryk. The Chariot of Souls approaches."

"Don't you go dying on me, monk; I still have many debts that need repaying," said Ro smiling at his friend, unable to hide the first tears as they escaped the corner of his eyes.

"Don't worry, our adventures don't end here," said Arlen almost in a whisper.

Ro looked up as two men came and crouched down beside him. One wore the uniform of the Order of Goresh, the same as Arlen and the other, whom Ro assumed was the healer, wore simple Silevian civilian clothing.

"Arlen, the…" Ro cut himself short when he realised that his friend had already slipped away. He started to weep openly then and rested his forehead against his friend's, cradling his now lifeless body close to his own, before lightly brushing Arlen's eyes closed with his fingers.

Behind him Ro heard the sound of several horses approaching, but he did not bother to turn. Such was his grief that in that moment in time, he no longer cared whether it was friend or foe.

Nothing mattered any longer.

Chapter 20

Their plan couldn't have worked any better if they'd spent all summer preparing. The Narmidian cavalry which had been relentlessly pursuing Teren's largely infantry force finally caught them up en masse in the early afternoon. By the time their commander had organised them into battle formation, however, the shadows were already growing long.

Teren's men were arrayed in two long lines atop a small grassy ridge, nothing that would have worried an attacking infantry force let alone light cavalry. As far as the Narmidian commander had been concerned, the allied force was too exhausted to run any further and had decided to make a last desperate stand rather than be caught strung out in column.

The Narmidian commander didn't doubt that the allies had some archers and fully expected to suffer quite heavy losses on the approach, but men he was not short of; a victory at any cost was what his king demanded and he had no intention of failing him. It was with a quiet confidence then that he sent his first wave of cavalry forward. When they were a hundred paces ahead, he sent his second wave after them and then when the same size gap was opened, he sent his third wave, holding his final wave in reserve with himself.

As expected the allies waited until the first wave of riders was practically on them before opening fire with their bowmen and as expected, losses at that range were heavy. However, the commander knew that the second wave would soon be upon the enemy and with so many rider less horses wandering around, targets would not come easily to the enemy. Then his men would be amongst them. Once the enemy lines were breached, the third wave would pour through and exploit the gaps and attack the enemy in the rear. It was a simple plan but an effective one and the commander fully expected it to work.

What he didn't expect, however, was what happened next. The second wave of cavalry were just about to break on the enemy front line when suddenly the men in the allied front two ranks who had been kneeling down in front of their archers, stood up lifting something as they did. The commander raised himself a little bit in the saddle, curious yet full of dread and then watched in horror as the shouts of alarm and squeals of pain from both men and horses, drifted across the battlefield. The enemy had been hiding long wooden poles sharpened to a brutal point at the end. The men in the first two ranks were now holding these at an angle towards the onrushing cavalry and unable to stop in time once they realised the danger, horse after horse was running on to the staves, their riders dropping to the ground where they were then butchered. Some horses did manage to pull up in time but invariably their riders were then thrown from their mounts either landing at the end of a Remadan sword point or worse still, finding themselves impaled on one of the poles.

It was a disaster and the commander watched as his first two waves of men were butchered in front of his eyes. Moments later the third wave of cavalry arrived. Unable to see clearly what was going on, they arrived in poor order amongst the chaos and confusion and suddenly found themselves under attack from the entire allied force which had been ordered forward to intercept them. Meanwhile the allied archers waited with arrows nocked to fire at the Narmidian reserves should they attempt to join the fight.

They were losing of that there was no doubt. Even from his position several hundred paces away the Narmidian commander could see that. Those of his men that had not been butchered milled around amongst the confusion unsure whether to press forward with the attack or to retreat. Everywhere there was chaos. Horses and men staggered around in a maelstrom of violence as the vengeful allies ran amongst them hacking and slicing. Killing. Some of the Narmidians did manage to turn their horses around and try to retreat, but many of those were cut down by a wave of arrows from the allied archers.

The Narmidian commander turned his horse and muttered for the small gaggle of officers sat around him, to follow with the soldiers he had held in reserve and slowly started to make his way west leaving his men to die.

"They're leaving, Teren, look," said Brak beaming and pointing towards the far ridge from where the Narmidian commander and his staff officers had been coordinating the attack.

Teren followed Brak's pointing finger and then nodded slowly.

"You're right, lad. Looks like they've had enough." He rested his sword on his right shoulder and gazed around the battlefield before him. Here and there the odd skirmish was still going ahead but mostly the violence had come to an end. The ground was littered with the dead and the dying, both men and horses. Teren was pleased to see that the Narmidian dead far outnumbered his own men.

To his right a horse lay on the ground whinnying and trying to right itself, a javelin embedded deep in its side. Teren watched the horse, a beautiful chestnut mare, for a few moments until he could no longer bear its pitiful crying and then knelt beside the creature. He whispered some quiet soothing words into the creature's ear whilst he stroked its head and then gently opened the big artery in its neck with his knife. The horse twitched a couple of times and then let out a long breath. Then it was still. Teren sat with the animal for a short while longer, the sounds of battle receding with every passing breath until eventually Teren heard someone run up and stop next to Brak, though he couldn't hear what they said. A few moments later Brak came and stood alongside Teren who was slowly getting to his feet, wincing as his right knee cracked. Brak saved his friend's blushes by pretending not to have noticed his friend's pain.

"We have the field, Teren."

Teren looked at his friend and then at the carnage around him. The fighting had stopped and there were no mounted men left. Here and there Teren's men walked amongst the dead and put the seriously wounded out of their misery, easing their passing. It seemed to a watching Teren that his men showed more compassion when putting a horse down than they did an enemy soldier. He couldn't blame them. There was not a man there who had not suffered a loss as a result of the war and all had reason to hate the invader.

Teren doubted that it was just the severely wounded who were being sent on their way, but also those with non-fatal wounds.

"Do you want me to get some of our men mounted and pursue the survivors?" asked Brak.

"No. Let them go. They're no threat to us now, but do send half a dozen lads to watch them for a while, just in case their commander suddenly grows a spine and turns round to harry our rear."

Brak nodded thinking that was a good idea and strolled off to find men who could ride a horse.

"We've won a great victory, Remadan," said the booming voice of Yarik.

Teren turned to face his friend and initially baulked at the sight that greeted him. Yarik was literally covered in blood and gore from his long matted hair and face down to his boots.

"It looks like you've been to Kaden and back," said Teren astonished.

"Tanith would never let me into Kaden as I would frighten his demons too much," replied Yarik grinning.

"So what did happen to you?" asked Teren.

"Whilst you were here tying your boots and finding things to keep you from the fight, real men were in the thick of the action. I must have killed fifty at least."

Teren doubted it but there could be no doubt many a Narmidian son would never see home again after crossing the big Delarite.

"Our plan worked well then?" said Teren.

"Aye it did at that. I never thought a pure infantry force could turn a mounted attack like that let alone rout and butcher them." Yarik glanced round at the piles of dead carpeting the ground in every direction. "It was a great victory."

"And we shall drink our fill of wine and ale tonight in celebration and in honour of those of our brothers who no longer draw breath," replied Teren solemnly.

"That we will, Remadan, that we will."

***

The scouts Brak had sent out to shadow and follow the

Narmidian survivors, arrived back at camp just before dusk and reported that the Narmidians were still riding due west and didn't look like stopping any time soon. They had seen their shadows on at least one occasion but no effort had been made to chase them off. Teren took that as a sign that they just wanted to put as much distance between themselves and the allies as soon as they could.

Clearing the battlefield of the wounded had been hard and tiring work, but by the middle of the evening all of the severely wounded from both sides had been despatched and the less wounded allied soldiers were being seen to by some of their comrades who had battlefield medical training albeit rudimentary. The less severely wounded Narmidians, who Teren's men had not yet put to the sword, knelt in a huddle in the centre of the camp. When he had finished his evening meal, Teren, Brak and Yarik strolled over to where the frightened looking Narmidians were kneeling and stopped a few paces in front of them and just stared for a while. Most if not all of them knew about the great Teren Rad and of his prowess in battle, but it was to Yarik that their frightened gazes turned, though none had the courage to look him in the eyes. Although he had cleaned himself up somewhat, some evidence of their comrades' blood remained on his boots and other clothes but most had seen the terrifying looking Delarite covered in blood earlier in the evening. The fear they felt in his presence was almost palpable. The way he grinned as he toyed with his axe chilled them to the bone.

It was a surprise then when after a minute or so's deliberation, Teren ordered that they be escorted from the camp and then set free and pointed in the direction of their comrades.

"Are you mad, Remadan? Why do you set them free?" snarled Yarik. He wasn't happy and had been sure that his axe was going to drink more Narmidian blood before the night was through.

"Haven't you had enough killing for one day, Delarite?" snapped Teren.

"Not where these dogs are concerned no. It is madness to let them go."

"What harm can they do us, Yarik? They've got no horses and no weapons and there are what... twenty of them?"

"And if they make it back to their own lines?"

"Vesla is likely to execute them himself for failing him," said Teren sighing.

"Then let's save him the trouble and do it for him." A number of men standing around him cheered, but they were mostly Delarites and Datians, Teren noted. Brak and some other men had surreptitiously moved to stand behind Teren ready to come to his aid if things turned ugly.

"Let them go, Yarik; they are of no consequence. I have spoken."

"You have spoken but perhaps we are no longer listening."

"And what's that supposed to mean?" asked Teren taking a step closer to Yarik.

"Maybe we are tired of following your orders. Maybe it is time for a change." Yarik took a step closer to Teren and now the two men were facing off virtually toe to toe. The crowd around them had multiplied but there was a hush as everyone wondered what would happen next.

"This is madness. Teren has just led us to a great victory, a victory that many of you thought wasn't possible," said Brak stepping forward and addressing the gathered crowd. "We had no right to win today's battle but we didn't just win, we routed the enemy and we did so with the loss of only two hundred and seventeen men. I would not have believed it had I not witnessed it with my own eyes. And now, later on that very same day you are questioning perhaps even challenging Teren's right to lead us? It is madness. Without him many of us would be food for the carrion birds by now." Brak could see by the look in some of the men's eyes in the dancing firelight that his words had hit home.

"I still say that we should kill every enemy soldier wherever we find them," snarled Yarik. Again there was a murmuring of support but it was much weaker this time, many of his supporters having deserted him in the light of Brak's words.

"I think you are missing a great opportunity, my friend," Brak said turning to face Yarik and smiling.

"Oh and how is that so?" asked Yarik never taking his eyes off Teren. He knew that Brak was smarter than he and suspected a trick.

"Look at their faces, Yarik, they're petrified. By letting them live and return to their comrades you're sending twenty terrified messengers back to the enemy camp. Their tales of the mad Delarite who slew ten..."

"Fifty," corrected Yarik.

"...fifty of their comrades single handed, will spread like wildfire and soon panic and terror will fill their hearts. A fearful man is a beaten man."

"I see what you're saying, northerner," said Yarik as he stroked his beard which was still caked in dried blood.

Brak turned to Teren and winked and the Remadan nodded almost imperceptibly back.

"Very well, northerner, I see the wisdom of your words. It will be of Yarik of Delarite that they will speak and not Teren of Remada."

"That's right," said Brak.

"So be it. You get what you want, Remadan, but not because I am bending to your will, but because it makes good sense."

"And has nothing to do with your ego I suppose?" asked Teren.

Yarik looked angrily at Teren and Brak flashed his friend a look that told him to back off and leave it alone lest he undo all the good he had just worked for.

"Get the prisoners up. Marot, pick twenty men and escort our guests a league to the west, then cut them free and return to camp," said Brak taking charge of the situation before things erupted again.

After giving firstly the captives and then Teren one last venomous look, Yarik turned and stomped off grabbing a flagon of ale from one of the soldiers he pushed past. The Datian soldier wisely didn't complain.

"Nicely done, Brak. You're going to make a fine king one day," said Teren.

"Thank you. I just hope there's somewhere left to be king of."

"And someone to rule over, eh?" said Teren slapping his friend on the shoulder.

"Yes, that would also be nice. But first there is the small matter of defeating the Narmidians and then wrestling the kingdom away from my brother."

"Well I don't know about the second problem, lad, but I think the first problem will soon be coming to a head."

"How do you mean?"

"I mean that we only have enough strength for one last battle. It's do or die."

"I'm sure you said that before the last two battles," replied Brak smiling.

"Aye, I probably did, but this time I really mean it. We've got to somehow draw Vesla into one pitched battle and give his army such a mauling that he has no choice but to run for home."

"I thought we just did."

"True, but he wasn't here to see it. The next one must be against the full strength of his army."

"But we'd never win such a battle, Teren, you know that. We have what, fewer than three thousand men; he has many and most of those are mounted."

"He has a lot less now I'd say. Besides, if we can make it to the northern kingdoms and persuade them to join us, that would boost our numbers, especially with horse soldiers."

"That's if they haven't already been overrun."

"They won't have. I also refuse to believe that the men with us here are all that's left of the free peoples of Arkadia. Somewhere, someone else is building a force to try and do the same thing we are."

"It's a nice thought, Teren, but a desperate one. Even if such a force existed, how would we find it? They could be anywhere."

"I haven't figured that part out yet."

Brak laughed. "And there I was worrying."

Teren slapped his friend on the shoulder again and laughed heartily.

"Come, my friend, let's go and see if that big ox of a Delarite is still being obnoxious."

Chapter 21

The Narmidians under Prince Balok had been completely routed and only a few dozen had managed to escape. As Ro looked out over the body laden battlefield he realised that but for the intervention and timely arrival of Arlen and the Silevians, things would have been so very different. The Lotari had been beaten and would in all likelihood have been massacred down to the last man, but the surprise arrival of two thousand mounted Silevians had turned the tide. With their lines cut and enemies availing them from all sides, Narmidian discipline had broken down and men had panicked. That panic had rippled out through the army until all but the prince's bodyguard had turned and tried to run. Disgusted with the cowardice shown by his men, the prince in one last wanton act of brutality had ordered some of his bodyguard to kill any of their men that turned and tried to run, whilst he and the rest of his guards, tried to flee the battlefield. The Silevians and Lotari had the enemy well sewn up though and there had been nowhere left to run. No escape. A few riders had managed to break through the cordon but most had been killed including Prince Balok. It had been a slaughter and Ro suddenly felt sick to the pit of his stomach at the sheer scale of human life that had been lost, one of whom had been his close friend, Arlen Meric whose actions had once again saved the Remadan's life. Now he would never be able to repay the debt which had been accumulating since their fateful meeting in some distant forest two years previously.

"You fought well today, my friend." The voice startled him and Ro spun round to see the smiling face of his friend, Emperor Zerut, of the Lotari. Ro bowed deeply, pulling himself together.

"As did you, your majesty. I watched you lead the charge of your elite guards."

"I couldn't let you have all the glory, Ro."

"I fear there is little glory to be had here in this charnel house, your majesty," said Ro glancing around at the dead bodies stretching as far as he could see in every direction.

"A battlefield is never a pretty sight, my friend, not even one where you emerge the winner. But we did win and you should be grateful for that."

"I am your majesty. Had it not been for the timely arrival of our friends from Silevia and your Northern Army I fear we would all be dead now."

"Yes, I know. I would speak with their leader. Can you point him out to me?"

Ro's gaze dropped to the ground momentarily.

"I regret that he was killed during the battle, your majesty. His body lies over there."

"This man was your friend was he not?"

"He was."

"Then I am truly sorry, Ro. His death and those of his comrades will not have been in vain. I hope that this joint action heralds a new era of cooperation and friendship between our two nations."

Ro smiled. "He would have been pleased to hear that, your majesty. It was his dream that all of the northern kingdoms become closer and cooperate economically and militarily."

"Then we will have to try and honour him by making this come to pass. Who now speaks for the Silevians?"

A few of the Silevians who had been stood around listening to the exchange, glanced at one another until eventually a man with grey hair and wearing what Ro knew was an officer's uniform in Arlen's newly reorganised army, stepped forward.

"I am Galand Farith, senior general in Silevia's new army. Until a new leader can be elected I will speak for the people of Silevia."

"It is good to meet you, General Farith," said the emperor, climbing down from his horse and extending a hand towards the general.

The general looked stunned that the emperor had lowered himself to look at him as an equal and hesitated before clasping the emperor's hand.

"Please, if we are to be friends, I would greet you as such," said the emperor.

The general clasped the emperor's hand and shook it vigorously and all the men around cheered.

"Tell me, General, is the army of Silevia willing to continue the fight beyond their borders?"

"We already have, your majesty, the moment we crossed into your lands, but yes, we are willing to join whatever other forces still stand against this scourge from the east. Today we have proved they can be beaten and word will spread."

"Excellent, General. We are to be allies then. As you say, word of our victory will soon spread and sooner or later Vesla will turn his attention north to seek vengeance. Better to take the fight to him in the company of friends than to stand alone and weak," said the emperor.

"It is agreed then. However, as commander of the Silevian forces I would make one request."

"And what is that, General?" asked the emperor.

"That Mister Aryk is allowed to lead our forces. I know that he and Arlen were close friends and Ro here was instrumental in helping to free our people from the tyranny of the Order. I would be honoured if you would lead our forces in this war, Ro," he added turning to face Ro.

"But it is your army, General. Arlen made you his second in command," said Ro.

"Yes, he did and there will be plenty of time for me to repay that honour when this is done and dusted. For now it seems appropriate that you lead us. After all, you trained most of us including me and although I'm a general we both know that I've never fought in a battle before this one. If we are to survive, then we need a man with experience leading us. We need you."

Ro looked over at the emperor.

"Is that okay with you?"

"It is not my concern but what the general says makes a great deal of sense. We will all need experienced men to lead us now. I will rest easy knowing that one such person leads my allies."

"So be it," said Ro.

"And what do you think we ought to do first, Ro?" asked the emperor.

"The men are tired, your majesty, especially yours. I suggest that we send out patrols to make sure there isn't another Narmidian army about to surprise us and to chase off the few who survived this massacre. Then once our wounded have been seen to we should make sure that everyone, the archers in particular, are re-armed. Then after a hot meal and a good night's rest we should head south west and look to find any other allied forces still in the fight. Even with Arlen's…I mean my men, our combined force is not strong enough to fight another pitched battle. Do you agree?"

"I do, but I would request that we march to Overa before heading south west."

"Overa. That's several leagues to the south is it not?"

"It is."

"May I ask why?" asked Ro curious.

"I am expecting company."

"Care to elaborate?"

The emperor was smiling. "Why not wait and enjoy the surprise?"

"As you wish," replied Ro. He glanced at General Farith hoping that perhaps he could shed some light on the matter, but the older man merely shrugged.

The emperor started to laugh. "Don't worry, my friend. It is the kind of surprise that you will enjoy. Now come, we have much to do," and with that the emperor nimbly remounted his horse and rode off followed by his entourage. After a few moments reflection, Ro followed him. There was indeed much to do.

***

Overa was typical of all Lotari towns. Small and well situated near two streams with rich meadows surrounding it on three sides, it was nothing special to look at. However, it wasn't the town which caught Ro's attention as his horse breasted the top of a small ridge about half a league away. Instead it was the mass of soldiers and horses sat around a myriad of cooking fires in front of the town which caught him by surprise.

Just before they climbed the short slope upon which he now stood, a small group of Lotari riders had approached the head of their column. One of the officers had spoken briskly to the emperor who had replied in his own tongue. Ro had not managed to make out more than a handful of words and the emperor had shown no inclination to translate for him. Thinking that it was something that the emperor did not want the Silevians to hear, he did not push the matter and instead had climbed the slope. Now he realised what the emperor had been so coy about.

"Are those your men?" Ro asked as the emperor rode alongside him.

"Some are. The rest are from the other northern kingdoms. All have answered my call to arms: Kalids, Tulans, Vahirans and Carliri."

"How many?" asked Ro grinning, unable to hide his obvious delight.

"At the last count, fourteen thousand foot and horse. But more are arriving every day."

"But how is this possible? There is much enmity between some of you northern kingdoms is there not?"

"There is. But some things transcend petty squabbles. What is the point continuing to argue over border infringements when if we don't unify there won't be any borders as we'll all be Narmidian provinces?" said the emperor.

"I take your point. Will they cooperate?"

"There will be much posturing and puffing out of chests, but at the end of the day they will fight and die together," replied the emperor smiling.

"We'll need a unified command. Also we'll…"

"Ro, relax, it is all taken care of. There is to be a meeting of the heads of state tonight at which the decisions will be ratified, but it has already been agreed that I will be in overall command. The only force not already party to that agreement is the Silevians."

"I'm sure that they will be in agreement," replied Ro earnestly.

"I think as their appointed leader that decision will be yours, Ro," replied the emperor smiling.

"Yes, of course, sorry. I forgot. I still can't believe Arlen is no longer with us."

"I am sure that he is watching, my friend and keen for you to avenge him."

"I hope so, I…" Ro stopped mid-sentence. "Those men down there in green are they…"

"Lydians, yes," replied the emperor.

Ro's heart soared at the thought of seeing Queen Cala again, but his hopes were soon crushed when he recalled her falling during the battle in the east.

"How did Lydians get here?"

"When I told you that I sent riders out to the northern kingdoms I probably forgot to mention that I also sent some south, west and east."

"But why? As far as I knew the Lydians, Remadans, Datians, Delarites and everyone else for that matter, were defeated and those that survived fled west with Teren."

"That is true; I had heard the same tales. But survivors of defeated armies have a habit of just melting away; it is just a matter of finding them again. You will be surprised to hear I think, that Remada has another army in the field, but at the moment we are unable to find it. But down there are Lydians and Laryssans and men from every nation. Not everyone followed Teren Rad west."

Ro stroked his beard thoughtfully.

"If we could find this missing Remadan army and join with Teren's force, we would have an army strong enough to not only challenge Vesla's force, but maybe even defeat it."

"Yes, I agree, but only if we can find them. Hopefully some of my scouts have run into them."

"But we can't wait here indefinitely for an army that may never come," said Ro dejectedly.

"No, that is also true. My scouts were instructed to tell everyone that they run into that we will wait here until the next full moon, in seven days' time; then we march south west to engage Vesla. Any longer and I may not be able to maintain this coalition of the northern kingdoms. Boredom and inactivity breeds indiscipline and indiscipline as I'm sure you know, leads to trouble. We can't afford any trouble. The sooner we march to fight the better."

"Then let us hope that your scouts have met with success,"

said Ro before turning in his saddle and signalling for the column to follow him down the slope.

***

The meeting later that evening went pretty much as the emperor had predicted. In addition to the emperor there were two kings, a queen and a princess along with a number of generals and other dignitaries. After formal introductions had been made, Emperor Zerut had addressed the assembly and thanked them for coming. He briefed them on what the current situation was with regard to the war as far as he knew. He also then invited Ro to add anything he wanted to though Ro had to admit that having been in Silevia for so long his information might be out of date. Still, some of the other leaders were pleased and surprised to hear that as far as Ro knew, Teren Rad still drew breath and continued to fight. Ro had made it sound like Teren had marched west to try and persuade the northerners to join the fight, rather than the truth which as far as Ro knew, was that the defeated allies had fled west after a heavy defeat and were seeking sanctuary with the northerners.

After Ro had finished each of the leaders was invited to speak. All were keen to fight the enemy and each one who spoke sought to outdo their predecessor with promises of what their army was going to achieve. Talk, however, was cheap, Ro reflected and the proof would come when their forces were drawn up in a battle line facing down thousands of Narmidian horsemen. Still, they all appeared eager to prosecute the war and that could only be a good thing. When the subject of who should be in overall command was finally raised, Ro immediately spoke up and offered his wholehearted support to Emperor Zerut. It wasn't just because the man was his friend or even because he commanded the largest army there, but simply because he was the best man for the job. He was young in years but he was an astute tactician and a brave man; his men would follow him anywhere. His courage would inspire others.

One or two of the other leaders skirted round the edge of approval, hinting that somebody else might be better suited yet without stating whom. In the end, however, the vote carried unanimously.

The rest of the meeting was spent deciding how much longer to wait for any others who might be heading to the rendezvous point. In the end, despite the protestations of Ro's old friend, General Larit commanding the Lydians, who claimed that he had heard credible information about a large Remadan force still in the field, the assembly decided to march out of camp two days early. Ro had supported the general's stance but they had been out voted by seven to three.

Over the next five days, little more than a few hundred men arrived at the camp, none of whom claimed to have seen a Remadan army although a few said that they had heard of its existence. The combined strength of the army was now around sixteen thousand men and was unlikely to get significantly stronger if they continued to wait, so two days before the allotted date, the allies last hope of victory marched south west away from Overa, led by Emperor Zerut.

News of the existence of a large army marching south west would have by now reached Vesla's camp and both Emperor Zerut and Ro knew that he would have to march east to confront it. The final battle for Arkadia's future would soon be upon them.

Chapter 22

The gold goblet struck the messenger squarely above his right eye, causing a gash which instantly began to stream blood, before falling to the heavily rugged floor. The messenger stumbled back a pace or two but then regained his composure and continued to stare straight ahead. To do otherwise was to draw further attention to himself and that could be bad for his life expectancy.

"The fool! The incompetent, arrogant fool," raved Vesla as he kicked a cushion across the floor, his eyes darting around the confines of his tent looking for something else to abuse and assuage his rage. Nobody dared meet his eyes. "Am I the only one around here with a brain? Idiot!"

"I am sorry for the loss of the prince, great King," said Genereal Zibla taking a step forward and raising his eyes.

"You think that is why I am upset?"

"I just thought…"

"Well don't, General. From now on let me do the thinking. I seem to be the only one around here capable of doing so with a clear head. I do not care about the loss of my son, General; he was a scheming dog, who has been conniving to overthrow me, whispering in the shadows, sowing the seeds of discontent. His sole purpose in invading the north was to seek glory for himself…himself, not me. Then he was going to use the wealth of the conquered nations to buy the loyalty of my northern army. No, it is not him I mourn; it is the thousands of men who have died as a result of his reckless actions and inadequacies as a leader. Worse still, our reputation for being invincible is now in tatters. With one stroke of his sword, he has given hope to those who continue to resist us. Others will rally to their flag now that hope is restored. No, General I do not mourn the loss of my son; I welcome it."

"It is a disappointing setback, my King, I agree, but surely that is all it is? You will still be victorious in the war."

Starik Vesla stared at his senior general for a few moments as if weighing the truth in the man's words.

"You are right of course, General Zibla. It is a setback and nothing more. The removal of my scheming son and his dissenters is a bonus and should be viewed such. Wine, bring me more wine and wine for the general and all my officers." Behind him, half a dozen slaves hurriedly scurried around retrieving jugs of wine and new goblets and quickly filling them before handing them out to each man stood around the king.

The last goblet was just being filled and Vesla's officers were just starting to relax as the tension slowly ebbed away from their leader, when the tent flap opened and one of Vesla's bodyguards showed another Narmidian soldier in. Both men stood still waiting for Vesla to signal for them to approach and after a few moments of laughing and joking with some of his officers, Vesla finally noticed them and beckoned for them to approach.

"Who is this?" Vesla asked General Zibla as he took another swallow of his wine.

"He is the leader of one of the patrols I sent out this morning, my King."

The messenger swallowed nervously and cautiously approached where the king was sat, the gaggle of officers in front of him parting slightly to let him through. When he was half a dozen paces from the king, he bowed his head and went down on one knee.

"Speak," ordered Vesla. "You have news of our victory over Rad?"

"My King. My patrol was about to turn back to camp after scouting in the direction General Zibla ordered, when we ran into some of Colonel Marek's men," began the messenger.

"Go on."

"They were riding due west when we ran into them."

Vesla's expression had turned to one of controlled anger and the knuckles of the hand holding the goblet had turned white. The messenger glanced nervously towards General Zibla and the older officer nodded imperceptibly for the messenger to continue.

193

"The men we ran into were the only survivors from the force you sent to destroy Rad."

"That can't be possible," said General Zibla. "How?"

"Apparently Rad's men chose to make a stand on a low ridge and awaited Colonel Marek's riders. They destroyed the first wave with arrows and then produced long poles which had been sharpened at the end, which they had hidden in the tall grass. By the time the second wave realised what they were charging towards it was already too late and many of the men and horses were impaled. Then Rad's men charged and butchered those caught by the poles."

Vesla was shaking with rage.

"And what of Colonel Marek? Did he have the good sense to die with the majority of his men?"

"No, my King. He fled with the survivors but was apparently killed by his own men for failing them."

"A pity. I should like to have had a discussion with Colonel Marek regarding his failings. What of his men?"

"Those that did not take part in the attack and which were held in reserve are back inside camp, my King."

"Do you want some of them executed as an example, my King?" asked General Zibla.

Vesla seemed to consider his general's suggestion for a few moments before speaking.

"These men took no part in the fighting?" he asked the messenger.

"No, my King. According to Captain Shular they were held in reserve as the fourth wave but before he had committed them to the fight, Colonel Marek realised what was happening and gave the order to withdraw."

"Then the fault is not theirs and Captain Shular showed good judgement in relieving me of Colonel Marek's incompetence." Vesla turned to face General Zibla. "Tell Captain Shular that he now has command of those men and a field promotion to major. Then allocate some more troops to bring his unit back up to strength."

"Yes, my King."

"You may go," Vesla said turning to face the messengers, but although the injured one hurried away, the second one made no effort to leave. "You have something else to add?"

The messenger licked his lips, his eyes darting nervously around the small group of officers all of whom were staring intently at him wondering what this latest bad news could be.

"Earlier in the day, my King, several leagues to the south east of where we met Colonel Marek's survivors, we saw a huge dust cloud in the distance. Thinking it was the men we were looking for, I sent three of my men to make contact whilst the rest of my patrol continued to skirt eastwards. None of my men returned and when we did meet Colonel Marek's survivors I knew that whoever was causing that dust cloud was either an enemy formation or reinforcements from the east."

He paused and drew breath and Vesla fixed him with a rigid stare and motioned for him to continue.

"After giving orders for most of the men to return here, I went to personally investigate. It was a column of Remadan infantry, my king, perhaps four thousand strong."

"In which direction were they headed?"

"North, my King."

Vesla glanced over at General Zibla.

"I thought that apart from Rad's rabble we had put the Remadans to the sword."

"As did I, my King. I can only assume that this is their elusive Eastern army, or what's left of it. It is of no consequence. We will swat this one out of the way as we have all others."

"Perhaps, but the subjugation of these lands is taking far longer than I anticipated. I thought that once we trapped Rad's men up against Breland and smashed them that would be the end of it. Now I find his force has escaped after inflicting a defeat on my cavalry, that there's a sizeable alliance of northern kingdom soldiers somewhere to my north and that there's a fresh Remadan regular force in the field as well. Who knows, there might be more out there. It's not looking quite so simple is it, General?"

"We still have the men to win this war, my King."

"Yes, but now they are spread too thinly."

"Perhaps it is time to send for our Southern army," suggested General Zibla.

"It would take weeks for them to arrive and besides, I received yet more troubling news from home earlier today."

That was news to Zibla.

"What has happened, my King?"

"The Salandori dogs are deserting their garrisons on our borders in droves and our enemies to the east and south are taking advantage of our army's absence. I have already sent orders for our Southern army to redeploy and put down these incursions. There will be no reinforcements for us, not yet anyway. We are going to have to win this war with what we have."

"Then I suggest, my King that we try and engage our enemies in one decisive battle and totally annihilate them so that they can never rise up again. If we continue to fight these smaller pitched battles we could be bogged down here for years."

"You think we have the strength to beat them in such a battle?"

"Yes, if we gather all our forces, including the garrisons in the conquered territories and so long as we find terrain which will be to our benefit."

"As always your counsel is wise, my friend." The general bowed his head slightly in gratitude for the compliment. "Where do we think this Remadan army is heading towards?" he asked turning to face the messenger who was still standing at attention in front of the two men, waiting to be dismissed.

"Overa, my King, a small town in southern Lotar."

"Overa. Do we know anything about this place?" asked Vesla glancing round at his officers.

They all shook their heads apologetically.

"I will send riders out immediately to scout the terrain, my King," said General Zibla. "It is my understanding that the army which defeated Prince Balok is also heading in that direction."

"Scouts have told you this?" asked Vesla.

"Yes, my King."

"It seems they are gathering their strength for one last battle. Perhaps Rad and his men are also heading there. Very well, make sure your scouts understand that they are not to be seen or to engage the enemy. They are to inspect the terrain, and spy on the enemy forces gathering there if possible, but under no circumstances are they to be seen or engage the enemy."

"Yes, my King," replied General Zibla. He immediately signalled to two of the more junior officers and they scurried off to carry out their king's orders.

***

There had to be at least two thousand of them, but from this distance, Eryn couldn't tell which army they belonged to. The Narmidians were mostly horsemen, but they did possess infantry regiments, some damned good ones, so it could still be them. If it wasn't, could it be his father's men? The last he had heard his father had fled northwest towards Breland and was trying to rally the men there. Why would he now be heading eastwards again? It didn't make sense. Eryn briefly considered the possibility that it was his old regiment, the one he had deserted from. He had not wanted to desert and leave his new friends, but the sight of the carnage on the battlefield had deeply affected him and all he had wanted to do was go after his father and to be with him.

After watching them for a little while longer he finally decided that it couldn't possibly be his old unit. He'd been heading due west ever since he'd deserted and it would have been impossible for a force that size to have passed him by unnoticed. Besides, their destination had been central Remada and there was no way they would have changed plans just to track him down.

He shielded his eyes against the sun once again and peered in their direction. They had closed the distance between him and them considerably in the last few minutes and were clearly moving at some speed. They were not marching in battle order or even in military columns, yet neither were they a rabble, spread out across the road in disorder. They were a very odd bunch indeed.

Eryn turned away and sat up to take a drink, confident that the treeline behind him would shield his presence from even the keenest of eyes amongst the approaching men. He would sit there and wait for the column to file past him and then he would resume his journey west in search of his father. Even if they were friendlies approaching he doubted that he could risk meeting them to ask of news about his father in case any of them recognised him. He was no longer dressed in his army uniform but in some ways the sheer fact that he was in civilian clothing would make him stand out as a deserter or worse still a coward. Every man of fighting age and even some of those too long in the tooth or too young had been pressed into the army in a last desperate attempt to prevail over the Narmidians.

Eryn lay back and closed his eyes, momentarily enjoying the warmth of the sun on his face. He was tired, more tired than he could ever remember being in his entire life and though the temptation to let his eyes remain closed and drift off into a deep sleep was great, he knew that to do so was not only foolish but extremely dangerous. It was with no small effort on his part that he eventually managed to will his eyes open. He rolled back onto his front and was suddenly alarmed at how quickly the men were moving. They also appeared to have changed direction slightly and were now on a direct path towards him, probably seeking the shelter of the trees with which to take a rest.

A slight noise behind Eryn caught his attention and he spun round just as a hare raced across the grass a few strides away from where he lay. Eryn watched him go, too slow and too tired to make any effort to catch it though he would have given almost anything for some meat.

He turned back around to watch the approaching men desperately trying to work out what his best options were. The vanguard of the force was much nearer now and Eryn could see that many of the men were carrying heavy fur jackets that they had either slung over their backs or were hanging from their kit. These men had obviously come from a cold climate. He was just considering the possibility that these were northerners coming down to join the fight against the Narmidians when he finally began to make out some of their uniforms and was relieved to see Remadan blue, Delarite black and Lydian green amongst a myriad of others.

Then he saw him emerge from somewhere within the mass

of men. Flanked by two other men, one of whom looked northern and the other a huge fierce looking man, who Eryn suspected was either Datian or Delarite, stood his father, Teren Rad. After weeks of wandering around the Arkadian countryside in a fruitless search for him, he had now by pure chance stumbled across him in the middle of nowhere, for at that moment in time Eryn had no idea where exactly he was.

He was just about to stand and make his way down to greet his father who he assumed would be as surprised by their reunion as he was, when another faint rustling noise behind him, drew his attention. The hare was back.

Turning to face it he said, "It's your lucky day, my friend, as I have more important things to do than hunt you, that's my..." The rest of the sentence stuck in his throat when he found two sword points at his throat and four men in different uniforms glaring down at him.

"What do we have here then?" said a young soldier wearing a Cardellan lieutenant's uniform. "A deserter? A spy?"

"I'm on your side," said Eryn nervously.

"That's why you're skulking away up here trying to stay out of sight is it? You're a collaborator spying for the Narmidians more like."

"No, I'm a Remadan soldier, or I was," replied Eryn sheepishly.

"So not a collaborator, a deserter," replied the officer smirking. "The general doesn't like deserters much."

"He'll like this one I think," said Eryn.

"I ought to cut your throat now myself for your insolence, but I can't deny the general that pleasure." Turning to the men stood next to him he said, "Bring him."

They hauled Eryn to his feet and took hold of an arm each and were about to start dragging him down the slope towards Teren and the fast closing mass of men, when another soldier in a Remadan sergeant's uniform came striding over. He looked from the officer to Eryn and then back to the officer, smiling almost imperceptibly as he did so.

"Begging your pardon, sir, but I'd let this young man go if I were you."

"And why would I want to do that, Sergeant? The man's a deserter at best or even a spy," replied the lieutenant.

"I doubt that very much, sir."

"I beg your pardon, Sergeant? I don't know how you deal with things in what's left of your army, but we Cardellans take deserters and spies very seriously."

"That may be so, Lieutenant, but I suggest that you let this one go, for the good of your own health, sir," replied the grizzled old sergeant, clearly unfazed by the young officer's blustering.

"Are you threatening me, Sergeant?"

"No, sir."

"Good, because if you did you would find yourself up on a charge."

"I was merely trying to do you a favour, sir and save you some pain," replied the sergeant.

"Pain? What are you on about, man?"

"Pain is what you'll get if any harm comes to this young man, sir, I can guarantee it."

"And why is that?" The lieutenant's patience had all but run out.

"Because this here is Eryn Rad, Teren's son," replied the sergeant grinning. "It's good to see you again, son," he added turning back to face Eryn.

"You too, Sergeant Ranul. It's been a long time."

The lieutenant looked dumbfounded and stared at both of them open mouthed. The two men holding Eryn's arms looked uncomfortable awaiting the order to release him and although they maintained their hold, the pressure eased considerably. Behind them, Teren and the front of the column had almost breasted the hill and were looking at the small group with interest. Eryn and the two men holding his arms had their backs to the fast approaching Teren and his companions.

"Now might be a good time to give the order to release him," the sergeant said quietly to the Cardellan officer.

"What?" The sergeant inclined his head towards Eryn's arms. "Yes, of course. Well don't just stand there, let him go," the lieutenant snapped at the two men loosely holding his arms. They instantly let go and looked thoroughly relieved to have done so.

"What's going on here, Lieutenant?" Eryn instantly recognised his father's gruff voice behind him.

"We found someone you'll be pleased to see I think, General," replied the lieutenant thinking quickly.

The sergeant winked at Eryn who was grinning, whilst the young lieutenant flushed red and tried to melt away into the background. Very slowly, Eryn turned round to face his father.

Teren stopped dead in his tracks and his jaw dropped in surprise. Then after a few moments he said, "Eryn! By all the gods," and then ran forward and embraced his son. He hoped that no one could see the solitary tear than ran the length of his cheek.

Chapter 23

Ro patted his horse's neck as he watched the long column of soldiers snake by. He had no idea what the combined strength of the army was, but it had to number in the thousands and more men were joining them every day from the nearby towns and villages.

"It is a fine sight is it not, Ro?" said Emperor Zerut as he walked his horse up alongside the Remadan.

Ro bowed slightly and then nodded.

"It is indeed, your majesty."

"Strong enough to beat these eastern barbarians?"

"Alone, no, but if we can find Teren's men or the Remadan army, then I think so, yes."

"That's if Rad still lives," replied the emperor cautiously.

"He is not that easy to kill, your majesty. Many have tried, few live to tell the tale."

"Indeed, I have heard the stories and look forward to meeting the man."

"You have never met him?" asked Ro surprised.

"Seen him, but not met him. I saw him when he fought at my father's side in the Northern Wars alongside men like Kam Martel and Jeral Tae."

"Great men responsible for great deeds."

"Yes, but now it is our time I think. Come, let us go make our own history and seize our own glory," and with that the emperor kicked his horse forward towards the head of the column followed closely by his personal bodyguard. After a few seconds' hesitation, Ro followed.

The journey west from Overa to Aliba, a small town in south western Lotar, took several days to complete and was largely uneventful. Although the guard was called out several times to investigate clusters of men seen in the distance, more often than not these turned out to be men making their way towards the column to join up. Only twice did it turn out to be enemy patrols. Once they managed to escape without contact but on the second occasion, Colonel Ulikath managed to trap them but instead of surrendering the beleaguered Narmidians fought to the last man rather than letting themselves be taken prisoner. When Ro had been shown one of the bodies later he had explained to the emperor and his gaggle of officers that the Narmidians had been from the Wotogi regiment, King Vesla's crack cavalry, fanatics who would follow him without question and who would lay down their lives without a second's thought. It was these men who would be guarding Vesla.

Both the emperor and Colonel Ulikath had expressed their disappointment at not being able to question the men as to Vesla's strength and disposition, but Ro had doubted very much that even if they had managed to take one of the riders alive, that he would have told them anything at all.

Other than those two instances, the column did not encounter the enemy again and early in the afternoon of the eighth day after leaving Overa, their army, which had swelled by nearly fifteen hundred men, arrived on the plains to the east of Aliba. But they were too late it seemed as the enemy was already there and drawn up in battle formation. Clearly they'd been aware of the approach of a large force of men from the north and had prepared.

"This is an unfortunate turn of events," said the emperor to Ro after surveying the force deployed in front of him less than a mile away.

"So it would appear," replied Ro, his gaze sweeping across the plains in front of him. "This small force cannot be all that remains of Vesla's army; where has he hidden the others?"

The emperor gazed around the terrain but when he had no answer to give he eventually said, "Shall I give the order to deploy?" Although the emperor was in overall command, he was a wise man and knew that Ro had far more battle experience than he and had already decided that he was going to rely heavily on Ro's advice and guidance whilst maintaining the overall air of being in command. To have done otherwise in front of his men would have been unthinkable.

"Do you notice anything unusual about them, your

majesty?" asked Ro completely ignoring the emperor's question.

The emperor looked quizzically at his Remadan friend and then stared intently at the mass of men spread out across the plain before him. If he didn't know better he would have sworn that their numbers had multiplied.

"That there appears to be a lot more of them than there was just a few minutes ago," said the emperor.

"There isn't. That's just a clever trick, an illusion created by the constant redeploying of the forces. Keeping them on the move makes it appear that there are a lot more men than there actually is."

The emperor looked again and raised his eyebrows in surprise. The enemy's reserves were indeed constantly altering formation whilst their front lines maintained their stance in case of a sudden attack. It was indeed a clever ploy and would have fooled a less experienced commander.

"Then what is it?" asked the emperor.

"Unless my eyes deceive me, with the exception of a few officers, all of those men down there are foot soldiers," replied Ro.

The emperor looked from Ro back down to the enemy formation, trying hard not to let himself be concerned by their apparent swelling numbers now that he knew it was just a clever illusion.

"You are right. Why would the Narmidians who are famed for fighting on horseback, choose to fight on foot? It makes no sense."

"It does to me," replied Ro grinning.

"It does? How?" asked the emperor.

"Because they're not Narmidians; they're Remadans, Delarites, Cardellans and everything inbetween. It also explains why they were executing that manoeuvre so well a minute ago."

"I'm sorry, Ro, I am not following any of this," replied the emperor quietly so that no one else could hear him. "Please explain."

"Unless I'm very much mistaken, your majesty, I think we've just found Teren Rad and his men," and even as he said it, he watched as a small group of men detached themselves from the formations opposite and started to walk out into the land between the opposing forces. It was too far to make out, but Ro had no doubt that one member of the group was in fact his old friend Teren.

"Rad?" said the emperor. He too had now seen the small group which had detached itself from the bulk of the army. "Should we ride out to meet them?"

"Colonel Ulikath and I will ride out with a couple of guards. You should probably stay here your majesty, just in case."

"In case what?"

"In case I'm mistaken and this is some deception by the enemy and several hundred horsemen come racing from behind the town walls and cut us off. This alliance would disintegrate without you. We should only risk my life."

The emperor glanced towards the small knot of his officers nearby and the senior most general amongst them nodded his agreement, though the emperor clearly wasn't happy.

"Very well. Ride out and learn the truth, Ro. I pray that you are right and those are indeed friends down there, but in the meantime I will give orders to deploy our men into battle formation as a precaution."

Ro nodded his assent and after gesturing for Colonel Ulikath to follow him, nudged his horse forward to intercept the small group of men walking towards them. Colonel Ulikath signalled for two of the emperor's bodyguard to follow him and then trotted after Ro.

It was normal in these circumstances for the two parties to meet at a point halfway between the two opposing forces, but as one was on foot and the other on horseback, Ro decided to ride all the way out to meet the men on foot despite the anxious looks the colonel was giving him. If Ro was wrong and these were Narmidians they would soon be within bow range, but as soon as Ro got within a hundred paces of the other men, he knew that his instincts had been right and allowed himself a small smile when he recognised the Remadan legend leading the other group towards him.

Ro reined in a few paces in front of Teren, Colonel Ulikath

and the two guards arriving just moments later, still unsure whether the hostile and fearsome looking men in front of them with their beards, war axes and tunics which invariably had dried blood splattered across them, were friends or enemies.

"Ro! By all the gods it's good to see you," said Teren when he recognised his friend.

"And I you, Teren. We thought you were the enemy," replied Ro climbing off his horse and embracing an embarrassed looking Teren.

"That's enough of that, lad, especially in front of the Delarite."

"Too late, I already witnessed it, Remadan," chuckled Yarik from a couple of paces behind Teren.

"See what you've done? He'll never let me hear the end of it now," grumbled Teren. "But it is good to see you. We thought you were the enemy too." He looked behind Ro and saw the three Lotari warriors still nervously sat upon their horses. "Lotari? I thought you and Arlen went back to Silevia. Come to think of it, where is that fat monk; I've missed his cooking?"

Ro glanced down at the ground as he searched for the words hoping that the lump in his throat would not betray his emotions. In the end he decided to just say it how it was.

"He's dead, Teren."

"What! Dead! How?" asked Teren taken aback.

"Killed in a battle. He died a hero and took many enemy soldiers with him."

"I would have expected nothing less. He was a game lad and I grieve with you, my friend."

"Thank you."

"Where was this battle of which you speak?" asked Teren.

"In Lotar, further to the north, near Qui'tang. The Narmidians had sent a large force to invade the smaller northern kingdoms and Emperor Zerut decided to ride out and engage them rather than allow a series of costly sieges. The Lotari fought like mountain lions but there were just too many of the Narmidians. If Arlen had not arrived when he did with his Silevians, I and most of the men behind me would not be here now."

"Why were you with the Lotari and not the Silevians?" asked Teren.

"It is a lengthy tale, Teren and one I will gladly regal you with over a cup of ale, but I suggest it keeps for later. If I do not soon ride back and tell Emperor Zerut that everything is okay, he is likely to launch an attack. Is there room in your camp for us?"

"We're all billeted outside the town on the plains to the south. There's plenty of room there for your men. You ride with Lotari and Silevians then?"

"I do as well as men from other nations, as you yourself do."

"Given the history between Lotar and Silevia that should have made for an interesting journey and something else I shall look forward to hearing about. Go and tell your emperor he is most welcome."

After slapping his friend on the shoulder, Ro climbed back on his horse and gestured for the colonel and his men to follow him, before turning his horse and galloping back towards where their army was now arranged in battle order. Behind him, Teren and the others watched them go.

"Just as well they were friends, Teren, some of the men were slow to get into position," said Brak.

"I anticipated as much. That's why I had our men perform those manoeuvres to try and make it look as if there was a lot more of us than there really was. I wouldn't worry too much about it, Brak; the men are just tired."

"They're not the only ones," said Yarik. "I can't remember the last good night's sleep I had."

"Nor can I. It must have been before your arrival though, as your infernal snoring has kept me awake every night since," complained Brak.

"No one's forcing you to share my tent, northerner," growled Yarik. "You could always move."

"What and miss out on your scintillating after dinner conversation? I'd have to be mad."

"If you two can stop your bickering for a minute I think we should go and tell the lads they can stand down before they start shooting arrows at our guests who will be heading this way at any moment," said Teren. He then turned round and headed back towards the allied lines closely followed by Brak. A few moments later and still grumbling under his breath, Yarik followed suit.

The majority of the men with Ro and the emperor were found space on the plain to the south of the town, but the emperor and his immediate retinue were found lodgings within the confines of the town. The local Carliri dignitary whose house was commandeered was none too pleased at being asked to vacate his premises but did so more graciously when his palm was crossed with a generous helping of Lotari silver.

Later that evening, the emperor invited all of the allied leaders and senior military figures to attend his new residence for a banquet at which they could discuss strategy and their immediate plans. Not counting bodyguards and adjutants, there were thirty-three men sat around the room on various chairs, the comfort levels of which were commensurate with their rank, the emperor seated on a plush, deep quilted seat with ornate carvings on the arm rests. The least senior of the military officers found themselves perched on uncomfortable wooden chairs which had seen better days.

"Is it really necessary for so many people to be here?" Brak whispered in Ro's ear as he glanced around at the packed room. The noise levels were high, a variety of languages and dialects all competing to be heard above one another.

"I'm afraid so. There are nine different countries represented here, ten if I include you and they all want their say," replied Ro.

"But wouldn't it make more sense if just you, Teren, Colonel Varis, Yarik and the emperor make some sort of war council? Some of these nations don't have many fighting men in the camp whereas others command thousands. It would make sense that you make up the war council as you represent the largest forces."

"Perhaps, but every man here is a free man and every nation's contribution needs to be acknowledged. This is the best way to do it."

"But we can't have this many leaders; it'll never work. A complex command structure could be our downfall."

"Relax, my friend, all will be well," smiled Ro. He then looked over at the Lotari emperor and nodded slightly. The emperor nodded back and smiled.

"Gentlemen... friends... thank you for coming. I thought that it would be a good idea if we all met as soon as possible to discuss our strategy and to formulate our plans. However, my Lotari and Captain Aryk's Silevians are new to the camp and have no information about troop numbers and the enemy's disposition and I would therefore respectfully ask General Rad to open the meeting and tell us what he knows," said the emperor.

"*General* Rad?" whispered Ro in Brak's ear.

"Don't ask. He's loving it and you'll only inflate his ego and this room's crowded enough already," replied Brak.

Ro laughed quietly and turned his attention to an embarrassed looking Teren who had started to stand but had then thought better about it and decided to address the room from his seated position. Clearly he wasn't sure about etiquette where emperors were concerned.

It could turn out to be an entertaining evening after all, thought Ro.

Chapter 24

The picture Teren painted of their situation was brighter than Ro had dared to hope for. Their combined force now amounted to around twenty thousand men, their numbers swelled by the sudden and unexpected arrival at Aliba of three thousand Remadan soldiers led by Teren's old friend Major Koker. This, the major had told Teren was the last Remadan army in the field.

The Lotari and Silevians amounted to around a third of the total number, with the Remadan army and Teren's men accounting for roughly another third. The remainder was a hotchpotch of Delarites, Lydians, Cardellans, Datians, Laryssans and men from other distant countries, some of which had not yet been touched by the war but who wanted to help.

The force was predominantly made up of foot soldiers although the Lotari still possessed a number of cavalry as did the Silevians, though as Ro pointed out to Teren, these were in reality little more than foot soldiers that were lucky enough to have found a horse. There was also a small number of Lydian lancers, Queen Cala's old troops, the Sikali Horse. These were the best mounted soldiers in all of Arkadia, and Teren treasured them very highly though their numbers were so few that their combat effectiveness was questionable. There were also about five hundred men who could competently shoot a bow, something Teren in particular thought would be critical in the coming battle. The rest were made up of various infantry regiments from across all of the nations represented.

The meeting had dragged on into the small hours of the morning, much to Teren's annoyance and twice he had tried to bring proceedings to a halt. Some, however, the Lotari emperor in particular, had been keen to resolve everything that night and appeared to have the energy to sustain their participation. Teren had envied them their youth and energy and had begun to feel his age. He had taken heart though when he happened to glance across at Yarik only to find the big Delarite sound asleep in his seat despite the noise around him. The man could sleep anywhere and Teren envied him.

The debate had dragged on for two reasons. Firstly there was disagreement as to whether they should march out and confront the enemy or stay where they were gathering their strength and await his arrival and secondly who should be in overall command.

The whole conversation had reminded Teren of his time in Breland a few weeks earlier when he had escaped with his men and sought refuge in the northerners' homeland. Then there had been endless debates about whether to flee or stand and fight. It seemed that history was repeating itself.

Teren tried to stifle a yawn as some minor dignitary from Cardella argued passionately for staying in the vicinity of Aliba. Most, however, seemed in favour of marching out immediately and actively seeking out the enemy for a one time decisive battle before the winter rains come. Others believed that it would be foolish to leave their chosen ground and argued that if they remained where they were they could continue to gather their strength, prepare the land and most importantly of all, rest. In the end, with the help of a belligerent Yarik who had not taken well to being rudely awoken, those wishing to remain on the plains outside Aliba carried the argument.

Then the debate had focussed on who should lead them. The emperor of Lotar had announced that as the senior monarch there he should be in overall command but the Datians backed by the Delarites had refused to fight under those conditions and put forward their own men. The emperor naturally refused to agree to their plan on principle. Others had been put forward but one by one they were all discounted until as he knew it eventually would, the burden of overall command landed squarely on a weary Teren's shoulders. Although there were still one or two dissenting voices, they were not very loud and eventually based on a majority decision, Teren was voted in overall command with the emperor in command of his own men, Ro in command of the

Silevians, Major Koker in charge of the Remadans, Yarik the Delarites and General Larit of Lydia in charge of the remaining forces. Whilst each of these men would be in direct command of their own troops, the final say on all matters, would rest with Teren.

They had all finally retired to their beds for some much needed sleep, but it felt to Teren that he had no sooner lay his head down than Brak was shaking him awake.

"What's a man got to do around here to get some sleep?" snapped Teren.

"You're just a man! I thought you were a god," said Brak smiling.

"Be glad I'm not, northerner or you would be one of the first I would smite," said Teren sitting up and rubbing his weary eyes with his sore knuckles. "What hour is it?"

"Dawn is but a little while away."

"Then why by Sulat have you woken me so early? I don't know if you've noticed, Brak, but I'm not getting any younger."

"Or convivial. Yes, I know, but we may have company later," said Brak.

Teren was up in a shot. "Why didn't you say so?"

"I just did."

"What's happened then?"

"Orton's patrol rode in a short while ago and reported seeing a large mass of men to the west."

"How large?" asked Teren, anxiously.

"It's dark so he couldn't be certain, but judging by the number of torches and camp fires, he estimates between twenty and twenty-five thousand."

"That many? And he's sure they're Narmidians?"

"Nobody else it could be. It sounds like Vesla's brought his entire army. Looks like he also seeks one decisive last pitched battle," said Brak.

"It does and I intend on giving him one. How far away are they?"

"It took Orton's patrol several hours to return here at the gallop and they knew where they were heading. Based on that and assuming they break camp after dawn, I'd guess that the fastest of their cavalry units could be here by midday and the infantry sometime tomorrow afternoon."

"Then there is much to be done. Still wish you'd let me have a few hours more sleep though," said Teren.

"You can sleep all you want when you're dead," replied Brak.

"Dead? I don't intend on dying. Haven't you heard, Brak, I'm immortal," said Teren fastening his sword belt and striding out of the tent.

Brak watched him go and then shook his head. "Wouldn't surprise me one bit, not one bit," he muttered to himself before following the Remadan outside. The sky to the east was just beginning to lighten hinting at the prospect of another sunny if not warm day. Teren was right; there was much to be done before the enemy arrived.

After grabbing a hunk of bread, some dried biscuits and some salted pork, washed down with watered wine, Teren had called a meeting of the senior officers and royalty, most of whom had attended the meeting the previous evening. Teren was determined that this meeting would not drag on for anywhere near as long as the last one, partly because they couldn't afford the time but mostly because his head just couldn't take it. He had witnessed enough posturing and ego stroking the previous evening to last him a lifetime. They had voted him in overall command, so today they would listen to him and heed his words.

Whereas the previous evening he had waited for the various conversations and debates to peter out of their own accord, today he grabbed everyone's attention by firstly banging his dagger hilt on the old wooden table behind which he sat and then by bellowing at the top of his voice. It had the desired effect and although a few looked at him with either offended expressions or outright indignation, they all fell silent. He no longer cared what they thought of him and only cared that they followed his orders to the letter.

When he was certain that he had everyone's unbridled attention he had passed on the news that the long range patrol had brought back to camp earlier. Some didn't look surprised and Teren found himself wondering whether some members of the patrol had opened their mouths to tent mates or their own commanders out of some mis-placed loyalty. That wasn't a good situation but probably an inevitable one he realised.

This time as everyone started to shout and offer their opinion Teren nipped it in the bud and shouted them all down.

"There is no need to panic. We knew it would not be long until Vesla arrived and we made plans long into the early hours last night."

"We didn't know that they were so close," said a small man wearing a Datian colonel's uniform. Teren tried to recall the man's name but couldn't.

"That is true. He obviously stole a march on us, but it changes nothing."

"Changes nothing? How can you say that when there is so much to do?" asked a Laryssan officer.

"It just means that we have got to work harder and faster. I will be doubling the number of patrols that we send out so we won't get caught with our breeches down, and will have the Lydian cavalry on standby to ride out and screen us should it become necessary." Teren looked at General Larit who merely nodded his acknowledgment to Teren's instructions. He had no way of knowing whether the man agreed with him, but he was a good soldier who would follow orders regardless. He wished his attitude would rub off on some of the others, in particular the Datians and Cardellans.

"You mean you still plan to stand and fight now that you know they're practically breathing down our necks?" asked the Datian officer incredulously.

"Of course. Not only do I plan to stand and fight but I also plan on winning."

"You're going to get us all killed," moaned the Datian colonel.

"Forgive me, Colonel, but weren't you fervently supporting our Cardellan colleague's stance about remaining here and awaiting the enemy, a mere handful of hours ago?" asked Teren.

"I was, but I thought we'd have longer to prepare. If you still plan on making your stand here you're mad and unfit to command."

Out of the corner of his eye Teren saw Yarik bridle at the insult and was quietly amused by the fact that someone who was not so long ago a sworn enemy, was now prepared to defend his honour.

"And what would you have us do, Colonel; run?" asked Teren.

"Retreat, yes. Retreat to the east and regroup."

"Retreat? Were you not paying attention to anything I said? There is a force of perhaps twenty-five thousand Narmidians bearing down on us, at least half of whom are skilled horsemen. You would have us retreat and be cut down in column? Besides, regroup! Regroup what? What we have here is all that we're going to get. There are no further reinforcements marching to join us. We either stop them here, or we die. If I have to die then I for one intend on dying with a wound to my front not my rear."

The tent exploded with noise as the vast majority began howling their approval and banging their weapons on the tables around them. Even the Cardellans were caught up in the moment leaving the Datian contingent exposed and alone.

"Now I suggest, gentlemen that you go and brief your men and get them started on the defences we discussed last night. General Larit if you could organise your Lydian riders so that we always have at least half your strength ready to ride out at a moment's notice." The Lydian general nodded, turned and left. "Ro, perhaps your Silevians could form the patrols? I want eyes and ears out there covering all possible approaches all the time. Don't just assume they are going to come at us from due west, although I agree that is most likely. This Vesla is no fool and it would be unwise to underestimate him."

"As you command," said Ro solemnly before also turning and striding out of the tent.

"That's it, gentlemen, dismissed. You all have your orders."

Slowly, in ones and twos, the royalty and officers comprising the allied force began to file out of the command tent to begin their preparations. Teren hoped that they would be enough and prayed that his men would not set eyes on the enemy until late afternoon at the earliest.

215

Chapter 25

It was a little after noon when the first warning was sounded. Teren had been sat around a small fire enjoying some pork, bread and cheese and listening to his son, Eryn, as he regaled Ro, Brak and Yarik with tales of his adventures since he had last seen his father. By the time that the messenger came running over to where Teren had been sat, Teren was already on his feet and strapping on his sword belt as were those around him.

"They're here, Teren," said the messenger his eyes darting from one man to another.

Teren thought about reprimanding the man for an unspecific report but then changed his mind. The man was obviously frightened and with good reason. The whole Narmidian army was likely bearing down on them and they had no chance of any aid reaching them. They would either stop the enemy here once and for all, or they would all perish. There was no other outcome.

"From which direction do they approach?"

"West," replied the man. "One of our patrols returned to warn us but by the time they arrived, the vanguard of the enemy force was already in sight."

"How in Kaden did they let them get so close?" asked Yarik. The patrols had been given specific instructions to observe and then report back to camp as soon as a positive sighting of the enemy was made.

The messenger merely shrugged in response to the Delarite's question.

"All right, soldier, have the signaller sound 'stand to'," said Teren. The messenger nodded and hurried away and a few moments later the sound of several horns playing the call to arms, drifted throughout the camp.

At once the camp became a hive of activity as men bustled about and assumed their designated positions. Most had already grabbed their weapons and shields when the initial alarm sounded but now that the stand-to had been ordered, they raced to form their units.

"It seems our company has arrived earlier than expected, gentlemen," said Teren as he turned and smiled at the small knot of men around him. "Best we don't keep them waiting. You all know your roles so there's nothing more to be said other than good fortune be with you."

The others all repeated the words and after a few brief handshakes, the men bustled off to assume their various commands leaving just Eryn and Teren behind.

"Where do you want me, Father?" asked Eryn.

Teren drew a long breath as he considered his son's question.

"You're a free man but it would be nice if you chose to fight alongside me."

Eryn winced at the term 'free man'. The previous evening he had confessed to his father about deserting the army after the battle in the east so that he could go looking for him. Knowing how much his father despised deserters he wasn't sure what his father's reaction would be, but was pretty sure it wouldn't be good. However, if he was to die the next day, Eryn wanted it to be with a clear conscience. After staring at his son for a while, Teren had then announced that he already knew about his desertion, Major Koker having informed him not long before Eryn himself came clean. Teren had been disappointed, but consoled himself in the knowledge that his son was no coward, having witnessed how bravely he fought at Vangor against the Delarites. He had also shown courage in admitting to his crime. In the end it had been Major Koker who had made the decision. Desperate for men, any deserters that his army had encountered on their march east had been pardoned once they swore allegiance to the army again. Major Koker had seen no reason why Eryn should be treated any differently and once Eryn had voluntarily approached the major and wholeheartedly apologised, he had suggested that the matter be dropped and never mentioned again. They had bigger things to worry about.

"So that you can keep an eye on me?" Eryn eventually replied to his father's suggestion.

"So you can watch my back. It is always well to have someone you know and trust guarding your side. Normally it would be Brak or Yarik but both have their own commands and are needed elsewhere."

"Then that is where I shall stand," said Eryn grinning.

Teren nodded. "Come, let us join the others or we might miss all the fun," and with that he strode over to the small incline upon which the Remadan infantry were now formed up in battle formation.

By the time that he joined Major Koker, the allied force was already completely dispersed as they had planned and as Teren glanced along their lines either side of him, he let a small whistle of appreciation escape his lips. They might represent a dozen nations all with competing priorities and with a less than ideal command structure, but spread out in battle order they still looked a force to be reckoned with. Unfortunately, Teren noted, so did the mass of Narmidians spread out on the plains before him. Divided into their various regiments, each regiment dressed in a different coloured tunic, they made for a very colourful and awe inspiring sight. Worse still, more men were arriving every minute and Teren suddenly began to wonder whether the enemy's numbers had been badly underestimated or whether reinforcements from the east had somehow arrived and bypassed the allies.

"There are a lot of them," said Eryn unnecessarily.

"Aye, there is, but that just makes it harder for our archers to miss," replied his father.

"Can we win this fight?" asked Eryn.

Teren turned to face his son hoping that no one else around heard the question.

"We can't afford to lose it, son, that's for sure."

"That doesn't answer my question."

"It's the only answer you're getting." Teren looked at the worried expression on his son's face and sought to ease his anxiety. "There are many of them, Eryn, but they can only use so many at a time. I have dispersed our men so that any outflanking manoeuvre by them is almost impossible so their battle line can only be as long as ours. Do you understand?"

"I do. But their lines will be many men deeper than ours."

218

"They will, but sometimes that can work against you as much as for you."

"But…" began Eryn.

"Enough questions, Eryn, they're sending out some riders. It looks as if the enemy want to talk."

"Perhaps they want to surrender," said Eryn matter-of-factly as he peered down at the plain below where a small group of horsemen were indeed approaching under a white flag of truce.

Teren looked at his son and laughed at his last comment.

"Perhaps. Let's go and find out," and with that Teren strode forward with Eryn and four men including Major Koker. They met the riders fifty paces from the allies' front line.

"That's far enough, lad. Say whatever it is you've got to say and then be on your way, I've got a busy day ahead of me," said Teren disinterestedly. The expression on the lead horseman's face clearly illustrated that Teren's attitude had rankled him.

"Do you command this rabble?" asked the rider imperiously.

"I do," said Teren dismissively.

"So you are the great Teren Rad about whom we have heard so much?"

"I am Teren Rad, that's for sure, but as to what you've heard, friend, I cannot comment."

The rider stared at Teren for a few moments longer and then seemed to remember what he was there for and suddenly sat upright in his horse.

"Starik Vesla, King of Kings and Lord of all Arkadia, invites you to save your lives. If you are prepared to lay down your arms and return to your home countries, he is prepared to let you march out of here unmolested, once you have sworn an oath of fealty to him of course. What say you?"

"Well that's mighty kind of him to offer us such generous terms but I'm afraid on this occasion I'm going to have to decline," said Teren grinning.

"What? Why? Are you mad? Do you not see the king's army spread out before you? This is the mightiest army ever raised and you would choose to defy it?"

"No, I would choose to destroy it."

The men stood around Teren chuckled to themselves antagonising the rider who fidgeted in his saddle almost incandescent with rage.

"You think you can beat us? You are truly mad, Remadan."

"So people keep telling me. Besides, I don't think we can beat you, I know, so why don't you ride back to your little king and give him our answer. Oh, and whilst you're at it, you might want to point out to him that he's not king of all Arkadia, not yet. There's a little piece of land here occupied by thousands of armed men who will take issue with his claim. He's free to come and discuss it with us any time he wants."

Teren's companions started to laugh again and the lead rider visibly coloured with rage.

"Then you choose death."

"Every man must face death at some point," replied Teren fixing the man with an icy stare.

"Yes, but yours, all of yours, are coming soon," and with that the rider turned his horse and galloped away, discarding the white flag as he did so. Moments later his companions did likewise.

"Did anyone ever tell you that you need to work on your diplomatic skills?" asked Major Koker with a smirk.

"Only my wife."

"And how did that work out for you?"

Teren's face clouded over. "Considering that she's dead at Vesla's hands, I'd say not well, wouldn't you?Come, let's return to our lines; something tells me it won't be long before we've got company."

"You think he'll attack today?" asked Major Koker as they made their way smartly back to the small escarpment from where'd they set off.

"Wouldn't you? He's got his men nicely arrayed in battle formation and from what I can see his heavy cavalry and infantry are already here. Somewhere in amongst that throng will be his archers. How he's got his men here so quickly I don't know, but he has. He's got enough men to sustain an attack, so yes I think he'll make his move this afternoon, once they've rested a bit."

Even as he spoke a horn sounded from behind him and Teren turned just in time to see the Narmidian ranks open smoothly and hundreds of archers fan through the gaps before forming ranks in front of the main army. Then through the channels left between the blocks of archers, hundreds of horsemen began to slowly filter.

"Apparently Vesla doesn't think they need rest. I guess what I said to his messenger upset him," said Teren.

"Indeed. Looks like they're going to hit us in the same old way," replied Major Koker.

"The trouble is we don't have enough horsemen to meet them in the same old way. We're just going to have to hope that some of our traps slow them up and cull their numbers."

In front of the Narmidian lines, two long rows of riders had formed up with weapons drawn. From what Teren could see the first line comprised Vesla's beloved lancers and the second line men armed with curved swords. If the lancers were to get amongst the allies' densely packed formations, they would cause havoc and could even turn their lines. He had to break their attack at the first attempt.

Teren turned to a man holding a signal flag to his right.

"Send the first signal, lad," said Teren calmly.

The young soldier nodded, stepped forward a few paces so that he could be seen all along the line and then began to wave the flag in a pre-determined fashion sending a clear signal to all the commanders along the allied line. Instantly there were a number of shouted orders being relayed to the various bodies of men and the hiss of swords being drawn from scabbards. The tension was palpable. Then very slowly, several hundred men along the line began to move forward. Those in the front were lightly armed infantry but behind them hopefully concealed to watching Narmidian eyes, were a couple of hundred pikemen carrying long sharpened poles.

Almost as soon as these men began moving forward, the Narmidian cavalry began to firstly walk then trot before finally charging forward towards the allied troops. The sight of several hundred mounted soldiers, many of whom were lancers, racing towards them was a terrifying sight and all a watching Teren could do was hope that the courage of his men would not fail. If they stayed the course there was a chance, albeit a small one, but a chance nonetheless, that they might just carry the day.

When they were no more than forty paces in front of their starting position the allied soldiers stopped and waited as the charging cavalry were no more than two hundred paces away. Thinking that the courage of the allied soldiers was faltering, the Narmidian cavalry commander urged his men forward, hollering and waving their swords above their heads.

When they were no more than a hundred paces from the allies he signalled for his lancers to lower lances and with a gleeful look in his eye, waved his men forward for the kill. He had no idea why the allies had stopped so suddenly and assumed it was fear, but he did not care. Soon his men would be amongst the enemy and many would die on the end of lance points and those who remained would be easy prey for the swordsmen who rode behind the lancers.

When they were no more than seventy-five paces from the enemy the Narmidian commander realised that the enemy were performing a brisk manoeuvre and he watched in horror as scores of men suddenly appeared at the front ranks brandishing long sharpened poles which they now lowered to rider height. It was too late to sound the retreat and even if he could he doubted that his men would heed the call and he watched in horror as the first wave of his men slammed into the sharpened points at the gallop. The screams and cries of wounded men and horses rent the air as rider after rider impaled themselves on the deadly poles. Those in front had simply been unable to stop in time even after they realised the danger, but those behind had been unable to see what was going on and had simply followed their comrades in.

The better horsemen amongst them like the commander did manage to veer away mere strides away from the deadly points but their momentum had carried them into a channel deliberately left by the allies. Unable to rein in before they had travelled some distance inside the channel, the surviving Narmidians suddenly found themselves assailed by enemy soldiers on both sides as well as in front.

Teren didn't need to give the order to close on the horsemen as his men instinctively followed the plan. Panic swept through the surviving riders and as they were assaulted on three sides they desperately tried to turn their mounts and flee the way they had come. But even as they tried to turn and run, the dreaded pike men wheeled round behind them and closed their escape route; Teren's trap was sprung and the horsemen were completely surrounded. What followed was a slaughter.

Unable to flee back towards their own lines through a forest of pike points, the riders had turned once again and tried to force their way through another direction, but the allies were well-prepared and there was nowhere for them to go.

Within a few hundred heartbeats, all of the Narmidian riders lay dead or dying. It was a successful start to the battle but it wasn't a sight Teren took any pleasure in seeing.

***

"It seems they don't learn from their mistakes, Teren," said Brak referring to the fact that they had used the same tactic to rout hundreds of Narmidian riders in their last engagement.

"Be grateful for that fact, Brak," replied Teren. "It just shows the level of the man's arrogance. Have you suffered many casualties?"

"Barely any."

"Good. Return to your position."

Brak nodded and then scurried away.

Buoyed by their success, cheering allied soldiers suddenly started to abandon their positions and stepped forward intent on finishing off any wounded Narmidians and looting their dead comrades.

Instantly Teren saw the danger but despite his shouted warnings and those of Ro and some of the other officers around, they were unable to recall all of the men in time and those who had wandered too far into the battlefield, suddenly found themselves beneath a storm of arrows as the Narmidian archers loosed volley after volley, intent on avenging their dead brothers.

Teren watched helplessly as several dozen men were mowed down needlessly, devaluing his victory.

"Idiots! Stay in your lines and don't move or I'll kill you myself," roared Teren as he stomped up and down the front line, disregarding his own safety. Those who had not been injured by an arrow or had not left the safety of their lines immediately began to fall back into position, whilst sergeants and the like marched up and down taking their lead from Teren and berating them and trying to dress the line. None of the men who had broken ranks and survived could look Teren in the eye such was his rage at that moment.

Across the plain, Starik Vesla had watched in anger as his beloved lancers had been butchered by the hated Remadans in what he considered to be a cowardly trap. His rage had only been partially assuaged by the vengeance his archers had visited upon the foolish allied soldiers who had broken ranks to loot the dead and kill the wounded.

"What are your orders, my King?" asked General Zibla as he manoeuvred his horse alongside Vesla.

"Send in the light infantry. Provided they have no more little traps set up for us we will simply overwhelm them with our numbers."

"What about cavalry support, my King?"

"What about it? I've lost enough of my riders already this day. There are enough light infantry to carry the day without cavalry support."

The general nodded but his expression suggested that he didn't agree with his king's assessment, though he knew better than to give voice to his concerns.

A short while later, under the harsh notes of a series of horns, hundreds of lightly armed Narmidian infantry, most of whom were drawn from the far reaches of the eastern empire, began to move forward as one, weapons at the ready. Behind them the archers took up their positions.

Teren watched them forming up and after quickly assessing their strength, signalled for his pike men to retire to the rear of the allied lines, replaced by swordsmen and axe wielders.

Ro had left his command position and walked over to Teren and now stood at his friend's side watching the enemy deploy.

"It seems this time he plans a massed attack," said Ro.

"Aye, without cavalry support by the looks of it. Seems he doesn't wish to lose any more of his precious riders."

"They're lightly armoured and poorly equipped men he sends against us now and should be no match for disciplined soldiers."

"Perhaps. Return to your command, Ro. The way he has deployed his men it would appear that he is going to hit your section of the line the hardest," said Teren.

"If he thinks that the Silevians are weak, he's in for a rude awakening."

"Will they hold under a sustained attack, Ro?"

"They will."

"Then make it happen. Break this attack where it falls."

Ro nodded curtly and then hurried back to his position a hundred or so paces to Teren's left.

To the thrum of drums, the Narmidians poured forward in neatly formed blocks of men. Around him Teren could sense his mens' tension and anxiety. Many wanted to break ranks and rush forward to meet the enemy, overwhelmed by adrenaline. But that was not the way. Only by remaining disciplined and steady would they manage to turn this tide of men.

When the enemy were only a hundred paces away Teren gave the signal for the archers to fire and scores of arrows raced into the sky before dropping onto the packed Narmidian formations. Most of the allied archers were just men with rudimentary training in using the bow, but even they found it hard to miss their targets so densely packed were the enemy formations.

Whereas professional trained archers would have managed at least three volleys in the time it took the enemy to cross the plain, Teren's men only managed two and a lot of the second volley missed as the men started to panic at the proximity of the enemy swords. The Narmidian archers had immediately replied and scores of arrows fell with almost pinpoint precision amongst the allied archers. In frustration Teren signalled for the archers, or at least what was left of them, to retire. Now was the time for men with blades to go to work.

The Narmidians were a mere forty or so paces away when

one of their officers gave the order to charge and with a chorus of blood curdling war cries, the Narmidians charged forward slamming into the front rank of the allies. Realising that the fighting was going to be close and personal with little room to manoeuvre, Teren had discarded his long sword and had instead decided to fight with his two Carliri war axes. Both were less than an arm's length but were blessed with a razor sharp double-bladed head. In this sort of fight they would be ideal for chopping and hacking, a fact Teren adeptly demonstrated to the first three men who were unfortunate enough to be in the part of the enemy line facing him.

The first man was slashed across the neck whilst the second felt one of the axe blades dig deep into his shoulder before Teren yanked the blade free and kicked the man backwards and away from the fight. The third man who came snarling into the gap in front of Teren found an axe blade biting into either side of his neck before his head leapt into the air above a spurt of bright red blood. Again Teren merely kicked the man's headless torso out of his way and prepared to meet his next challenger though none were stepping forward eager to fill the void.

A hundred or so paces to Teren's left, Ro was encouraging his men to hold the line. As Teren had correctly predicted, whether by chance or design the Narmidians had hit his section of the allied line the hardest and his men were hard pressed. It seemed that every time they killed a Narmidian another two stepped forward to take his place and whilst these men weren't Vesla's elite, sooner or later sheer weight of numbers would tell.

"Hold the line! Hold the line! Renley, take six men and move over and support Ilik, his men look ready to fold," Ro called to a small shaven headed man standing to his left, but even as he did so, a lance thrown by someone in the throng of enemy soldiers, struck Renley in the neck. For a few horrifying moments he stood there looking at Ro, the lance protruding from either side of his neck and then he collapsed to his knees before eventually toppling over dead.

Silently cursing, Ro looked around for someone else to carry out his instructions, but a young boy not much older than

Eryn was already pulling men out of the line and telling them to follow him having overheard Ro's orders and witnessed Renley's death.

Ro nodded his gratitude to the young lad as he glanced his way and then turned back to the fight just as a snarling warrior clad all in white with a red sash, came racing towards him, his sword poised to strike. Ro blocked the man's downward chop, rolled his wrist and slashed the man across his unprotected midriff. Another warrior dressed in the same garb rushed towards Ro carrying a lance he had obviously picked up from one of his dead comrades. He thrust at Ro's stomach but Ro managed to step back and sway out of the way at just the right moment and the man's momentum carried him forward. Ro wasted no time in slicing his sword down into the man's back giving him a ferocious cut that if it didn't kill him outright, would surely cause him to bleed out.

Ro took a step back to assess the situation. His men were holding and the breach he had worried about had been plugged by the timely intervention of the young lad and the men he took with him. The ground was slick with blood and gore and everywhere you looked were the dead and dying. And still the enemy came on. It was difficult to see much of the rest of the line from where he was standing, but he could just about make out Teren swinging his war axes and cleaving men all around him.

To his right a small group of Narmidians suddenly burst through the perilously thin line and confronted two Silevians, one a young lad and the other an older man who had once been a leader of the Order of Goresh and a friend of Arlen's. Whilst the older man could clearly handle himself the young lad was out of his depth and outnumbered five to two, they would soon be overwhelmed.

Ro grasped his sword with both hands and holding it out in front of him, charged. The Narmidian warrior on the right of the small group noticed Ro's approach too late and by the time he had turned and raised his sword to try and stave off the inevitable thrust, he was already dead, he just didn't know it. Ro withdrew his sword from deep inside the man's guts and then slashed at the next man's thigh, severing his leg just above the knee. He collapsed to the ground howling with pain and out of the fight.

The other Narmidians had become distracted by the surprise assault on their flank and the older of the two Silevians took full advantage and opened the throat of the man directly in front of him. But the Narmidians had not been the only ones surprised by Ro's arrival. The young Silevian soldier who just moments before had been sure that his life was about to end in a hail of sword thrusts, was heartened by Ro's sudden arrival and had taken his eyes off the men in front of him to watch the fearsome Remadan. It was to be his undoing as a burly Narmidian had seen an opportunity for an easy kill and had thrust his sword deep into the youth's stomach.

His own grin soon turned to a grimace of pain though when Ro pierced his side with his sword just as the last Narmidian was despatched by the older Silevian.

The remaining Silevian withdrew his sword and after nodding his thanks to Ro and checking that they were in no immediate danger, knelt down by the young boy's side. He put one arm under the lad's shoulders and gently lifted him up, but it was clear to a watching Ro that the lad was already dead.

"Did you know the boy?" asked Ro, touched by the grizzled old warrior's tenderness.

"He was my eldest," replied the older man without lifting his head.

"I am so sorry," whispered Ro genuinely. "He died bravely and at his father's side."

"He died needlessly," replied the other man.

Unsure what else to say, Ro lightly placed a hand on the man's shoulder and then stood and walked away to leave the man to grieve. He was just trying to assess the situation around him when a great cheer suddenly went up from behind him somewhere. Ro turned to look in the direction from which he had just come and although there were still isolated fights going on here and there, many of his men seemed to be watching something a little way in front of them.

Ro jogged over to where the young lad who had stepped in for Renley and plugged the gap, was standing and looked in the direction in which most everyone else was looking. Ten or so paces in front of the allied front line and deep amongst the shocked but still numerous enemy soldiers, was the old Silevian who had just lost a son. In a pique of rage or grief, he had raced out of the allied line deep into the enemy's ground and had started cutting and slashing at those around him like a mad man. Five or six men were already lying on the blood soaked ground around him whilst seven or eight others circled him warily waiting for their opportunity. For his part the Silevian appeared to have been wounded in at least three different places though from that distance Ro couldn't tell the severity of the wounds.

Behind him the old man's comrades began chanting his name as they watched him carve his way through the enemy seemingly without fear or regard for his own safety.

The Silevian suddenly roared with rage and leapt forward swinging his sword. His first slice was easily blocked by one of the men facing him and whilst his sword was high in the air and away from his body, two more of the enemy took the opportunity to thrust their blades into him, one piercing his side the other his chest. The Silevian immediately responded by back swiping his sword slashing one of the Narmidians across the back. The other Narmidians immediately poured forward and began hacking and slicing at the Silevian but even as he finally succumbed to the multitude of blows, he managed to thrust his sword deep into the groin of the Narmidian standing directly in front of him. Then without uttering another sound he collapsed face first into the blood soaked ground.

For a few short breaths nothing happened. The Narmidians seemed relieved that they had finally killed the mad man who had killed or wounded at least eight of their men and just stood looking at his ruined body.

No more than a dozen or so paces away, the Silevians who had watched and cheered as their comrade hacked a path through the enemy lines, looked on silently. When one of the Narmidians suddenly hacked the old Silevian's head off before lifting it into the air and spitting on it, that all changed. With a collective roar the Silevians raced forward, all thoughts of discipline scattered on the wind. Ro understood their fury and their base desire for revenge, but the soldier in him knew that to lose discipline like this was to risk losing everything, but despite his shouted orders, the Silevians poured forward.

Chapter 26

Distracted by the sudden cheering, Teren had watched as the lone Silevian warrior had raced forward into the enemy soldiers and started hacking and killing anyone around him. Teren had no idea why the man had chosen to die in that fashion, for it was clearly a suicide mission for all its daring, and although he had admired the man's bravery, Teren had a pretty good idea what would follow. He had known that when the man died those behind him would do one of two things. They would either turn tail and run, disheartened by the loss of their impromptu champion, or battle rage would overtake them and a desire for revenge would send them surging forward harder and braver than any amount of berating from a sergeant could have done. Either reaction would potentially be a disaster for the allies.

Teren watched in dismay as his fears came true and the Silevian section of the allied line burst forward to engage the enemy and avenge their dead comrade. The man's bravery had been rewarded by the Narmidian dogs with the indignity of having his head chopped savagely from his shoulders and then spat upon. Teren could understand the man's comrades' anger.

He could see and hear Ro and one or two of his officers urging his men to stand and return to the line, but Teren could see that it was already too late; most of the Silevians were already amongst the surprised Narmidians. There would be no order to that battle now it would merely be brute force against brute force, man against man, courage against courage. Teren's biggest fear was that emboldened by the actions of their comrades, the rest of the allied line would also surge forward. Teren didn't doubt that they would probably reap some early victories and possibly even turn the Narmidian attack, but he was still of the belief that for the time being at least, their best hope of victory was to remain disciplined and to hold the line. He just hoped that the other commanders were of the same opinion and didn't act unilaterally.

"Stay where you are, boys," said Teren above the roar of battle. He could see it in the eyes of some of the men around him that they longed to emulate their Silevian allies and rush forward to engage the enemy.

In front and behind the men, sergeants and officers strode purposefully along, ordering the men to remain where they were.

Just when Teren dared to hope that the impending disaster could be averted or at least curtailed, a shout to his right alerted him to something happening further along the line. He looked up just in time to see the Lotari who were positioned to the left of the Silevians, spill forward from their previously neatly ordered ranks and join the melee.

"Damn it!" screamed Teren as he watched what appeared to be the entire Lotari contingent surge forward.

The Remadan soldiers around him looked at him hoping that he would give the order to join them, but he merely shook his head at them and told them in no uncertain terms to dress their lines. In truth he had briefly considered ordering everybody forward in one huge gamble; sometimes fortune favours the bold, but in the end caution won out.

The fighting was brutal and bloody and it was hard for Teren to tell which side if any held the upper hand. Virtually the whole left flank of the allied army was committed to the fight and if Vesla were now to commit his cavalry to attack what remained of the left flank, the small force of Lydian cavalry and Laryssan archers would be annihilated. If that were to happen he would have to quickly manoeuvre most of his Remadans to turn and face the cavalry.

He was still contemplating that possibility when a horn sounded from somewhere over in the Narmidian reserve lines and then to his great relief, the masses of infantry that had marched across the plain to attack the allies began to slowly disengage and retreat in good order towards their own lines.

Teren released a breath he didn't realise he'd been holding onto. They were going to survive and some of the men at least, more than he had hoped for, were going to be able to return to their lines. Vesla had missed his opportunity. A more daring commander would have tried to turn the allied left flank and roll up their lines, a move that was sure to bring victory, but either Vesla had not realised the golden opportunity that lay before him or he didn't possess the courage to execute the plan. Either way it was a gift from the gods as far as Teren was concerned and the foolishness of those Silevians and Lotari would not cost them everything after all.

In a matter of a few heartbeats, Teren's hopes were dashed. Misreading the Narmidians' organised withdrawal as a rout or perhaps just lost in the battle haze, the surviving Silevians and the Lotari, urged on by Emperor Zerut, decided to pursue and harry the retreating enemy.

Allied horns desperately sounded the recall but the pursuers were in no mind to return and be denied the victory which they thought was theirs for the taking. Teren, Ro and some of the other officers shouted themselves hoarse in an attempt to draw their men back, but it was no use; the Silevians and Lotari, encouraged by their emperor who to his credit led the pursuit, were committed.

The retreating Narmidians were closer to their own front lines now than the allies and continued to withdraw in good order. Teren watched as they edged ever closer to safety and silently prayed for his men to see sense and start to back away and disengage.

"I'm sorry, Teren, I couldn't stop them," said Ro panting hard as he came and stood alongside his friend.

"I know, lad. They were of no mind to listen."

"We could have lost the whole battle because of their stupidity."

"We could have, but Vesla missed his chance," replied Teren.

"We're still going to miss their numbers."

"Maybe some of them will make it back," said Teren sombrely though in truth he knew they were probably all lost.

Suddenly one Narmidian voice rang out above all others, loud and coarse and almost as one the retreating Narmidians dropped to the ground.

Ro and Teren stared wondering what was happening but then realised the true reason for the Narmidians' actions. Lined up in two long ranks, one kneeling and one standing and previously concealed by the retreating infantry, were a couple of hundred Narmidian archers. Another shout went up and scores of arrows flew through the air at the startled and momentarily motionless allies. Being no more than fifty paces away from their targets, it was almost impossible for the skilled archers to miss and for what seemed an eternity, they continued to fire arrows into the now panic stricken and disorganised allies. Some turned and finally tried to run, but they were too far away from their own lines and in clear sight of the archers. It was a massacre and in no more than a hundred heartbeats what had briefly been a confident army pursuing a supposedly beaten enemy, became food for the carrion birds. The field between the two opposing forces was suddenly quiet and empty save for the odd flailing arm from a wounded soldier but these were quickly despatched by the Narmidian infantry who had got to their feet again. The entire Narmidian army began to jeer and mock the allies and Teren could feel his own rage rising. He turned to face the Remadan soldiers behind him and shouted as loud as he could so that as many of his men as possible could hear.

"That is why we have to obey orders. That is why we have discipline. You can either follow my orders and possibly live to see another sun rise or you can disobey your officers and throw your lives away needlessly like those fools. Hundreds of good men have just lost their lives; and for what? Now we are all going to have to fight twice as hard just to have an outside chance of victory. There will be no more stupidity. No more false bravado. We will fight and die if necessary as one unit not as a collection of rabbles." He waited a few moments for his words to sink in before continuing. "Are you with me then?" A half-hearted cheer went up. "I said are you with me then?" Another cheer, louder this time. "I can't hear you and neither can that barbarian scum over there, so tell me again; are you with me?"

This time an enormous roar filled the air, those further down the line who couldn't hear what Teren was saying joining in anyway. To Teren's right, Yarik Holte stepped out in front of his command of Delarites and Datians and after picking up a shield lying discarded on the ground, began to rhythmically bang his sword against it. Instantly his action was mimicked firstly by dozens of men and then by everyone who had a shield, so that by the time that everyone was cheering or banging, the noise was deafening and boomed across the plains to the watching Narmidians.

Starik Vesla king of Narmidia watched from the back of his horse and shook his head slowly.

"Don't these Arkadians know when they are beaten? We have killed several thousand of Rad's men today and weakened his force greatly, yet still they continue to show us nothing but defiance."

"A hollow gesture, my King. We will finish them in the next attack. Shall I give the order?" said General Zibla.

Vesla looked at his most trusted general and shook his head.

"No, there has been enough killing for one day and the shadows grow long. We will rest now and renew the attack at dawn."

"As you command, my King."

"I shall retire to the royal tent now. Have the men stand down but make sure that plenty of sentries are posted. Rad is a treacherous dog and I don't trust him."

"You think he might attack us during the night, my King?" asked the general incredulously.

"I think that man is capable of anything and is not to be underestimated. I have done so once and paid the price. I will not be caught out again. Do as I say and make sure that there are plenty of guards and rotate them often. Anyone caught falling asleep on duty is to be summarily executed, do you understand?"

"I do, my King and it will be as you command."

Satisfied, Vesla gave the still cheering Remadans one last glance and then turned his horse away and rode slowly back to where the royal tent had been erected. He doubted Rad would be as foolish as to attack but you could never be certain with that man. Either way, tomorrow would be a bloody day.

**

Teren had watched Vesla retire from the battlefield and then the gradual stand down of his men. To Teren, Vesla had just made another mistake. With the allies still reeling from the virtual annihilation of the Lotari and Silevians, this was an ideal opportunity to press home the attack. In fact, Teren was sure that had Vesla ordered an all-out attack as soon as his archers had finished their bloody work, the allies would have folded. In the fading light, with decimated numbers and morale low despite Teren's impromptu cheer leading, they had been there for the taking. But Vesla had missed his chance. Again. Even so, Teren made the allies stand to for another hour or so before he was finally satisfied that there would be no further Narmidian attacks that day. Then he had given the order for the men to fall out and to get something to eat and drink. Sleep was going to be scarce and on a rotational basis so that at least one third of what remained of his army were ready to repulse any attack at a moment's notice.

There would be little if any sleep for him and the other commanders though and after greedily consuming some meat, bread and cheese brought to him by Brak, Teren called an immediate meeting of the senior commanders.

Accurate head counts and roll calls had not been carried out due to the more pressing need for rest and food, but based on the rough figures provided by the men sat around the fire with him Teren estimated that the afternoon's battle had cost them perhaps as many as four thousand men. What had started out as a morale boosting victory with the destruction of Vesla's lancers and cavalry had ended up being more costly to the allies.

"So what now?" asked the colonel commanding the Datians.

"Now we have to kill twice as many men each as we did this afternoon," replied Yarik gruffly. "I'm okay with that by the way."

"I wish it were that simple, my friend, but it isn't," replied Teren.

"Sure it is. There are more of them than us, so now every man has to kill at least three of the enemy. What could be simpler?"

"In a pitched battle you'd be right and I'd perhaps back us to be victorious, but Vesla isn't going to present his army in nice columns for us to hack our way through. He's got more cavalry than us, more archers than us and more swordsmen than us and a lot of open plain on which to deploy them. Our line will be much shorter and thinner tomorrow. If he's got any sense he's going to make the battlefield as wide as possible and stretch our forces to breaking point. He'll use his archers to pin us down whilst his cavalry outflank us and try to roll up our weakened flanks."

"Then all is lost," said Colonel Bree who commanded the Cardellan contingent.

"Whilst I don't agree with our Cardellan friend's assessment of the situation, as your friend, Teren I have to tell you that as motivational speeches go this isn't one of your best," said Brak smiling.

The men around the camp fire all laughed, except for the Cardellan.

"So given what you have just said, what do you propose we do, Teren? Do you have a plan?" asked Ro.

"I always have a plan, Ro."

"I was afraid of that," said Brak as he took a swig of wine from his flagon.

"And what is this plan, Remadan? It better not involve running away and hiding," said Yarik examining his fearsome looking knife blade.

"On the contrary, my barbarian friend. I plan on attacking."

"I'm sorry, what?" asked Major Koker.

"I must be tired. For a moment there it sounded like you just suggested that we attack the Narmidians," said Brak incredulously.

"That's right. We do what they least expect and attack them. We hit them quick and we hit them hard," said Teren grinning.

"He's lost his mind. Who's second in command here?" said Brak glancing around at the other faces. His gaze fell on Ro. "Ro, say something; surely you can't be seriously considering this?"

"I don't know, Brak; it's crazy enough that it might just work. Teren's right; in an open battle on this sort of terrain Vesla's going to be able to out-manoeuvre us and keep us pinned down with his Skythian archers. Taking the fight to him might be the only way to secure victory."

"And how do you propose that this plan works, Teren?" asked General Larit of the Lydians. Out of all the royalty and senior officers, the only casualties that day had been Emperor Zerut of Lotar who had been badly wounded and a Laryssan prince who had died from an arrow to the heart.

Teren scratched his unruly beard and then took a swig of wine from his drinking flagon. In truth he hadn't given much thought to the plan and had just blurted his idea out. Now that he had their attention he was going to have to come up with something and fast. He took another deep swallow of wine buying himself a few more seconds before finally speaking.

"I reckon that they're probably planning on attacking us a little after dawn so I'm thinking we'll hit them whilst it's still dark. I plan on sending a small force of men to go ahead of the main force, to neutralise the sentries and then cause as much mayhem as possible."

"Berserkers?" asked a Laryssan officer.

"Don't like the name myself, but yes, essentially berserkers," replied Teren. "At the same time our Lydian friends will circle round behind the enemy and try and stampede and disperse their horses, neutralising their cavalry threat. What remains of our archers will fire torches into the other flank of the enemy camp causing yet more panic and confusion."

"And the infantry, where will they be?" asked Ro.

"Half of the Remadan force will follow the berserkers in and try and exploit the havoc that they cause. The Datians and Cardellans will form up on the right flank behind the archers and the remaining Remadans and everyone else will form up in front of the tree line on the left flank and cover the Lydian cavalry's retreat. If we can drive a deep enough wedge into their camp, splitting their force and scattering their horses, thereby stopping their greatest threat, I believe we can win this fight and with it the war."

"If your plan fails, the men in the middle will be annihilated," said the Cardellan, Colonel Bree.

"I know. That is why I shall be leading what our friend has

called the berserkers and Ro will lead the force following up behind."

"I don't think so, Remadan," said Yarik staring coldly at Teren. This is your plan so you need to be in control not leading some suicide mission from the front. Leave that to a real warrior."

"Like you, you mean?" asked Teren wryly.

"Can you think of anyone better suited?" asked Yarik.

Teren had to admit he couldn't.

"Very well. Yarik will lead our berserkers and I will command the follow up force. Ro, you will take command of the force on the left flank. Once the Lydians have scattered their horses and we have split their forces I intend on driving their men towards you. We will catch them in a vice in front of the forest and crush them."

"And what of their men on the right hand side of this division; they're not going to stand there idly and watch as we crush their comrades?" asked Colonel Bree.

"When enough damage has been done, Yarik will turn his men to face the enemy on the right and drive them back towards the combined force of Cardellans and Datians which you will be commanding, Colonel. That side of the camp will be awash with burning tents if our archers have done their job and the enemy will be in total disarray. Confronted by Yarik's madmen they will try and flee to the east towards you. Your force along with the archers must stand strong and try and deal with them in the same vice action that we will be executing on the left flank. General Larit," Teren said turning to face the Lydian cavalry commander, "once you have scattered the enemy horses as best you can, you are to circle back around behind our lines and aid the Cardellans and Datians from the south. With Yarik behind them, the Cardellans and Datians in front and your cavalry to their right, I suspect that the fight will go out of them very quickly."

"What's to stop them fleeing north?" asked the general.

"Nothing, nothing at all, but that would just take them further away from home and I don't think that it's an option very many will take. Anybody any questions?"

"Where will I be?" asked Brak.

"You'll be with me leading the infantry ready to exploit Yarik's success. When we've split their forces, you'll take a small force and support Yarik's push towards the right."

Brak nodded his understanding and then said, "We don't have long to organise this, Teren."

"I know. I suggest that you all go now and debrief your junior officers, then try and get a few hours' sleep. Yarik, I assume you'll be taking your Delarites with you?"

"I will, but there are a few other handy lads I wouldn't mind tagging along. There's even a couple of Remadans who might do, so long as they don't start crying for their mothers."

"Take whoever you need. I figure about a couple of hundred men should do it."

Yarik nodded. "Sounds about right."

"Don't you ever get tired of suicide missions?" Brak asked Yarik.

Yarik snorted. "That is why people will always remember the name Yarik Holte but will never remember your name. I go where the glory is to be had."

Brak glanced at Teren who merely shrugged in response.

"Right, well if there's nothing else, gentlemen? Dawn will soon be here and by then we'll either be well on our way to victory or on our backs staring up at the sky."

The men all began to stand and one by one they filed away until eventually only Ro was left standing next to Teren.

"Something on your mind, Ro?"

"This plan of yours, Teren, it's…"

"Bold? Daring?"

"Actually I was going to say fraught with danger."

"You think I don't know that, lad?"

"If everything goes according to plan, our chances of victory are slim, you know that don't you? But if one simple thing goes wrong, it's likely to be a massacre."

"I know. We'll just have to make sure nothing goes wrong," said Teren.

"We have no control over things like that, Teren."

"Then what in Kaden do you want me to do, Ro? Do you have a better plan? Did any of you? No, you're all looking to me for guidance. Well this is it. This is all I could come up with. It will either work and we'll be victorious and breathing the air of a free Arkadia this time tomorrow, or we'll all be dead and nothing will matter anymore."

"Perhaps you're right. I'm tired, Teren, tired of endless war and death."

"I know, lad, I feel it too. But I've got to know; are you with me tomorrow? Can I count on you?"

Ro smiled and some of the tension which had been building between them eased.

"Always and to my dying breath," replied Ro, slowly turning and walking away.

"Well let's hope that it doesn't come to that," replied Teren quietly as he watched his friend disappear into the dark of the camp.

Chapter 27

If he was honest Teren would have admitted that he didn't really expect to be able to get everyone in position without alerting the Narmidians, so it was a somewhat surprised Teren who now hunkered down in front of his men halfway across the plain between the two armies. General Larit's Lydians had ridden out some time earlier and by now should have been arcing round behind the enemy camp ready to strike at their rear and scatter the horses. Similarly, the Datians, Cardellans and every archer Teren could muster, would now be in position beyond the enemy's right flank.

A hundred paces or so further on from where Teren knelt, the two hundred men under Yarik's command lay flat on the trampled grass waiting for the order to attack. Just ahead of them, a score of men, men skilled in stealth, were crawling their way towards the enemy lines ready to take out the sentries. Everything was going according to plan.

Teren turned to look behind him and Major Koker gave him the thumbs up. They were ready. Dawn was just a matter of a few minutes away. Teren peered into the darkness ahead of him and for a moment thought he saw movement, but then it was gone. Teren hoped that it was Yarik's assassins off to despatch the guards, but with his failing eyesight he couldn't hope to see what was happening ahead of him.

A flash of light in the periphery of his vision to the right, and then another drew his attention and he glanced in that direction as a couple of dozen flaming arrows soared into the air towards the enemy camp. A solitary shout went up from the Narmidian camp but this was quickly muffled, though it was clear that a few men had heard it.

Teren cursed to himself. That fool of a Cardellan colonel had given the order to fire the arrows too soon. Not all of the sentries had been dealt with by Yarik's men. The plan was that once all of the sentries had been quietly taken care of, Yarik would wave a torch towards the archers and they would open fire on the right side of the Narmidian camp whilst Yarik's men went to work causing havoc in the middle. Now they had lost the element of surprise.

Ahead of him, Teren heard Yarik roar with anger, before leaping to his feet and charging towards the Narmidian camp, closely followed by his two hundred men. To the right of them, flaming arrows had caught many tents alight, but the enemy were awake and although there was still some surprise and panic amongst them, they were starting to arm.

"What happened?" asked Major Koker who had sidled up alongside Teren.

"That fool of a Cardellan gave the order to fire too early. Not all of the sentries have been dealt with and Yarik's men aren't in the camp yet," replied a surly Teren.

"Do we go now?"

"No, let's give Yarik and his boys a chance to do what they came here for."

"But the Narmidians have been alerted; they've lost the element of surprise."

"Not entirely. Besides, half-awake and disorientated with half of their camp on fire, I don't think they're going to react too well to seeing Yarik and the others." The major didn't look convinced. "Don't worry, Major, he can look after himself. Now go and get the men ready, it won't be long before I give the signal."

The major hurried back to where the large force of Remadans waited patiently to enter the fight as Teren turned his attention back to the camp ahead of him. He had to get this next phase just right. If he went too early his men could get in the way of Yarik's berserkers and do more harm than good and blunt their effectiveness. But if he left it too late he could be signing their death warrants as they could become surrounded and cut off. Teren looked to his right again and was pleased to see that much of the camp was now aflame. There may have only been a few score archers, but they were making every arrow count.

Just then half a dozen horses came galloping past Teren causing a brief panic in the men behind who had to quickly scamper out of their way. A few more horses appeared and also galloped past them and then some more. They were running in every direction except towards the fires. Teren smiled. The Lydians had done their job and had scattered the Narmidian horses at least for now. That had levelled the odds considerably. Now it was up to him and his men to support Yarik and then peel left and drive the bewildered Narmidians onto the swords and spears of Ro's men waiting in front of the treeline up the slope to the left. Teren stood and turned to face the expectant sea of faces waiting behind him in the fast evaporating gloom.

"Now, Remadans now is your time. Make these heathens pay," shouted Teren and after briefly smiling at his son Eryn, he issued a mighty roar, took out his Carliri war axes and raced towards the enemy camp. Moments later nearly four thousand Remadan soldiers rose to their feet and charged after him. The fate of Arkadia was about to be settled once and for all.

***

The muscles in Yarik's arms were burning from the exertion of swinging his axe. He was already covered virtually from head to toe in blood and gore, but he didn't care; he was already lost in the battle haze, the feeling that comes over a warrior when they can focus on nothing else but the butchering of the men in front of them. That glorious feeling a warrior gets when the weapon in his hands is so in tune with his body that it feels like an extension of his arm.

Yarik had felt like storming over to the right flank and tearing the throat out of the cowardly Cardellan colonel who had clearly lost his nerve and given the order to loose arrows too early. Maybe he would once the battle was over. The fool's incompetence had meant that only some of the sentries posted by the Narmidians had been taken out and as a consequence, some had been able to raise the alarm when the fire arrows started raining down on the camp.

As soon as the first shout of warning had gone up, Yarik had given the order for his men to attack and as one they had burst into the centre of the camp and started slicing and stabbing anyone they saw. Most of the Narmidians had come stumbling out of their tents, half-dressed and bleary eyed and had quickly been despatched by Yarik and his comrades. But now the camp was filling up with Narmidians, the element of surprise slowly dissipating.

Still Yarik and his men fought on, slashing and cutting, roaring their war cries and doing everything in their power to unsettle and frighten the enemy. Most were by now covered in blood like their leader and were a terrifying prospect for the weary men who came staggering out of their tents half-awake to find out what was going on. Slowly though a few of the Narmidian officers were managing to organise their troops into small formations better equipped to deal with the snarling, blood soaked madmen who were assailing them.

Whenever Yarik saw any sign of organised resistance he would order one or two of his men to just hurl themselves into the throng like shrieking banshees. Some of the enemy would flee in terror, some would die and a few would stand and fight and eventually overpower and kill their attacker, but by then their job was done.

Yarik parried a blow from a sword, swept the man's weapon to one side and then brought his axe crashing down into the man's shoulder and through to his collar bone. The warrior crumpled in front of him and Yarik placed a foot on the man's midriff and pushed him away at the same time as yanking his axe free. The ground around the Delarite was carpeted with dead Narmidians, but still they kept coming. But now his men were dying. Exhausted and outnumbered by an increasingly confident enemy, his men were now being picked off one at a time by small knots of Narmidians.

A burning pain like he'd never experienced before suddenly flared in his right thigh and he looked down to see the shaft of an arrow embedded just above the knee. He looked around for the coward who had fired it, his gaze falling on a small olive skinned man with a long moustache about twenty paces away. He was nocking another arrow.

Yarik made to approach the man but just then another warrior come racing towards him with his sword poised to strike. Yarik cleverly swayed out of harm's way and then punched the man in the face with the blunt end of his axe, breaking the man's jaw and sending teeth flying everywhere in a haze of blood. He then nimbly took a step back and removed the man's head with a powerful slice of his axe.

Something struck him in the left shoulder and he stumbled back a pace. Anger rather than pain swept over him when he saw another arrow protruding from his flesh and with a roar he began to run towards the bowman. Panic threatened to paralyse the Narmidian archer as he struggled to nock another arrow. Normally it was an action he could do blindfolded, but now with the terrifying looking axe man bearing down on him, it was as if he had never done it before and his trembling fingers fumbled and refused to obey him.

Finally the arrow was ready and grinning with relief the archer started to raise his bow, but to his horror the warrior was right in front of him and he never felt the cruel axe blade as it bit deep into his face almost splitting his head like a melon.

Yarik grunted with satisfaction as he struggled to yank his axe free of the man's head and when after a few moments he realised that it wasn't coming free any time soon, he drew his sword instead. Out of frustration he then kicked the dead Narmidian.

"That's my favourite axe, Narmidian, so don't be going anywhere," growled Yarik.

A roar from behind him drew Yarik's attention and he whirled round just in time to confront two sword wielding warriors. Yarik managed to parry the first man's strike and swerve out of the way of his comrade's thrust before launching his own back handed swipe which raked across the chest of the warrior to his right, leaving a terrible gash. But even as he did so, Yarik knew that he'd made a mistake and had over extended himself leaving his own left side completely vulnerable and a few moments later he felt the cold bite of steel as the other warrior's sword pierced his side. Quick as a flash and doing his best to ignore the pain, Yarik reached out and to the warrior's surprise, grabbed him by the throat and began to crush his windpipe. The warrior automatically let go of his sword, letting it fall to the ground and tried to prise Yarik's left hand away from his throat leaving his own midriff exposed. Moments later he realised his mistake as Yarik slowly pushed his blade deep into the man's guts and watched as his face turned to purple and his eyes began to bulge. When he felt the blade pierce the man's back he gave it a vicious twist and then slowly withdrew it, revelling in the pain he could see in the man's eyes. Then, when his blade was free again, he let go of the man's throat and let him drop to the ground, where he died moments later.

Suddenly the world began to spin and Yarik's legs felt unsteady as if he were hopelessly drunk. He stumbled around briefly and then slowly fell backwards onto the ground, landing on top of the dead archer. Then everything went dark.

***

Teren had waited as long as he dared before giving the order for his men to advance, but when he had, like a tightly coiled spring, they had sprung forward into the opening that Yarik's men had created and continued the killing. The dazed Narmidians had just about begun to organise themselves and overwhelm the berserkers when they were suddenly confronted by a tide of fresh troops flooding into their camp. For some it was too much and they turned and fled, but most stood their ground and the real battle for Arkadia began.

Despite the fact that their approach had been seen before they had fully infiltrated the camp, Yarik's men had done a fantastic job of causing death and mayhem and the ground was carpeted with dead and dying Narmidians, Teren noted. Now it was time for the Remadans to push home the advantage and give the beleaguered Delarites time to recuperate. They would not have long, however, before they had to turn and try and push some of the Narmidians back through their burning camp towards the combined force of Datians and Cardellans who by now should have been joined by the Lydian cavalry.

As his men fanned out and began trying to drive a wedge between the Narmidian force, Teren looked around for Yarik. He'd expected to find him at the front of the fight, cleaving Narmidians left, right and centre, but he was nowhere to be seen. None of the resting Delarites he asked claimed to have seen their leader for some time and Teren was just beginning to fear that he had ventured too deep into the Narmidian camp and got himself cut off, when he spotted the big man lying on the ground about twenty paces away surrounded by dead Narmidians.

After dispatching two Narmidians who came running towards him, one carrying a sword, the other a spear, Teren ran over to where the Delarite lay on top of a dead Narmidian. Yarik's eyes were closed and for a moment Teren thought the man was dead until he saw the shallow rise and fall of his chest. He gently rocked the Delarite's body back and forth with his right foot until Yarik finally showed signs of coming to. It was now light and Teren could see that Yarik had been wounded in the shoulder and thigh, but neither looked life threatening.

"I take it I'm dead and in Kaden? Why else would I still be seeing your ugly face?" said Yarik when his eyes finally focussed on Teren.

"Sorry, Delarite, you're still alive I'm afraid, but if you carry on lying around here that might not be the case for much longer," replied Teren. He extended a hand to help pull his friend up. "That's if you can bear to leave your new friend," he added nodding towards the dead Narmidian archer upon whose legs Yarik's head and shoulders were resting.

"This is the whoreson who put the arrows in me," said Yarik clasping Teren's hand and allowing himself to be pulled up.

"I guess he won't be doing that again any time soon," said Teren grinning. "And these lads?" he asked gesturing towards the other dead Narmidians lying nearby.

"I figured he might need some company in the afterlife."

"Very thoughtful of you. You ready to resume the fight and lead the push to the right, or do you want some plump Cardellan nurse to see to these scratches of yours?"

"Of course," replied Yarik indignantly.

Teren noticed the pained wince as the big Delarite leant forward to pick up his sword and thought that he looked like he was in a lot more pain than he ought to be from the two arrow wounds. Then he noticed the deep looking wound in his friend's side. It needed urgent medical attention or the big Delarite risked bleeding out.

"Good, then let's..." Teren never finished his sentence as

he was roughly shoved to one side as Yarik lifted his sword and pulled it back ready to thrust.

When Teren regained his balance and turned to look behind him he saw a large Narmidian warrior with Yarik's sword thrust deep into his mouth and protruding from the back of his head. Teren grimaced as the Delarite withdrew his sword and the dead Narmidian collapsed forward, his face now a gaping bloody maw.

"I knew he was there," said Teren, "but thanks anyway."

"Bet that hurt," said Yarik, "thanking me I mean?" Teren mumbled something unintelligible under his breath and Yarik laughed despite the pain he was in. The wound in his side was agonising and felt like it was bleeding profusely, but if he told the Remadan about it he would order him to stand down and get medical help, maybe even withdraw from the fight altogether. He wasn't about to let that happen. There was glory to be had this day and he'd be damned if he was going to let the Remadan steal it all.

"Right, let's get going," said Teren. "Watch out!" Yarik turned sharply to look in the direction from which Teren had indicated there was danger, his sword poised to strike, but there was nobody there. He was about to ask Teren what in Kaden he was playing at when something struck him hard on the back of the head. He remained upright for a few moments and then collapsed backwards towards the ground.

For one terrifying moment after he'd struck his friend on the back of the head, Teren feared that he hadn't hit the man hard enough and that he was going to turn round and clatter him. He knew the Delarite was thick headed but to have withstood a blow like that would have been unbelievable. He was just on the verge of panic when Yarik had suddenly started to topple backwards and Teren had quickly moved directly behind him and caught him, breaking his fall. The man weighed the equivalent of a bull and Teren felt a twinge in his back as he tried to arrest his friend's fall. Eventually though he managed to lay him gently down on the ground. He started to look around him and was gratified to see that there appeared to be no more enemy soldiers anywhere near. Instead four startled looking Delarite soldiers stood staring at Teren and most had their hands on their weapons unsure what they had just witnessed and clearly trying to work out whether they should attack the Remadan who had just knocked their leader unconscious.

Teren quickly assessed their mood and after hastily explaining why he'd done it, the four men agreed to lug Yarik back to their own camp where some of the camp followers would be able to attend to his wounds. Satisfied that his friend was going to be safe at least for now, Teren then went looking for Major Koker.

He found the major leading a group of fifty men as they tried to drive a similar number of Narmidians to the west towards the woods and the force of men waiting there led by Ro. Teren immediately weighed into the fight and had killed two and severely wounded another before they even knew what had hit them. Emboldened by the courage and strength of their leader, the Remadan soldiers doubled their efforts and slowly they began to drive the Narmidians backwards. When with a mighty roar Teren removed the head of the warrior in front of him, the Narmidians finally broke and ran.

"Perfect timing as ever, Teren," said the major panting from the exertion of the fight, something Teren didn't fail to notice.

"You going to be all right, old man, or do you need a lie down?" asked Teren grinning.

"Don't you old man me, Rad, I'll out last you don't you worry. Just as soon as I get my breath back that is."

"Good. You have command of the men on this side. Push them hard towards Ro. They must be crushed between your two forces, you understand?"

"I'm tired, Rad, not senile. Of course I understand," said the major indignantly. "I thought you were leading this side."

"Yarik's down. I've got to lead the push towards the Cardellans."

"So be it. Good fortune, Teren."

"You too, Davik." Teren glanced around for Eryn but his son was nowhere in sight. Neither was Brak. He hoped that they were both okay though there was nothing he could do about it at that moment in time; he would have to look for them later. After nodding at the major, Teren turned and bellowed to the Delarites around him to form up on him. Then, supported by some Remadan infantry, they began to slowly advance amongst the burning tents, driving the now increasingly disheartened Narmidians back and out of the camp. Behind him Teren heard Major Koker give a similar order and begin his push west.

Chapter 28

From his position in front of the forest to the west of the Narmidian camp, Ro watched as Teren's plan unfolded. He hadn't seen the signal from Yarik's men for the archers to start firing arrows into the camp, but perhaps he had missed it, or perhaps the Cardellan colonel had lost his nerve and started firing too soon. If that were the case he had no doubt that Yarik would be having a quiet word with the man once this was all over, especially if his premature action had cost Delarite lives which it almost certainly will have. Regardless of what happened, the Narmidian camp was now well and truly afire and one Kaden of a battle was raging down there. It had been difficult to see in the half-light what damage Yarik's men had caused, but now that the sun was up, Ro could see the battle raging below and waited his turn.

With the trees at their back, Ro had ordered his first two ranks of men to lie down in the grass just in front of the wood whilst the others remained concealed within the tree line. He wanted to draw the fleeing enemy as close to him as possible, but if they saw his men waiting for them as they fled the camp, they might turn north and avoid engagement. Teren's plan was centred on destroying Vesla's army there today in one final battle. There was no secondary plan which involved chasing down any soldiers that managed to flee. They had to finish it once and for all that day.

Ro dropped to the ground in front of his men at the first sign of enemy soldiers fleeing their way. He had to get his timing right. Let them come up the slope as far as possible and then attack. Any that then turned and fled back towards the camp would then run straight onto the swords of Teren's men following them out of the camp.

Ro turned to the officer next to him and grinned.

"Tell the lads to get ready. It's nearly time."

The captain nodded and then turned and passed the message on to the next man and so on down the line until finally by the time Ro gave the order to stand, they were virtually all ready and expecting it.

The fleeing Narmidians were panting hard from the exertion of the climb and had not expected to be confronted by more allied soldiers to their front, believing that if they made it to the wood they had a chance to survive. Instead of looking to their front they had instead been anxiously looking over their shoulders at the Remadan soldiers slowly pursuing them up the hill. When Ro and several hundred men suddenly stood up in front of them no more than thirty paces away from the leading Narmidians, it came as a complete shock to them.

Ro desperately wished that Teren had spared him some archers, but there were too few left in the allied army and they had been needed to support the right flank of the pincer. Instead he was going to have to make do with the couple of score Lotari that had survived the earlier annihilation, who on his command, released their *jemtak* from virtually point blank range, taking down many of the Narmidians' vanguard.

Exhausted and caught between a hail of deadly metal stars and several hundred sword wielding men to their front and another force of pursuing Remadans just down the slope, panic broke out amongst the Narmidians. Despite the best efforts of a handful of their officers that remained, the men who represented a myriad of different nations from across Vesla's empire, lost their discipline. Some decided to attack the men in front; some turned to flee north, whilst others threw down their weapons and dropped to their knees pleading for mercy.

What followed was a massacre. Lacking coordination and discipline, the Narmidians were easy prey as Ro's men slowly advanced down the slope in good order. The men had been instructed to take prisoners if the enemy threw down their arms but as Ro glanced about him it was clear that particular order was being ignored. Good men, good soldiers, were now butchering the enemy whether they offered resistance or not; clearly the memories of previous defeats were still fresh in the minds of many. There was nothing he could do about it Ro realised and he found himself silently praying that nobody would try and surrender to him.

Within a few minutes it was all over and the once lush

green slope leading up to the forest had turned red with the blood of the dead and the dying.

"Well met, Ro," said Major Koker as he stepped in front of his compatriot and extended his arm.

"Well met indeed, Major," said Ro grasping his arm in the warriors' embrace. "Where is Teren, I thought he was leading this advance?"

"He should have been, but Yarik Holte was wounded, so Teren took over the right flank."

"How bad is Yarik?"

"I don't know, but for him to have persuaded Yarik to withdraw from the fight I'm guessing the Delarite must be in a bad way."

Ro nodded. The major was right; Yarik would have to be virtually dead before he'd pull out of the fighting.

"Well we've done our part, now it's up to the Cardellans and Teren."

"Some of the Narmidians have escaped to the north, Ro, should we pursue them?" asked the major.

Ro glanced in that direction and could indeed see a couple of score men fleeing to the north, many of whom had discarded their weapons.

"No, let them go. We knew that some would manage to evade us; there just weren't enough of us to close that escape route off. They're beaten and I don't think they'll be back. Besides, I think there's been enough killing around here for one day don't you?"

Both men glanced around the battlefield where Remadan soldiers were now going around and finishing off Narmidian wounded whether their wounds were severe or not.

"It was always going to happen like this, Ro, it's not your fault. Many of these men have lost family and their need for vengeance is strong."

"Perhaps," said Ro turning back to watch the handful of Narmidians fleeing northwards. His gaze suddenly settled on something in the distance and he peered hard to try and make it out. "Who's that do you suppose, Major?"

The major followed his gaze and after staring in that direction for a minute or so he finally answered.

"That's Vesla's royal standard. The coward's left his men and run north with his senior officers and a few guards. Now he's watching his men being slaughtered from a safe distance. Do you think we should go after him?"

"They're on horse and we're on foot. They'll wait for us to get so near and then bolt. I think we should support Teren's attack instead."

Both men turned to see how the attack on the other flank was progressing and cursed when they saw that far from driving the Narmidians down towards Teren's force, the Cardellans and Datians were instead themselves being pushed back despite the arrival of the remaining Lydian cavalry. Some of the Narmidians had even managed to acquire horses and were now engaging the Lydians on equal terms.

"That isn't how this is supposed to be playing out," said the major.

"No, it isn't," said Ro anxiously.

Even as they watched the Narmidians took control of the summit on the right slope driving off the remaining Lydian cavalry before forming up to face Teren's force of Delarites which was climbing the slope behind them.

"What in Kaden has gone wrong over there?" asked the major.

"I don't know, Major, but if we don't do something and quick, Teren and his men are going to be smashed if the Narmidians send their cavalry charging down the slope."

Teren was now about halfway up the slope and caught in a difficult position. He could either retreat and hope that his men didn't break and run, form some sort of defensive circle where they stood and hope to fight the attack off or carry on up the slope and try and press home their own attack. Given that they had just tasted victory Ro doubted that the Narmidians would cooperate and run if he did try to press home their attack.

"Get the men fell in quickly, Major, we've got to get over there and support Teren before it's too late," said Ro.

"And Vesla?" asked the major.

"Will have to wait," said Ro glancing briefly towards where the small huddle of Narmidian officers and guards were watching proceedings.

The major immediately shouted for the men to fall in, a cry instantly taken up by the other officers and soon Ro found that he was at the head of a decent sized column of men, having suffered few casualties in the battle just finished. Then with one last glance towards Vesla he ordered the column forward at double time.

***

"Prepare to receive cavalry," bellowed Teren and the Delarites began to form a circle, but the Narmidians were already thundering down the slope towards them. "Come on, lads, come on," roared Teren but he could already see that it was too late and that not everyone was moving quickly enough. Some would inevitably be caught out in the open.

Moments later the front riders of the Narmidian cavalry were amongst the stragglers, chopping and hacking at exposed backs and heads. Those within the defensive circle who had spears tried to aid their comrades by throwing at the incoming riders but they were too few and did little to slow the killing. Some even lost their discipline and broke from the circle and raced to attack the riders. One or two succeeded in bringing a rider down but most were slaughtered where they stood.

"Stay where you are you whoresons," roared Teren angry at the breakdown in discipline, the fury in his expression enough to give any others thinking of breaking ranks, pause for thought.

After finishing off the lone men outside the defensive formation, the Narmidian cavalry began to circle the Delarites probing for weaknesses, but the Delarites stayed strong and the cavalry could not find a way inside their defences. Eventually horns sounded from behind the riders and in one smooth movement they veered away to the north revealing a large body of Narmidian soldiers standing behind them in battle formation. Whilst screened by their cavalry the Narmidian commander fresh from his victory over the Cardellans and Datians, had marched his men down to confront the Delarites.

"Battle line, now," screamed Teren and the Delarites immediately changed formation, quicker and more efficiently this time.

Teren didn't need a head count to tell him that the Narmidians outnumbered his men by at least two to one and he could feel the anxiety emanating from those around him.

"Steady, lads, they're just a bunch of goat botherers from the east, no match for Delarite's finest," said Teren. He felt rather than saw the line regain its resolve.

He was just about to say something else to stiffen their spines when the enemy attacked. There was no discipline to the attack, no finesse; just one mad rush at the Delarite line in an attempt to quickly overpower them, for the Narmidian commander had seen Ro's force of Remadans making their way down the opposite slope towards them.

Teren smashed his Carliri war axe into the head of the man in front of him before kicking the next man in the groin as he tried to force his way through. When this man doubled over he brought his other axe down into the base of his neck. A quick glance along the line told him that the Delarites were holding, but the Narmidians were more numerous than he'd expected and it could only be a matter of time until they were overrun. He hoped that Ro had fared better and even held out the hope that his friend would be able to come to his aid, though he doubted it.

A Narmidian soldier thrust his sword forward and Teren only just managed to sway out of the way and avoid being gutted, before chopping down with his right axe and cutting the man's sword arm off just above the wrist. The warrior staggered away clutching at his bloody stump. Another warrior, a large one wearing the uniform of one of Vesla's elite units, came snarling into the gap and sliced down with his curved sword. Teren cried out as the blade cut his upper arm before swinging the axe in his left hand and burying the head deep in the warrior's guts. The warrior groaned with pain but then thrust again with his sword, the point this time piercing Teren's right side. Unable to pull his axe free of the man's guts, Teren brought his other axe down with as much power as he could striking the man in the shoulder though his armour took most of the impact. A fist crashed into Teren's face and he stumbled backwards just as the warrior's sword blade swished in front of him. The tip caught Teren's left cheek causing a nasty gash and as he crashed to the ground he could feel blood starting to stream down his face.

The warrior lurched forward towards Teren sensing victory, his sword ready to plunge down into Teren's chest. With one axe still buried in the man's midriff and the other dropped somewhere, Teren looked round frantically for a weapon, his gaze settling on a lance lying just to his right. Just as the Narmidian went to thrust down with his sword, Teren thrust upwards with the lance. With its longer reach the lance pierced the man's stomach close to where Teren's axe remained buried and after coughing up thick red blood, the man collapsed to the ground, his sword dropping from his hands and cutting Teren's right thigh.

Exhausted and bleeding from at least three separate wounds, Teren lay there for a few moments and was suddenly distracted by what was a familiar noise but one he couldn't readily identify. It was only when the sky above him seemed to fill with arrows that he recognised the sound. The conniving Narmidians must have hidden archers somewhere and were now going to wipe his men out from distance. It had been a good fight and he was proud of his lads. They'd done all that anyone could ask of them and more. He could die proud. He just wished that he could have seen his son one last time.

Teren closed his eyes and waited for the arrow that would end his life.

Chapter 29

He could hear voices, distant and undefined. Gradually the voices got louder as if drawing nearer and one or two began to sound familiar. He tried to put faces to the voices but resisted the urge to open his eyes. It was nice in the dark. Peaceful. Calm. If he was dead then he had all eternity to figure out whose voices those were. At that moment in time all he wanted to do was stay safe in the quiet embrace of the dark.

But others had different ideas and as he laid there willing himself away from the light and back to unconsciousness, he could feel his body being shaken and somebody gently calling his name. It sounded like...Brik, Bryke...no *Brak,* the man speaking his name was Brak. He slowly and reluctantly opened his eyes and found himself looking up at the concerned faces of Brak and Ro.

"Can't a man get any peace even in death?" grumbled Teren, his voice raspy and hoarse.

Brak smiled, put a hand behind the Remadan's head and lifted him up gently before holding a cup of water to his lips. Teren took three or four sips and then lay back down.

"You had us worried there for a moment, Teren," said Brak.

"You mean I'm not dead? It looks like Kaden with all you lot standing around staring at me morbidly."

"No, my friend, you're not dead," said Ro smiling, "though you did your best to make it otherwise."

"I don't remember much of..." Teren's words were cut short by another familiar voice. Yarik! He sounded angry.

"You still alive, Remadan?"

Brak and Ro stepped aside to reveal Yarik lying in the cot next to Teren. He was wearing several bandages.

"Now I know I must be in Kaden. Yes, I'm still alive, Yarik," said Teren.

"Good, because I'm going to kill you." He tried to sit up in his cot, but winced from the pain and a woman who had been quietly checking his dressings, gently pushed him back down onto his cot with a stern look that brooked no argument. "Just as soon as I can sit up."

"Now what's got you all riled up, Delarite?" asked Teren.

"What's got me all riled up? How about the fact you whacked me over the back of the head for starters," said Yarik indignantly.

"You needed medical treatment."

"So you thought you'd just give me another injury is that it?"

"Would you have left the field if I asked you to? No, I didn't think so."

"You still should have asked me," said Yarik.

"I was trying to save your miserable life though try as I might I can't think why I bothered," grumbled Teren. "You're welcome by the way."

Both men glowered at one another for a long while and Ro was just about to say something to try and break the tension when both Teren and Yarik started laughing heartily, a fact both instantly regretted when the action caused their respective wounds to ache.

"Well I'm glad we got that sorted," said Brak.

Teren looked at his two friends and suddenly wondered why Ro was looking so glum. Something had to be the matter. Had they lost? Were they prisoners of the Narmidians? Then he remembered that the Narmidians didn't take prisoners and besides, Ro and Brak were armed. What then was the matter?

"So tell me, we won I assume? What happened after I went down?"

"Yes, we won, but at some cost. Your plan worked well on the left flank and we were able to completely rout the Narmidians, but on the right flank things did not go so well," said Ro.

"That much I know; I was there," said Teren bitterly.

"What you don't know is the reason why things went so wrong on that flank. After giving the order to set the Narmidian camp alight sooner than he should have done, compromising Yarik and his men, when the Narmidians started streaming up the hill towards him, the Cardellan colonel lost his nerve and turned and ran taking his men with him."

"Damned cowards," said Teren. "What about the Datians?"

"Surprisingly they stayed and fought and were supported by the remaining Lydian cavalry, but they were soon driven off and the Datians were annihilated."

"All of them?" asked Teren.

"To the man."

"What happened then?"

"That's when I looked across and saw that your men were halfway up the slope and that the Narmidians were massing for an attack. I quickly gathered our men, formed a column and began marching to your aid."

"I remember the Narmidians charging but we managed to beat them off. When they left the field, standing behind them were masses of infantry who suddenly charged our circle. There was some hard fighting and..." Teren's hand automatically travelled to where one of his wounds was bandaged. "I was wounded and collapsed to the ground and the last thing I remember was looking up at the sky and seeing scores of arrows. Where had the Narmidians been hiding their archers?"

"Those weren't Narmidian archers, Teren," said Ro.

"They weren't? Explains why I'm still drawing breath I suppose. Whose were they? I thought all of ours were wiped out along with the Datians."

"Perhaps I'd better let one of their leaders explain what happened," said Ro.

"Is he here?" asked Teren.

"She is, yes," said Ro stepping aside and grinning broadly.

Teren couldn't believe what he was seeing when a girl in her late teens and dressed in the colours of the forest, stepped forward and smiled at him.

"Hello, Father."

"Keira! Keira is that really you?"

She leant forward and carefully hugged her father, before kissing him on the forehead.

"It is."

"But how? The last time that I saw you was in the forest with that lad...Cal."

"Col. Yes, I'm still with him. We remained in the forest for some weeks, months; I don't really know, gathering our strength and numbers. Then one day we intercepted a Remadan rider who told us that you were back from the west and planning a last stand at Overa. We decided that we'd sat the war out too long and marched there as quickly as we could with nearly two hundred archers, but when we got there you'd moved on. It was easy to follow your trail to Aliba though. It seems like we arrived just in the nick of time."

"If it had not been for Keira and her people's timely arrival, I fear the outcome today would have been much different," said Ro. "They took the Narmidians completely by surprise and thinned their numbers down so that by the time my column arrived, we had numerical advantage. The enemy soon broke then."

"Did any escape?"

"Some, but not many. It was a total victory, Teren and you should be proud."

"We all should," said Teren. He turned to look at his daughter again and briefly caught a glimpse of the sad expression that flitted across her face before the smile returned. It was the same look that Ro was wearing. There was something they weren't telling him. Teren glanced round and finally realised somebody was missing. "Where's Eryn?" Nobody answered. "Keira, where's your brother?"

Keira's eyes moistened and she looked down unable to meet her father's gaze.

"I'm sorry, Teren, he didn't make it," said Ro reaching out and placing a hand on his friend's shoulder.

Teren just stared at his friend for a few moments unable to comprehend what he'd just been told.

"What do you mean he didn't make it? He was fine the last time I saw him."

"According to witnesses, when he saw you fall, he lost his head and advanced deep into the enemy. They say he killed many a warrior in his battle rage, though I know that is poor compensation for your loss. You must understand grief and anguish had overtaken him, Teren, he didn't know what he was doing," said Ro.

"Was it quick?"

"It was. I saw him fall. It was a clean strike. He would have felt no pain," said Brak joining in. "I am sorry, my friend, I tried to reach him, but the enemy were too many and his rage too great. He would not heed our shouts to withdraw."

"I doubt you would have been able to stop him, Brak," said Teren sighing. "He was a stubborn fool at times."

"Can't imagine where he got that from," said Yarik from his cot. "He was a brave boy, Teren. My men say he fought like a demon after you fell."

Teren nodded and an awkward silence fell over the group until Keira spoke again.

"At least I know my sister is safe," said Keira.

Teren's head shot up. "You have seen Marta?"

"No, but I heard from someone reliable that she is with the Ryd family in Hedeira. She's been looked after by them since they fled Lentor."

"That is good news. Is she well?" asked Teren as he tried to recall the last time that he saw his youngest daughter. She had been a baby and did not know him.

"They say that she's growing up into a fine young lady. Mother would be proud." This time it was Keira's turn to watch a strange expression cross the others' faces. "She's dead isn't she?"

"I'm sorry, Keira, yes, she is," replied Teren. "Vesla killed her for helping Eryn to escape."

For a moment it looked like Keira's legs were going to buckle under her and Ro moved to catch her, but then she seemed to get hold of her emotions and straightened her back. Teren looked on proudly. Like his dead son, Eryn, she was truly a Rad.

"Well at least he got what was coming to him although I would have liked to have been the one to send him to Kaden," said Keira.

"You'd have to join a very long line, girl," said Yarik from his cot.

"Vesla's dead?" asked Teren incredulously. "I'd have thought that being the coward he is he would have fled the field at the first sign that he was beaten. He's done it before."

"He did," said Ro, "but what was left of the Lydian cavalry gave chase. Vesla ordered some of his personal guard to intercept them and then carried on running with the other lesser kings. The Lydians killed the guards and then resumed the pursuit. They found Vesla's body lying in the dirt about four leagues further on to the east. He had been stabbed about a dozen times. It seems his own nobles had tired of him and saw the opportunity to be rid of a tyrant and turned on him."

"A fitting death then."

"So it would seem," said Ro.

"And what of these other nobles?"

"They were long gone and the Lydians were too exhausted to pursue them any further. Besides, they're no longer a problem. The Narmidian empire is about to disintegrate and there's likely to be years of in fighting as the other kings battle for dominance. Arkadia is safe once more."

"At least for now," said Brak.

"Then it is finally over," said Teren suddenly looking and feeling his age.

"Not yet it isn't," growled Yarik. They all turned to look at the big Delarite. "Many a good Delarite soldier lost his life today because of Cardellan cowardice. This must be answered in blood."

"I suspect the Datians would feel the same way," added Brak. "Had any survived Cardellan treachery."

"They will be brought to account, Yarik, don't worry," said Ro, "but not just yet. Now is a time for recovery and rebuilding. We will never forget what the Cardellans did this day and we will never forgive and at some point I promise you they will be made to pay."

Teren was surprised Yarik didn't argue the point and instead merely nodded his agreement. The Delarite must be in more pain than Teren realised.

"Now, let's leave the injured to get their rest," said Ro. "I'll see you soon, Teren," and after a cursory nod at Yarik, Ro turned and strode out followed by Brak and the other officers. Keira went to follow but Teren gently caught hold of her arm and stopped her.

"Will you stay a while? We've so much to talk about."

Keira smiled, pulled up a rickety wooden chair and plonked herself wearily down by his cot.

"Of course."

"Good. Now why don't you start by telling me everything that's happened since we left you in the forest?"

Keira nodded and began to talk.

Epilogue

"Are you sure that I can't get you to reconsider?" said Ro as he gently stroked the neck of Teren's horse.

"Not this time, my friend."

"Remada needs men like you more than ever, Teren."

"No, Remada needs men like me in times of war, not in peace. Rebuilding Remada… Arkadia, is a young man's caper, men with energy and vision. I have neither. All I've got is an aching back, pains in my fingers and a desire to sleep most of the day."

"But you more than anybody won the peace for us, it's surely only right you are here to shape the new world," said Ro.

"Maybe ten years ago, but not now. I've done my part."

"So where will you go?"

"I'm going to head for a Laryssan port and board a ship headed for the southern continent. I've heard it's a beautiful place with a warm climate which will be good for my aching joints. They say there are plenty of opportunities for a man with my abilities," said Teren.

"Have you not had enough of war?"

"Enough to last several lifetimes but when it comes right down to it, it's all I know and I'm good at it," replied Teren ruefully.

"What happened to your dream of returning to your cabin in the Lonely Mountains?"

"Too much has happened. I've lost too much. Living in sight of Lentor would just remind me of everything that this war has cost me. Maybe one day I'll return, but not yet. The events of the last three years have given me a hankering for one last adventure and I've always wanted to see the southern continent. I had three weeks lying in that hospital cot to think about it."

Ro knew that Teren was lying. He was running away from the memories, but who could blame him when he had lost so much?

"And how does Keira feel about that?" asked Ro. "She's recently learned that she's lost a mother and a brother; now she's to lose her father all over again?"

"You don't need to remind me what we've lost, Ro, I'm all too aware of that. I have spoken at length with Keira and she is disappointed but supportive of my plans. Besides, she's happy in Col's company and they plan on travelling to find Marta and then settling down on a small farm somewhere. She's got her own life to live and doesn't need an old man with a failing body and a mind full of guilt holding her back."

"Then your mind is set?"

"It is," said Teren checking that the straps on his saddle were tight.

"Then I wish you good fortune, Teren."

Teren held out his arm for Ro to clasp, but Ro just grinned and instead hugged his friend in a warm embrace.

"Easy, lad, you'll open my wounds if you're not careful," said Teren hugging Ro back.

They parted and smiled at one another.

"Farewell, Ro," said Teren taking his horse by the reins and turning to leave.

"And just where do you think you're going?" said the booming voice of Yarik behind him. He too had been laid up in hospital for the best part of three weeks. He was holding the reins of his horse.

"South to one of the ports where I'm going to catch a ship to the southern continent," replied Teren.

"Is that right?"

"It is."

"And you weren't even going to say goodbye? I'm hurt, Remadan."

"You know I don't like tearful scenes, Yarik," said Teren. "Now if you'll excuse me I have a long journey and I'd better be going."

"Just you?" asked Yarik.

"Yes, I'm going alone."

"Of course you are," said Brak who suddenly appeared leading his own horse, "and we're coming with you."

"Now wait a minute, nobody asked you to come, your

places are here," said Teren. "Men like you will be needed to rebuild Delarite, Yarik and as for you, isn't there a throne waiting for you in Breland?" he added turning to face Brak.

"What did I just hear you say to Ro? Oh, yes, men like us are only needed in times of war, not peace. Delarite doesn't need an old man like me any more than Remada needs you. Besides, if I don't come who else is going to keep you out of trouble?" said Yarik grinning.

"And as for me, I've heard being a king isn't all it's cracked up to be," said Brak smiling. "Maybe one day, but not just yet. There's still a lot more of this world I want to see before I settle down. Anyway, I've received word from Tharl Marit that a reliable witness has come forward saying that he overheard my brother giving orders to assassinate the king and then us. My brother and his cronies on the Council have either been executed or exiled and the Council now rules instead. Tharl Marit says the crown is mine when I want it."

"That is good news," said Teren and the others nodded their agreement.

"Anyway, it's like the big Delarite said, if we don't accompany you who's going to watch your back?" said Brak smiling.

Teren stared at his two friends and then nodded.

"Is there nothing I can say to dissuade you both?" asked Teren.

"Not a thing," replied Brak grinning broadly.

"So be it! This must be my penance for leading the life I have. What about you, Ro, do you want to join us now?"

"I've had enough adventure for now, thank you. Besides, somebody's got to stay and make sure things don't fall apart. Silevia is leaderless as is Lydia and Lotar's emperor is severely wounded but expected to live. Other nations are also in political turmoil. We may have won the war but now we have to win the peace. It won't be easy."

"Perhaps not, but I can't think of a better man to oversee the transition from war to peace," said Teren.

Brak and Yarik hugged Ro and then sidled up alongside Teren.

"This isn't the end, Ro, we'll see you again, don't worry," said Teren before turning and walking away.

Brak and Yarik both nodded at him and then followed.

Ro stood for some time watching his friends disappear into the distance. It was going to be a different world without those three legends around and certainly not a better one. He hoped that they found what they were looking for in their travels and that one day they would return. He turned to look behind him when he heard footsteps and smiled when he saw Major Koker approaching. When he looked back towards the horizon in front of him, his friends had disappeared. With a heavy heart, Ro turned and strode towards the major.

There was much to be done.

Lightning Source UK Ltd.
Milton Keynes UK
UKOW04f1107230615

253974UK00001B/8/P